A VALENTINE WALTZ

"I think we have done enough for today," Justin announced.

Belinda, at the pianoforte, shook her head. "One more of the simpler dances, then we shall be done. Lorissa must learn the waltz."

Justin didn't like the idea of anyone holding Lorissa in such an intimate manner, then realized he was being ridiculous. Everyone danced the waltz these days. "Very well."

With that he stepped closer to Lorissa. Taking her hand, he put his other at her waist. He heard her issue a small gasp; then she gazed up into his eyes with alarm. Soon her expression melted into one of total trust. The music started and they began to move gracefully into the three-count rhythm as if she had been born waltzing.

Justin twirled her slowly about the room, but his mind was not on the dance. For the first time he really saw his old friend. Gone was the child of memory. Here was a beautiful, tempting female. What startled him the most in his revelation was the rush of desire he experienced for her. How could this be? She was little Lori. His gaze swept over her. The child he'd fished from the river had passed into history. Before him stood a woman . . . and a very desirable one.

—from "The Ruby Heart" by Lynn Collum

BOOK YOUR PLACE ON OUR WEBSITE AND MAKE THE READING CONNECTION!

We've created a customized website just for our very special readers, where you can get the inside scoop on everything that's going on with Zebra, Pinnacle and Kensington books.

When you come online, you'll have the exciting opportunity to:

- View covers of upcoming books
- Read sample chapters
- Learn about our future publishing schedule (listed by publication month *and author*)
- Find out when your favorite authors will be visiting a city near you
- Search for and order backlist books from our online catalog
- Check out author bios and background information
- Send e-mail to your favorite authors
- Meet the Kensington staff online
- Join us in weekly chats with authors, readers and other guests
- Get writing guidelines
- AND MUCH MORE!

**Visit our website at
http://www.zebrabooks.com**

VALENTINE KISSES

DONNA BELL
CATHERINE BLAIR
LYNN COLLUM

Zebra Books
Kensington Publishing Corp.

http://www.zebrabooks.com

ZEBRA BOOKS are published by

Kensington Publishing Corp.
850 Third Avenue
New York, NY 10022

First Printing: January, 2000
10 9 8 7 6 5 4 3 2 1

Printed in the United States of America

Contents

A VALENTINE COURTSHIP

by

Donna Bell

PART ONE
THE DAWNING

"I tell you, Miranda, I have made my promise and shall keep it."

"But Adam, marrying just to please your mother!"

"You know me better than that! I must acknowledge that it is time for me to think of setting up my nursery. I need an heir."

"You are hardly in your dotage, Adam."

"Were I a female, I would be considered on the shelf, past all hope," he said with a drawl.

"Like me?"

Adam Hunter, Earl of Marsden, hastily retreated behind his winning smile. Running one hand through his dark curls, he said, "You, my dear Miranda, cannot be considered on the shelf when you have been wed before. A beautiful widow can never be considered on the shelf."

Miranda Sinclair laughed, a light, airy sound that filled the box they shared at the opera. "You were always so easy to torment," she whispered, rapping his arm with her painted fan.

"And you have always been eager to torment me," he replied. "But you have dragged me away from the original point of our conversation. Have you any advice for me? Any particular ladies you think I should consider? You know I value your opinion, Mir."

Miranda smiled, but the light did not reach her eyes as she suggested, "Why not wait until the Season in the spring? January is hardly the time to find a bride in London."

"True, but I promised I would make my choice by my thirtieth birthday, and that, as you know, is the fourteenth of next month. I thought I would announce my betrothal at Mother's annual St. Valentine's Day ball," said Adam, his dark eyes growing serious.

"So soon?" she asked.

"You know me, now that I have made up my mind, I want to take action!"

The lights dimmed and the curtain rose. The two friends, unlike many in the audience, turned to the stage to give it their undivided attention.

As the evening wore on, Miranda found it increasingly difficult to concentrate on the action taking place on the stage. Despite the play being one of her favorites, and Adam's also, tonight's performance of *The Taming of the Shrew* was proving impossible to follow.

She had always known that one day Adam would marry. He was so conscientious about his position, his family; of course he would do his duty and produce the next heir. But why now? She wasn't ready to give up her friend! And his marriage would mean just that; no bride would accept another woman as Adam's best friend.

Miranda could see only loneliness looming before her. She had other friends, certainly, but they were all married ladies and busy with children. Miranda sighed.

"Oh, that was good!" exclaimed Adam as the curtain fell at the end of Act I. "Didn't you think so?" he asked when he received no response to his first enthusiastic comment.

"Yes, certainly," she said, loathe to give up her thoughts and return to the present. "Perhaps not as good as the last time," she added, hoping he would not quiz her on particulars since she had no idea what she might say.

"Perhaps, but you must admit that new actress is excellent in the role of Katherine."

"Indeed, she makes a wonderful Kate," agreed Miranda.

"Would you care to walk around? I know you usually despise the kind of insipid conversation that these short intermissions allow, but . . ."

"By all means, let us join the assemblage," said Miranda, rising and eagerly making her way toward the corridor. She had no wish to carry on a probing conversation about the play with Adam.

Adam caught her up and took her hand, sending a surprising jolt of electricity coursing through her fingertips and up her arm before he tucked her hand into the crook of his elbow.

Leaning down, he whispered, "One would think that there is a particular reason for your eager flight, Mir. Some prospective swain awaits, perhaps?"

"Fustian," she replied, a trifle too sharply, for his eyes widened in surprise and his pace slowed. Relenting, Miranda lied, "I am just very thirsty of a sudden. Shall we?"

"Certainly, Miranda. What do you want? A glass of champagne? Ratafia?"

"A stout ale," she muttered before replying with forced enthusiasm, "A glass of champagne, if you please, Adam!"

Somehow, Miranda made it through the play without any tears or tantrums. She smiled and waved gaily when Adam dropped her at her elegant house on South Audley Street, off Grosvenor Square. But when the door had closed and she made her way to the salon, where her night-owl aunt was waiting, she dropped noisily onto the sofa, expelling a soft, "Damn."

"Miranda, really!" said her scrawny Aunt Sophie, laying aside her novel in anticipation of an explanation.

"You will never guess what I found out tonight!"

"Then why don't you tell me, my dear," came the blunt reply.

"Adam . . . I don't think I can say it," said Miranda, sitting forward with her elbows resting on her knees and frowning fiercely into the fire.

"Oh, dear, never tell me Marsden has decided to wed!" exclaimed her perceptive relative.

Miranda only stared, nodding her head in amazed affirmation.

"How did you guess?" she finally asked.

"It was bound to happen; after all, the boy is almost thirty."

"But I might have been speaking of a new horse, his mother, any number of things. How could you know?" asked Miranda.

"Quite easily explained. No other news would have produced that odd blush of color on your cheeks which instantly fled when you started to speak, leaving you a deathly white, my dear girl."

"I am not a girl," said Miranda automatically.

"Put your head between your legs, or you will faint," said Aunt Sophie, taking one surprisingly strong arm and pushing Miranda's head forward.

She struggled against it, and her aunt subsided as the color returned to her niece's complexion.

"It was bound to happen, love."

"But why now? And so quickly! He wants to announce his betrothal on his birthday!" she said.

"And who is the lucky girl?"

Miranda started to giggle, the sound rapidly transforming into a loud, long, wheezing laugh. Aunt Sophie rose and fetched a glass of port, thrusting it into Miranda's grasp and guiding the glass to her lips.

Coughing and sputtering, Miranda's laugh was replaced by a rasping noise that sounded suspiciously like a sob.

"What am I to do?" she asked when she had regained her voice and composure.

Her practical aunt was silent for a moment before declaring, "I suppose you will have to marry him yourself, Miranda."

"Me? Marry Adam? Why, that would be like marrying my brother—if I had one, that is! You must be mad, Aunt Sophie! Adam is my dearest, oldest friend, but marry him . . . ?"

"Sounds like a match made in heaven to me," said the old spinster. "As for it being like marrying your brother, when was the last time you and Adam Hunter behaved like brother and sister? For that matter, when was the last time you really thought of him as a brother?"

"Well, I . . . I can't remember. I suppose it was after Sinclair died, when Adam came to comfort me," she said, frowning thoughtfully. Then, ever one for honesty, Miranda shook her head. "I remember then, when he hugged me, I thought how warm and wonderful it was to have him back in my life." She shook her head. "But I was grieving; I couldn't possibly have felt—"

Aunt Sophie rose and walked to the door, her tread stately as ever, despite her sixty years. She paused and asked shrewdly, "I loved my own brother dearly, and he loved me. But we never felt the need to be in each other's pockets like you and Marsden. Think on it, girl. And if you want it, you must make it happen. In my experience, and I admit it is somewhat limited, a man finds it impossible to see what's in front of his face most of the time. He has to be shown!"

"Let's suppose I decide to marry him, I have no idea how to go about showing Adam I want to!" remarked

Miranda, who didn't have a single feminine wile in her body.

"That is one problem I was never able to solve, but you must think of something, and it had better be fast. Otherwise, my girl, you will lose Marsden forever."

When she was alone, Miranda set aside her confusion and tried to form her battle plan. If her aunt had little experience with men, Miranda had even less, for all that she had been wed for two years. Her marriage at eighteen to Nigel Sinclair had been arranged by her father. Her husband had been kind and had indulged her as he would a child. Except for learning to run a household and sharing his bed a few times, her life had changed very little during her two years of marriage before her husband had died, leaving her a wealthy widow with not a care in the world.

It had been eight years, she recalled, not without a sigh. She had never loved Sinclair, but she had liked him. The marriage had been suitable and had pleased her father, but there had never been a question of love.

What, she wondered, would it be like to wed a man like Adam, a man her own age, a man of passion?

Miranda hugged the thought to herself as she slipped off her shoes and tucked her feet beneath her. Marriage to Adam would be nothing like her first; Sinclair had been close to fifty years old when he took her for his child bride.

But she was no longer a child, and the thought of sharing Adam's bed brought a heated flush to her cheeks. Was that all it was? she asked herself. Was she merely curious about Adam in that way? Could she really love him as a wife should love her husband?

Miranda recalled how companionable their time together always was. They attended the same social affairs, leaving together most evenings and ending up at her house, sharing the tea tray with Aunt Sophie. She certainly felt comfortable enough with Adam to consider him for a husband.

But that was not enough, she realized. She wanted much more, and Adam deserved more, too.

Though company was thin in London, Parliament was in session, and enough of the members' families had returned from their country estates to make entertaining worthwhile. Several diversions were to be had, including a ball given by Lord and Lady Weymouth, who had twin daughters to present in the spring. Adam had agreed to escort his mother, Miranda, and her aunt.

Miranda chose a gown of rich lavender with a shawl of deep green. The high waist lent her height, and the skirt, fuller than most, swirled delightfully when she twirled around. In her hair, which she wore in a tight chignon on the crown of her head, she had placed lavender rosebuds made of silk. Her green eyes, fringed by thick black lashes, needed no artifice, and her lips were pink from biting at them with trepidation.

Never, she reflected, had she taken such care with her ensemble when she was merely attending a modest ball with Adam.

Her efforts paid off, however, when he expelled an appreciative whistle upon seeing her. Taking her hand in his, he turned her in a neat pirouette under his arm.

"Charming," pronounced his mother, who presented her cheek for a quick kiss.

Growing up on neighboring estates, Lady Marsden had filled the motherless Miranda's need for a maternal ear, while Miranda had been a surrogate daughter for the countess, who had produced three rowdy boys.

"Shall we go?" asked Adam, offering his arm to his mother, who ignored it and linked elbows with Aunt Sophie, one of her oldest friends. Bestowing on her a quizzical expression, Adam turned to Miranda. With a trembling hand she took his arm, and they followed the older women to the carriage.

The Weymouth town house was nearby, on Curzon Street, but it took thirty minutes to reach the door, there was such a crush of carriages. The brisk wind tore at Miranda's skirt as she descended to the street, and she gasped when it flew above her head. Adam caught the hem as it flew past his face and hauled it down to her ankles, laughing as he assured her that it was too dark for anyone to see.

When he had hurried her inside, he leaned over and whispered outrageously, "Except me, of course, and I won't tell a soul that your petticoats match your gown perfectly."

"Scoundrel!" she replied, feeling a blush rise but knowing he couldn't guess how his remark had affected her, since her cheeks were pink from the cold already.

"Lord Marsden, so happy you could come this evening. My son warned me that you might be out of town," said Lady Weymouth, wetting her lips as she turned to present her two marriageable daughters. "Make your curtsey to Lord Marsden and Lady Marsden," she added. The twins simpered and curtseyed; Adam bowed and moved along.

"There are two possible candidates for you, Adam," teased Miranda when they were standing on the edge of the ballroom looking at the throng of guests.

"Not until they grow up," said Adam. "There is Miss Allgood. What do you think of her?"

"She is quite pretty, though her hair, I believe, is a bright red normally and has been changed to a more subdued auburn."

"Indeed, I would not have guessed. Why would she do such a thing?" asked Adam.

"Red hair is not in fashion," replied Miranda.

"Ridiculous," said Adam, turning his attention elsewhere.

"Marsden, you divine creature! I had no idea you were still in town," gushed a willowy brunette, descending on them with a sweet smile for Adam and a smirk for Miranda. "I was in despair of finding anyone suitable for the next waltz until I saw you," said Lady Redmonton, whose husband had been killed two summers before at Waterloo.

"Good evening, my lady," said Adam, stepping back to include Miranda in their conversation when Lady Redmonton maneuvered her way to his side, supplanting Miranda. "You remember Mrs. Sinclair."

"Of course, hello," said the widow, allowing the merest smile to cross her lips before returning to the hunt. "So, Marsden, do you know the waltz?"

"Of course, my lady, and I would be honored if you would . . ." The quadrille ended, and Lady Redmonton led Adam onto the floor, joining the promenade with the previous dancers and leaving Miranda fuming.

"Almost as proprietary as a wife," murmured Aunt Sophie, watching the couples.

"She'll find herself mistaken if she thinks to trap Adam with such open tactics," commented the countess. "Adam can't abide a pushy female."

"But sometimes it is the tenacious ones who succeed."

Miranda favored her aunt with a scowl and stalked away.

"Has something upset Miranda?" asked Lady Marsden.

"Let us just say she has a great deal on her mind, what with Marsden announcing that he plans to wed," said Aunt Sophie.

"Don't tell me they are finally coming to their senses," remarked the countess, smiling with genuine pleasure when her friend nodded silently. "Perhaps I will forgo playing cards tonight, Sophie. This may be as good as a play!"

Miranda did not get far before Lord Weymouth, a country squire sort of man, sought her out for the next dance. While they waited for the waltz to end, he conversed easily about his family and latest horses. Miranda smiled politely as she watched Adam's progress around the dance floor, one hand at Lady Redmonton's waist and the other clasping her hand. Every few moments the lady would throw back her head and giggle, offering her long neck and indecently exposed breasts for Adam's perusal.

"I understand you are very fond of riding," said Lord Weymouth.

"I dote on it," replied Miranda.

"I thought as much; I have often seen you and Lord Marsden out of a morning."

"Indeed? You should join us, my lord," she replied, breathing a sigh of relief as the music ended and Adam made his way to her side after an extremely short promenade, leaving behind a disgruntled Lady Redmonton.

"Weymouth," he said, sketching a bow to his host before turning to Miranda and saying, "Next dance, Mir?"

"No, I'm sorry. I am already engaged," she replied airily. "Perhaps later."

"Beat you to it, old boy," said Weymouth. "Have to be a sight quicker to secure a dance with a lovely young lady like Mrs. Sinclair."

"To be sure. Perhaps you'll save the next waltz for me, Miranda," said Adam, turning away only to find Lady Weymouth presenting one of her daughters to him as a partner. Polite as always, Adam bowed and led Miss Weymouth onto the floor for the boulanger just forming.

Miranda watched Adam surreptitiously throughout the evening. Finally, just before supper was announced, the orchestra struck up the next waltz. Adam hurried to her side and led her onto the floor, placing his hand at her waist.

"Gadzooks, it's good to have a partner I can relax with!" exclaimed Adam in hushed tones, his breath teasing her ear.

"I know what you mean," she whispered, smiling up at his dear face and wondering how many times before, when they had waltzed, she had taken his affection for granted. What would happen to their friendship if he married elsewhere?

Their movements were as one; Adam danced superbly, and Miranda followed his lead with ease, her face turned up to meet his fond gaze, though neither uttered a word.

This is how it is supposed to be, thought Miranda, studying her old friend with purpose. His eyes danced under her regard, and he pulled her closer. Miranda laughed as they took their final steps together before the music ended.

Adam led her into dinner, a munificent buffet of tempting dishes, both hot and cold. One table, overflowing with hothouse fruits and light pastries, boasted an ice sculpture of two Grecian maidens.

When they were seated, Miranda whispered, "Do you suppose that is meant to be the Weymouth twins?"

"Surely not," said Adam, leaning closer and adding, "There was probably not enough ice in London to manage that!"

"Adam! Do not be unkind! The Misses Weymouth are not that, uh, robust."

"Not to look at, but just try waltzing with one and having your toes crushed every few seconds; then see if you don't agree with me!"

"Adam, you are . . ."

"Marsden! There you are!"

"Lady Redmonton," he said, half-rising from his chair.

The lady in question gestured to the man behind her, and he pulled up another chair. When she was settled, he motioned to a servant, who produced yet another chair, and Miranda found her tête-à-tête neatly ended.

"You know Lord Picton, I believe," said Lady Redmonton in an off-hand introduction.

Miranda looked up with genuine pleasure and welcomed the newcomer. "It is good to see you again, my lord."

"And you, Mrs. Sinclair. What has it been, three years?"

"Yes, I believe so. How are the children, especially my goddaughter?"

"They are all well, growing like weeds. Little Miranda is six years old now."

"Is she in London with you?"

"Yes, I hate to leave them at home with the servants. They fret if I am gone too long, and I didn't want to miss this session."

"May I call and visit them?" asked Miranda.

"I'm sure Picton would love it if you did, my dear," said Lady Redmonton, not bothering to disguise her boredom with the present conversation.

Adam covered the surprised silence with, "How is it you two know each other?"

"My late wife and Mrs. Sinclair were at school together," said Lord Picton.

"We were the best of friends. Sarah was a wonderful lady," added Miranda, patting Lord Picton's hand in sympathy.

"Thank you," he replied, covering her hand with his for a moment before shaking off the pall and asking, "Shall we eat?"

After supper, Adam was dragooned by Lady Redmonton for another set, and Miranda agreed to partner Lord Picton and join them. When the music finally ended, she was surprised to realize that Lord Picton's conversation had held her attention; not once had her eyes strayed to Adam.

Before parting, she promised Lord Picton that she would call on him and his children the next morning.

Another hour passed, and Aunt Sophie and the countess appeared, yawning and declaring they were ready for their beds.

"Your wish is my command, dear ladies," said Adam, offering an arm to each of them.

When they arrived home, Miranda asked Adam and the countess to join them for tea, but they politely declined.

"But I will see you in the morning, will I not?" asked Adam, taking her hand in his and holding it until she replied.

"I'll be ready, but I promised Lord Picton I would call by eleven o'clock, so we must make our ride quite early," said Miranda.

Adam bowed and touched the back of her gloved hand with his lips. Then he was gone. Miranda heaved a sigh and followed her aunt up the stairs.

Patiently, she waited for her maid to finish undressing her. When she was tucked up in bed, she allowed herself to reflect on the many emotions the evening had evoked in her breast—curiosity, jealousy, nostalgia, and, lastly, the realization of a deep affection.

Did she love Adam in the way a wife should? She was attracted to him, but she was still unsure about the depth of her love. She knew, however, that she would be miserable if he married another.

If that made her selfish, then so be it, she thought.

When they went riding in the morning, she would try to look on him in this new light, see if it was really possible that she could love him as a wife should.

Then she would make her decision.

* * *

"I say, is that a new hat?" asked Adam when she joined him in front of the house at ten the next day.

"No, it's one from last year, but I added a feather. Do you like it?" she asked as he threw her into the saddle.

"Very nice; it matches your eyes. You should always wear a touch of green. Where shall we ride this morning?" he asked, already mounting his gelding and signaling the groom to stand away.

"Hyde Park. It is practically deserted at this hour, and I feel the need for some quiet."

"Very well," said Adam, shooting her retreating back a quizzical look.

When they had reached the park, Adam inquired, "Was there something you wished to talk about, Miranda? For the past few days you have seemed rather distracted, and then wanting privacy and all, I thought perhaps . . ."

"Not really, Adam. I suppose it is just old age creeping up on me," she said with a false giggle, glancing his way but not looking directly at him.

He gave a crack of laughter before saying, "Yes, yes, you are the wisest, most ancient woman I know . . . apart from your Aunt Sophie. And I gather you mean to overtake her. What is all this nonsense about?"

"Oh, I was only teasing again. You know what I am," she said, silently cursing her babbling tongue; she had never been good at flirtation! "I didn't sleep very well, and sometimes the nannies in Green Park where we usually ride don't exercise any control over their charges. I didn't feel like listening to those childish squeals today."

"Hence your plan to visit Picton's children this morning," he said. "Never mind, you are suffering from a case of the megrims, and I shall give you something else to occupy your mind. Tell me, have you thought any more about my predicament since last night? What ladies should I consider? I know Miss All-good is a suitable prospect."

"Oh, no, Adam," moaned Miranda.

"I know, she is not exactly exciting, but she is all that is proper, despite her dyed locks, and she does come from a good family."

"So does your gelding, Shady Deal," said Miranda tartly. "Please, Adam, you must try to choose someone with a modicum of personality!"

"Such as . . . ?" he asked, reining in and facing her.

Miranda felt the slow blush rising up her neck and turning her cheeks red. Any other day, she would have had a witty rejoinder, but not now, not with Adam. She wanted to curse this sudden awkwardness!

Instead, she murmured, "I don't know. As I said, I didn't sleep well; I haven't really given your search any thought."

"Miranda, you know I value your opinion. Time is short; I need your help if I am to choose a bride by St. Valentine's."

"I promise to give it some thought this afternoon. It will occupy me while Aunt Sophie is having her at home. You know how deadly boring that can be, with all her old friends dropping by and staying for hours."

"I would love to rescue you, but I have an appoint-ment," lied her friend, ducking his head to avoid her hard gaze.

"Very well, if *you* are too busy to help *me* . . ." chal-lenged Miranda, never one to shy away from an ad-vantage.

"Oh, all right. I shall call at two o'clock to take you to . . . a fitting?"

"Good, I need to go to the dressmaker," said Mi-randa with a wicked smile.

Adam groaned.

"You may help me choose a costume for your mother's masquerade ball."

"But then I will know what you are wearing," said

Adam, the gleam of victory shining in his dark eyes as he concluded, "and I know how you like to surprise everyone."

"You may wait in the reception while I am closeted with Madame Celeste. I'm sure her shopgirls will make you comfortable," said Miranda.

"I can see I'll not win this tug of war. Very well, I will call for you at two o'clock," said Adam, touching his riding crop to the big gelding's neck and calling, "Race you to the end of the row!"

Adam escorted Miranda to Lord Picton's modest home in Hanover Square. After helping her dismount, he flipped a coin to a groom, saying, "See that you walk her mare and then escort her home when she is ready."

"Right you are, guvner," said the servant.

"Thank you, Adam. See you this afternoon," called Miranda as the door opened. Adam waved and rode away.

Lord Picton greeted her warmly and led her up to the nursery, where three children waited with wide eyes.

"Make your bows and curtsey to Mrs. Sinclair, children," urged their nurse.

Miranda curtseyed in return and sat down on a small chair, bringing herself down to their level.

"What have you been doing this morning?" she asked, nodding at the puzzles covering the table.

"I have been putting together a map," said the little girl solemnly. "They have been learning their shapes and colors."

"Now, which one of you is Andrew and which is Curtis?"

"Me!" they chorused, causing the adults to laugh.

"Andrew is four, and Curtis is three," announced their sister. "I am six," she added grandly.

"Oh, I know how old you are, Miranda."

"Yes, you are my godmama. Papa told me so."

"That's right, and I am very glad for this chance to become better acquainted with you."

"Thank you, Mrs. Sinclair," said the little girl. "Did you really know my mother?"

"Very well. You look very much like her, but I daresay your papa has told you that."

"No, Papa doesn't talk about Mama very much."

Lord Picton cleared his throat and said, "I think we have interrupted your lessons long enough, children. Perhaps Mrs. Sinclair will call again."

"Will you?" asked the child.

"I promise I shall. In the spring, perhaps we can plan a picnic in the park, if your papa and nurse agree."

"Can we, Papa?" asked the children. "Can we?"

"We shall see," said Lord Picton.

The little girl gave Miranda a shy hug and her brothers followed suit. Miranda felt a wave of affection for her old friend's offspring and had to swallow the lump in her throat before she could bid them farewell.

"They are charming children," she said when she was sharing a cup of tea with their father in the salon.

"Thank you. I worry that they have no female, except their nurse, to show them affection."

"Perhaps you should marry again," said Miranda impulsively before clapping her hand over her mouth. "My wretched tongue!" she exclaimed. "Please forgive me, my lord."

"No apology necessary, Mrs. Sinclair. I have thought much the same myself. But it is difficult. I don't know if my wife ever mentioned it, but ours was not an arranged marriage. I loved Sarah deeply, and I don't know if I am ready—indeed, if it is even possible—to replace her."

Miranda nodded, as if she understood his loss, and

he said quickly, "But you were wed yourself. You know what I am talking about better than most."

"Of course it is difficult, but perhaps for the children . . . Now, I really must be going."

"Certainly. I'll send my groom with you. I appreciate your taking the time to call," he said.

"It was my pleasure, and I warn you, I intend to take my role as godmother quite seriously."

"Thank you again for coming."

"You're welcome. Good-bye," she said.

Turning toward home, Miranda considered Lord Picton's assumption that she could understand his grief from personal experience. How terrible it must have been to lose his beloved wife so young.

And how terrible it was that she had lost a husband and grieved so little.

When Miranda was home again and had changed for their afternoon callers, she joined her aunt at the dining table for a light nuncheon.

"Well, have you come up with a plan to win Marsden?" demanded her forthright aunt when the servants had retreated.

Miranda shook her head and picked at the food on her plate.

"I suppose I was just being selfish last night," she said. "Adam should marry, and I have offered to help him find the right bride."

Her aunt's derisive snort made Miranda bristle.

"Have you any better ideas?" she demanded.

"If you can't tell him face to face, Miranda, then write him a letter."

"And say what, Aunt Sophie? 'Dear Adam, I don't know if I love you or not, but I am too selfish to allow anyone else to have you, so will you marry me?' "

"If that's the best you can do, my girl, you don't deserve him!" said her crusty aunt, glaring back at her.

"Don't you love him?" came the crucial question, shredding all of Miranda's armor in four short words.

"I . . . I don't know. I think so, but what if I am merely being selfish?" she asked, her green eyes dark with worry.

Her aunt smiled and asked, "In a year's time, suppose you return home for a visit and call at Marsden Hall. How will you feel dangling his child on your knee, knowing it could have been yours?"

Miranda bowed her head, closing her eyes and trying to envisage such a scene. A stab of pain, almost physical in its intensity, darted through her heart.

Dear God! I do love him! she thought.

"Impossible," she whispered fiercely, her haunted eyes meeting her aunt's.

"Then do something about it," said Aunt Sophie.

"Thank you so much for rescuing me, Adam. Lady Bartholomew was just launching into her favorite topic, her health. I would probably have suffered an apoplexy myself had I remained. She was there last week, too, and I endured an hour of politely acknowledging that she has the worst health of all Aunt Sophie's old dears."

"Sir Galahad is always happy to oblige a beautiful damsel-in-distress," he teased, flicking the tip of his whip close to his leader's ear and sending the curricle safely through a narrow opening in the traffic.

He pulled up outside Madame Celeste's establishment and jumped down, turning to receive her hands as she stepped out of the carriage. The tiger who had been clinging to the back of the vehicle hopped into the seat and pulled his cap when Adam instructed him to, "Walk 'em."

Madame Celeste greeted them at the door, ordering wine for the earl and showing him to a chair personally.

"What may I do for you today, Mrs. Sinclair?" she asked.

"I need to order several things, but mostly a costume for a masquerade."

"Ah, yes, the St. Valentine's masquerade of the Countess of Marsden. If you will step this way, madame," said the couturier, and Miranda waved at Adam and followed.

Madame Celeste indicated a straight-backed chair covered in striped satin, and Miranda sat down while the seamstress began pulling lengths of cloth from the overladen shelves.

"What did you have in mind for this year, Mrs. Sinclair? Last year I believe you went as a Greek goddess?"

"Yes, along with half the other ladies. This year I would like something truly different, perhaps even daring," said Miranda, rising and joining madame at the shelves. Removing her gloves, she touched a piece of scarlet velvet and sighed at the luxurious feel of the fabric.

Madame Celeste smiled and pulled out the material, laying it on the table. She turned back and chose another ell of fabric, this one a sheer organdy, white with delicately embroidered silver hearts. It joined the velvet, and Madame Celeste added another piece of white satin.

"This, for the skirt," she said, pointing to the white satin, "and the embroidered organdy for the overskirt. The velvet for the bodice, a scandalously low decolletage shaped like the top of a heart with a *V* at the waist. And around your neck, a choker of red velvet with a single heart-shaped diamond. *Quelle extase!*" breathed the dressmaker dramatically.

"I don't know, madame. It is not in my usual style," said Miranda, who favored more conservative colors and fashions.

"*Exactement!*" pronounced Madame Celeste, folding her arms as if the matter was settled. She turned to the table, reached underneath, and produced several fashion plates, seemingly from another era. "This one, I think. It will accent your tiny waist and give you height. You yourself will look like a Valentine heart!"

Miranda picked up the sketch. The dress had long sleeves and a waistline that actually fitted at the waist, an anomaly in the current age of high waists and tiny puffed sleeves. The neckline did not appear too scandalous, though it would certainly show off her curves. The skirts were full with wide panniers.

"I cannot like the stiffness of these wide skirts."

"Hm," said Madame Celeste, taking another piece of paper and sketching the dress with a different style of skirt. "There! It will be full, but there will be no difficult paniers or whalebone construction. You will be *ravissante!*"

"Ravishing?" said Miranda, picking up the scarlet-colored velvet and holding it to her face as she gazed in the mirror. The color brought out the green of her eyes and made her complexion glow with vitality.

What would Adam think? Would he like this new look? Not that it would matter, if his betrothal to someone else was announced at the ball. She simply couldn't allow that to happen! She would do something!

Suddenly, she smiled at her image as a plan began to brew in her mind. Turning to the dressmaker, Miranda said, "Very well, make it up for me. And will you see to the accessories also? I don't think I will have the time to search for everything. I will be quite busy between now and the masquerade."

"But of course!" agreed the seamstress.

Since his father's death, Adam's mother had insisted on living in London, leaving the large manor house in the country for her son, except for short visits at Christmas and during the warmest months of summer.

In the winter, the countess of Marsden was famous for her Tuesday evening "supper and card" parties, and they were well attended. Miranda's Aunt Sophie never missed one; she loved winning, and she was an expert at cards. Miranda, when Adam was in town, invariably attended with her aunt.

The day after their visit to Madame Celeste's, she waited for evening in a fever of impatience. Unable to explain her mood to Aunt Sophie, Miranda grew short-tempered, restlessly watching the clock and sighing from time to time.

Finally, they arrived at the Marsden town house; Miranda wore a dark green gown, its narrow hem embroidered with leaves of gold thread. In her hair, she wore a wreath of silk leaves entwined with a dainty gold chain. She had no need of artificial color, for her cheeks were rosy with anticipation.

Adam singled her out immediately, his usually keen attention to details missing her careful toilette completely. Miffed, Miranda followed him to the study, where he shut the door behind her before striding to the desk and opening a drawer.

"Adam, what is going on? Did you bring me in here to watch you write . . . oh," she said, her eyes widening as he withdrew a familiar red heart.

"Only look at what arrived this morning," he said, torn between pleasure and bewilderment.

Miranda picked up the heart and pretended to scan the familiar missive.

"Who is it from?" she asked.

"I haven't the faintest notion. Do you? I mean, it seems too odd a coincidence that someone is suddenly sending me love notes when I have just decided to wed. Did you tell anyone of our conversation?" he asked, taking the heart-shaped card and reading it again.

"No, of course I did not, Adam. Perhaps, as the message says, the person has simply decided this is the right time to reveal herself. She says she has long admired you."

"I don't know, Mir. It's rather havey-cavey, don't you think? I mean, can you imagine ever writing something like this? 'The time is ripe, the time is near, when love is in the air, for all to hear.'"

Miranda gave a nervous laugh. "What rubbish," she said, her heart turning cold with grief. She watched as Adam carefully put away the card.

"Still," he said, looking up at her and grinning, "even though the poetry is bad, the sentiment is rather flattering."

Feeling her heart thaw, Miranda teased, "So you will allow your head to be turned by a secret admirer?"

"Let us say, I am willing to see where it will lead. The writer indicates that this is just the first of many. We must both listen and pay attention; one of us may be able to guess the identity of this mystery writer. You know, Miranda, I think this winter, London may be a very interesting place indeed! I do wish I didn't need to go down to Marsden Manor tomorrow," mused Adam, offering her his arm and leading her back to the other guests.

"I didn't realize you were leaving town," said Miranda, her enjoyment of the evening turning flat.

"Yes, there is a problem with Harper, the new steward. He's a good man, but he's young and inexperienced. He wrote to tell me that he would have to evict the Yardleys."

"The Yardleys!" exclaimed Miranda. "But they have lived on the estate forever! He can't do that!"

"No, of course not. You remember that Mr. Yardley died last spring. The farm is going downhill, but the oldest boy, Donald, is trying."

"How old is he? Fifteen?"

"Sixteen, but he has had some of the most devilish luck. The barn roof collapsed last week. The fences are falling down, but that's because there was no money after that poor harvest."

"I thought you told your steward to see to the repairs on the fences."

"So I did, but he insists that the problems are due to laziness. I must go down and soothe everyone's feelings."

"Of course, you wouldn't want to be accused of being an absentee landowner," said Miranda. "But I will miss you, Adam. London is more amusing when you are here," she added rather self-consciously, despite the fact that what she said was true.

"You could come with me," he offered.

"No, I shouldn't leave Aunt Sophie alone," she said, thinking privately that what she really couldn't do was bear to travel all that distance alone with him now that she realized the true nature of her feelings for him.

"Come into the card room. I have purchased a new game; perhaps you have heard of it, Bagatelle."

"No, I'm not familiar with it. I hope it is not some sort of card game."

"No, it's a wooden board with numbers and slots," explained Adam, leading her to a table where an older man was trying his luck with the new game.

"See, how he pulls back that lever. It is attached to a spring, and you let it go like so. Good one, Mr. Quincy. See, Miranda, the ball landed in that slot, so he gets points for that."

"It looks rather too easy," said Miranda, her mind still on other matters, like the way the candlelight played on the highlights in Adam's hair.

"It certainly is not, Mrs. Sinclair," said the elderly Mr. Quincy, leaning over the board and pulling back the lever again. "It takes quite a bit of skill. There! What do you think of that!"

"Very good, Mr. Quincy," said Miranda.

"Here, you must try it, Miranda," said Adam as the older man moved away to join the other guests.

The last thing Miranda wanted was to master some ridiculous new game, but the opportunity to be with Adam, to have his undivided attention, was not to be missed.

She let fly the first ball, and it rapidly descended to the bottom of the board.

"Too hard," said Adam, taking her hand in his and guiding it back to release the next ball more gently. "Not bad!"

"Not bad," murmured Miranda, wishing he would put his hand over hers again, but knowing that such a request from her would shock him. Instead, she had to be content with his nearness, knowing he would be gone the next day.

That night, when Miranda was alone in her chamber, she pulled out a heavy volume of plays and began leafing through it. If he was leaving, it would give her more time to create his secret-admirer missives. She would send him one each day, from the first of February until the St. Valentine's masquerade, each one hinting at her identity and revealing the true nature of her feeling for him. Perhaps her words would enable him to see her in a different light.

She began skimming through one of their favorite plays, *All's Well That Ends Well*, searching for some line to borrow that would tease and intrigue Adam without giving him a disgust of her poetic ability.

The wind turned bitter, and the skies threatened rain for the next week; Miranda waited impatiently for Adam's return, filling the hours with her compositions, which she lined up in the drawer of her desk, one through fourteen. The first of February arrived amid a flurry of snowflakes and Adam's return. Taking the first of the anonymous letters, Miranda sent it to the Marsden town house and waited impatiently for him to call.

* * *

"Ladies, the Earl of Marsden and Lady Marsden," announced the butler that afternoon.

Miranda rose, crossing the room to take Adam's hands in hers, to pull him close, but she restrained herself and merely shook his hand before turning to his mother and leading her to the sofa.

"Good afternoon, Marsden, my lady," said Aunt Sophie, signaling to the butler to see that refreshments were served.

"Sophie, how are you managing with this terrible weather we have been having?" asked the countess.

"I stay inside by the fire," replied Aunt Sophie sensibly. "Though I cannot say the same for Miranda. She insists on venturing forth every day, bent on performing some sort of errand."

"I have my charity work," said Miranda, hoping she did not succumb to the usual blush. "And I have also furthered my acquaintance with my goddaughter."

"And her papa," said Aunt Sophie, earning a withering glare from her niece.

"Goddaughter?" asked the countess.

"Lord Picton's eldest, a sweet child of six. Her mother and I were quite close at school."

"So, Lord Picton is a widower," murmured the countess, exchanging a speaking glance with her friend. "Now, that leads to an interesting possibility."

"I'm sure it is nothing of the sort," declared Adam stoutly. "Is it, Miranda?"

Some devil took control, and she found herself smiling coyly and shrugging her shoulders. "I daresay you are right," she replied, adding, "Anyway, I also have my charity work."

In truth, she had been out every day, but her motive had been diversion rather than charity. Anticipating her campaign to win Adam, to have stayed cooped up in the house because of a little rain and cold would have driven her mad.

"And so do I," replied the countess, "but I draw the line at foul weather. Today, of course, Adam insisted that we pay you a visit, since he has been gone for a week," she added, smiling fondly on her son.

"One would think you'd want to stay by the fire with the snow falling," said Aunt Sophie.

"I am not so frail as that. Besides, do not let Mother hoodwink you. She was bored all to flinders staying home by the fire. It took very little persuasion to entice her out of doors."

Thinking a change of topic would be best, Miranda asked, "Did you have a successful trip, Marsden?"

"Yes, but most of the misunderstanding had been straightened out by the time I arrived."

"How so?"

Adam grinned and said, "I had written to Harper, instructing him to see that the barn roof was replaced. By the time I arrived, the work was finished, and Harper had decided to let the Yardleys stay."

"Wonderful! But why?" asked Miranda.

"It seems he had never met the eldest Miss Yardley until he began helping with the barn roof. Miss Yardley is a very sweet, very comely young woman. I believe Mr. Harper hopes to make a match of it," said Adam, laughing.

The ladies joined in, but Aunt Sophie silenced them with a pointed, "I understand you also hope to make a match, Marsden."

Adam raised one brow and turned to Miranda, who blushed a rosy pink and said contritely, "I am sorry, Adam, but you know I can keep nothing from Aunt Sophie."

He shook his head and laughed. "Never mind, it is not as urgent as it was."

"Yes, I persuaded Adam that he really should spend

more time choosing a wife than he would a horse,"
said the countess.

"And since I have been gone this past week, I have
come to realize that I probably won't be able to settle
on a suitable candidate by the masquerade. Still, it
would have been nice to have concluded the matter."

"You make it sound like a business transaction," said
Aunt Sophie, looking down her long nose at Adam
before turning to Miranda and skewering her with,
"Miranda can tell you it is nothing like!"

"Please, Aunt," said Miranda.

"How is your mysterious costume coming along?"
asked Adam, his deep, resonant voice commandeering
the conversation effectively.

"Very well," said Miranda gratefully. "It is almost finished."

"We are expecting a huge crush," confided the
countess with a smile. Her dark hair shimmered with
silver threads, but her lively eyes, so like her son's, and
smooth complexion belied her age. "I have hired Gunter's to assist with the food and a large orchestra to
provide the music."

"Your masquerade is always the highlight of the winter, Elizabeth," said Aunt Sophie. "I am looking forward to it immensely, especially this year."

Miranda shot her aunt a warning look, and Aunt
Sophie continued with wide-eyed innocence, "The
weather has been so terrible of late, the diversion of
your masquerade ball will carry me through to the
spring, when the Season begins!"

"You are too kind," said the countess, obviously
pleased.

"Marsden, I see Newsome has forgotten to include
some brandy on the tea tray," said Miranda. "Why
don't we go to the library and find something else for
you?"

"Thank you, I would like that," said Adam, rising
and escorting her from the room, keeping their ac-

tions formal until they had left their older relatives to a comfortable gossip.

"Is something wrong, my dear?" he asked when they were ensconced in the comfortable, book-lined room, seated on a dark green leather sofa.

"No, of course not, but I fear Aunt Sophie enjoys embarrassing people too much. I suppose she thinks her age gives her license to say anything she pleases," said Miranda.

"Well, I wanted to see you in private anyway," said Adam, reaching inside his coat pocket and handing her the card that she had sent to his house early that morning.

"It's another one," he said, grinning, "but the writer decided to quote a play instead of creating her own poetry."

"I don't recall the play," lied Miranda, who had spent days searching *All's Well That End's Well* and other works for some suitable lines.

Taking back the card, Adam read out loud:

> 'Twere all one
> that I should love a bright particular star
> And think to wed it, he is so above me.
> In his bright radiance and collateral light
> Must I be comforted, not in his sphere.

"A bright particular star . . . very flattering, but what does it mean, Adam?" asked Miranda, watching him closely.

He grinned and shook his head. "I blush to think. But you see, she continues and says all will be revealed at Mother's ball. I find I am quite looking forward to it! That is the main reason I have decided not to choose a bride yet . . . not until I can discover the identity of my mystery admirer."

"You have no idea who it could be?"

He laughed, "Probably some squint-eyed school-girl."

"Perhaps it is Miss Allgood," teased Miranda. "Or Lady Catherine Bingham? Miss Ingleswood?"

"More like your Aunt Sophie, doing this for a lark!" said Adam, making his friend squirm in her seat with his near-accuracy.

"No, it cannot be she. If I can keep nothing from her, then the same is true in reverse. I daresay it is some unexceptional lady who wants to attract your interest."

"She has certainly managed to do that. I couldn't wait to get back to town and see if more letters had been delivered. You will think me vain, but I was a little disappointed when there were none until the one came this morning."

"So you are flattered," she teased.

"A little, I admit. But I am mostly curious. Have you given it any thought? I haven't been able to come up with any possible suspects."

"Nor I."

"I thought it might be that little Miss Everett—you know the one who is not terribly intelligent. But after reading this one, I knew it could not be she. It is too clever for that."

Miranda turned pink with pleasure but agreed soberly with his rationale.

"I suppose you will just have to wait until the St. Valentine's masquerade to discover the identity of your secret admirer," said Miranda smugly.

"Oh, I shall do my best to discover her identity before that! It is two weeks away! You know how impatient I am! And my letter writer promises to give me hints as she progresses toward that date."

"Adam, are you ready to go?" asked the countess from the open doorway.

"Of course, Mother," he said, rising. "Good day, Miranda. The first day the weather turns fine, we'll go for a ride."

"I look forward to it," she said.

***

My lord,

I style my letter thus because I am yours to command. As the Miranda of Mr. Shakespeare's The Tempest *says of her Ferdinand:*

"I might call him a thing divine; for nothing natural I ever saw so noble."

Until we meet on St Valentine's night, when all will be made known to you.

Adieu,
Yr Secret Valentine

"I know what you are thinking, Miranda, and I agree. It is very sentimental, almost maudlin," said Adam, grinning self-consciously as he transferred the reins to his left hand and pocketed the card with his other.

"So now she is your secret Valentine, not just an admirer," teased Miranda, enjoying his discomfiture immensely. She had never known Adam to be unsure of himself. He had always been the leader in their childhood escapades.

Just as Adam had promised, on the first day of fine weather, they set out for a ride in the park. They had waited until afternoon so that the paths would have a chance to dry, and the park was filling with other people eager to escape after the week of dreary cold.

"Is that the latest?" asked Miranda, knowing full well it was not.

"I received another this morning," the earl admitted, watching Miranda out of the corner of his eye. "It was too personal."

Miranda felt a foolish flash of jealousy. She had written the letter, but she feared Adam was building up some vision of this secret admirer to which she could never measure up. He was definitely curious, but what would he say when he discovered that his romantic admirer was none other than his best friend—comfortable, old Miranda? In a rush of apprehension, Miranda realized she could lose Adam completely, as a potential lover *and* as a friend.

"Have there been any hints as to her identity?" she asked.

"Not really, though I do believe she is well acquainted with me; she knows where my home is and something of Somerset," said Adam, eyeing Miranda with some indefinable emotion.

Miranda gave a trill of laughter, and said, "Gudgeon, anyone with a guide book could obtain that information, and much more, if she travels in the same circles socially."

"Yes, I know, but there is something very intimate about the tone of the letters, especially the one I received this morning."

"Just what did it say that was so intimate?" asked Miranda, nodding to Lady Weymouth and her sister as they drove past.

"Nothing in particular," said Adam. How could he tell her that the writer had alluded to an incident that had occurred years ago, when he and some friends had drunk the wine kept in the church; the rector had chased them across a frozen pond and had been neatly upended. He recalled sharing the tale with Miranda long ago, and they had shared a merry laugh. He had instantly suspected her of penning the letter. Now, he studied her wide-eyed air and shook his head. Miranda probably didn't even remember him telling her about it. As for the other boys, several had sisters who might have learned about the incident.

Not that the letter had been specific; no, the writer had mentioned, "laughing until you cried when your father took a birchrod to your backside." If his admirer were one of his friends' sisters . . . The only one Adam could recall was recently married, and he did not trifle with married women. There were no other possibilities.

Except Miranda, of course, and he had at first thought she was making game of him, but what had followed in the letter could not possibly have been written by Miranda. Even now, he carried the card in his pocket; it was almost as if he could feel the card burning into his flesh. He didn't need to extract it in order to recall the words: "I can envision you out there, cold and damp, and I wish I was there to warm you."

"Adam?" said Miranda, bringing him back from his distraction.

"Sorry, Mir. Just trying to sort things out. I suppose we should get back. You're coming to my mother's card party tomorrow night, are you not?"

"Yes. I promised Aunt Sophie I would not embarrass her by asking to play spilikins instead of cards," laughed Miranda.

"I thought it was a jolly good idea," said Adam. "I know the young ladies present enjoyed themselves immensely."

"Yes, I thought so, too, but Aunt Sophie takes her cards seriously. She said that if someone else brought it up, fine, but she didn't want a niece of hers making such a nonsensical suggestion again!"

"Your aunt is an original," said Adam.

"And fortunately, she is also unique," said Miranda.

"Oh, I see quite a bit of her in you, Miranda," he teased. "Sometimes, you are almost as autocratic."

"And sometimes you are incredibly vexing," she retorted as they arrived in front of her modest town house, and a groom came out and grabbed her horse's bridle.

"That is part of my charm," he said, saluting her with his riding crop before cantering away.

Miranda's smile faded as he disappeared from sight.

With a discouraged tread, she made her way inside and joined her aunt in the salon.

"How was your ride?" asked her relative, barely glancing up from the book she was reading.

"Fine."

Aunt Sophie closed her book and set it aside, peering at Miranda over the top of her spectacles all the while.

"I have not inquired, Miranda, merely for the sake of polite conversation," said her aunt. "I only ask because I would like an honest answer. If you do not wish to discuss the matter, then you need merely tell me so."

"I'm sorry, Aunt. I am just out of sorts. You know I am writing to Adam as a secret admirer."

"Yes, and I have never heard of such an absurd notion!"

"But I told you I could not simply blurt out, 'Oh, by the way, I am in love with you.' "

"Very well, so what has happened?"

"I think Adam is becoming very interested in this mysterious letter writer."

"Then it is working better than I thought it would," came Aunt Sophie's grudging reply.

"No, no, it's not! Just because he is interested in *this* letter writer, it doesn't mean he will be delighted to discover *I* am the one writing them!"

"Miranda, you must tell him," said her sensible aunt.

Miranda was in no mood for rational advice. Shaking her head, she left the salon and sought refuge in her room.

She took out the letters she had so carefully planned and read each one, tossing them aside in disgust. What had she been thinking? she demanded.

Adam tore open the letter and quickly digested its contents, grunting in surprise as he read the last line.

"My lord, this will be my last letter; I fear my suit is

doomed to fail, and I will not be able to hide my broken heart."

"Wonder what prompted that." Adam sat up straight and pushed the card away in disgust. His eye fell on the note Miranda had sent his mother, saying she was too unwell to attend the card party that evening.

Sitting up straight, he placed Miranda's and the secret Valentine's letters side by side. Miranda's script was slanted in the opposite direction; still, there was something similar about the letters. He ran his fingers over the paper; both were from the finest stationers. He turned them over. Both had been sealed with red wax, a common enough occurrence.

Frowning, he held the letter close to Miranda's note; the *m*s were the same! Slanted in different directions they might be, but they were definitely the same: the same curls and lines, the same size.

Adam pulled out the other five notes and laid them out side by side by side. Every *m* was the same! With a whoosh of pent-up breath, Adam sat back in his chair and thought back over the past three weeks; since he had announced his intention to wed, Miranda had changed. He hadn't really noticed at first; then there had been a certain reserve in her manner. At times, she had been almost coy with him.

But why the secret letters? Why would she be teasing him so? Machinations were simply not Miranda's style. If she wanted something, she said so. If she had disapproved of his plans to wed, she would have said so. Wouldn't she? he wondered.

Unless . . .

But the thought was too preposterous! He simply couldn't, simply wouldn't, believe it! Miranda had never shown the slightest interest in him in that manner! Could she suddenly want more from him than friendship?

In a fever of curiosity, Adam drew on his overcoat and headed out the door, walking the two blocks to

Miranda's house only to be told that neither lady was at home.

He lingered at the door for a moment. Smiling suddenly, he began to whistle as he tripped down the steps, his pace jaunty as he returned home.

Too sick to attend his mother's card party? More like she was too fainthearted to face him!

He recalled how she had reacted when he had waltzed with Lady Redmonton; he had assumed her displeasure derived from her dislike of the forward widow. But what if she had been truly jealous? If Miranda was expressing her true feelings in the cards she had been writing, she would find it hard to mask them. One of the things he admired most about her was her honesty.

And if it was only a game, she would soon confess; he knew Miranda well enough to know that she couldn't possibly keep a secret for long.

And if it was more? There was only one way to find out. . . .

PART TWO
TURNING THE TABLES

"I tell you, Aunt Sophie, it is a lost cause. Adam will never look on me as a wife," said Miranda.

"But he has asked you to help him choose a costume for the Valentine's ball," said her aunt.

"He has asked me because he wants to appear dashing for his secret admirer when he discovers her identity," said Miranda.

"But that is you!" argued her aunt.

"But he doesn't know that! He'll feel a fool when he discovers that his secret admirer helped him choose a costume to impress her!" Miranda replaced the damp cloth on her forehead and groaned. "It sounds so stupid when I say it, but I do understand what I am saying!"

"Oddly enough, I understand, too," said her aunt, frowning as she pondered the problem besetting her great-niece. "If there is one thing a man cannot tolerate, it is being made to feel foolish. You must on all accounts avoid that!"

"Argh!" growled Miranda, sitting up on the sofa where she had been reclining and rising. The swift movement made her head reel, and she swayed uncertainly for a moment. "I am going to my room."

"The Earl of Marsden," announced Newsome, allowing Adam to pass into the room.

"Have I arrived at an inopportune time?" he asked, noticing Miranda's damp cloth and the slight frown on her brow.

"Not at all," said Miranda, returning to the sofa and indicating the place by her side.

"I was just going upstairs for my afternoon nap," announced Aunt Sophie loudly. "Good-bye."

"Good-bye, Aunt Sophie," said Adam. "Sleep well."

"What brings you this afternoon, Adam?" asked Miranda when they were alone.

"I was concerned about you when you wrote that you were too unwell to attend Mother's card party last night."

"I am better today," she said softly, tucking the damp cloth behind her skirts.

Adam reached around her and pulled it out, holding up the evidence with a raised brow.

"You never have been able to lie to me," he replied. "I will go if you are still unwell."

"No, no, I am merely feeling a little dispirited by this foul weather. I need some diversion to take my mind off, er, things."

"Good, because I want to ask your opinion. I think perhaps I have penetrated the identity of my secret admirer."

"Oh?" asked Miranda, stilling her hands, which she suddenly wanted to wring.

"Yes, I think it must be Lady Redmonton!" announced Adam with flair. "Think on it. You saw how particular she was in her attentions to me at the Weymouth ball. She practically swept me off my feet! I think it must be she! She even mentioned that she had a special costume planned for the Valentine's ball and said she hoped I would take care with my own costume."

"Really?" said Miranda, her downtrodden spirits slipping further toward a dark depression.

"Yes, you remember, I told you that the letters said I was to take special care selecting my costume. That is why I asked you to help. It must be something really dashing! After all, I may be announcing my betrothal!" he declared, pleased with this last bit as Miranda grimaced.

"Very well. What do you want to be? A pirate? Robin Hood?"

"I thought Henry the Eighth would be a good costume," quipped Adam, his remark causing Miranda to regard him in disbelief before she began to laugh hysterically.

"It nee . . . eeed . . . ed . . . only that!"

"Then you'll help?"

"I would be a fool not to do so!"

"Would you like to go for a ride? I know it is quite chilly, but the sun is shining today. We can discuss my costume," he added, as if promising some special treat.

"By all means, then. Just allow me to go upstairs to change."

When they had reached the park, Adam picked up the thread of their conversation, saying, "I wasn't certain until today."

"Why do you say that?" asked Miranda.

"It was the card I received this morning," he confided.

"This morning!" exclaimed Miranda, knowing she had not sent anything to Adam. Taking a deep breath, she strived for calm and asked, "What did it say that told you it was Lady Redmonton?"

"A gentleman never speaks of his conquests," he replied piously, ruining his pose by the wicked grin that followed.

"But by refusing to speak, you do just that," snapped Miranda, thinking she could cheerfully throttle him at the moment.

"Perhaps I overstated the case," he hedged. The last thing he wanted, thought Adam, was to alienate Miranda just when he thought he might be able to drive her to reveal the truth. "It was just something she said, a reference to the Weymouth ball and our waltz."

"Your wal . . ." His mention of that waltz made Miranda grind her teeth, and she added haughtily, "I'm sure I don't wish to know what was said."

"Good, because it would put me to the blush to reveal it," said Adam, gleefully consigning the overbearing Lady Redmonton to the rank of wanton. Let Miranda think on that for a bit, he concluded, kicking his heels and sending his gelding ahead at a trot.

Miranda curbed her mare's impatience and continued to progress at a walk, nibbling at her bottom lip as she digested Adam's disturbing revelation.

How had he received a card today? She certainly hadn't sent it! She pressed a hand to her head, which had suddenly begun to throb again.

Perhaps, she thought, she had forgotten. Perhaps she had given today's Valentine to the footman yesterday with instructions to deliver it this morning. Perhaps . . .

What did it matter? she demanded ruthlessly. Adam had settled on Lady Redmonton. Despite saying he would not rush to choose a bride before the countess's ball, he was doing just that. He was simply too caught up in his search for the author of those dratted cards. He wouldn't stop until he discovered, or thought he had discovered, the author's identity.

Miranda choked back a bitter laugh. How ironic that her letters had led him to Lady Redmonton! How disappointed he would be if he discovered that good old Miranda had written them!

It was just as Aunt Sophie had predicted: Adam couldn't see what was right under his nose!

More disheartened than ever, Miranda loosened her

grip on the reins, and the lively mare closed the gap, quickly catching up with Adam's gelding.

"I was about to ride back for you. Anything wrong, Mir?" he asked, a frown on his forehead as he studied her gloomy face.

"Not at all," said her voice, but the effort at cheerfulness brought tears to her eyes. "I think I should go home, Adam. I believe it was a mistake to come out this morning."

"Of course. I hope you are not coming down with the influenza, my dear," he said, puzzling over the flash of pleasure that touched her eyes, only to disappear quickly.

"No, no, I shall be fine. I suppose I have been burning the candle at both ends of late, and it has caught up with me," she lied, turning her face away from him as she spoke. She would have to store up that mild endearment; he would never dare to speak thus when he had wed the possessive Lady Redmonton.

"Then perhaps we should go home. I want you well enough to go with me to Letitia's ball tomorrow night."

"Lady Redmonton's?"

"Yes, you were invited, were you not?"

"Yes, but I declined," she said, relieved.

"A shame. I find I am quite looking forward to it. But perhaps a night at home, in bed, will put you to rights!" said Adam with that infuriating liveliness.

Fifteen minutes later, as Adam rode away from Miranda's door, he found his own mood had become curiously depressed.

He had been amused to discover the author of his mysterious Valentines was Miranda. If he had reserved any doubts, her odd reaction to his disclosure that he had received a card that morning had erased them. She had been shocked by this revelation. And still she refused to confess, he thought angrily. Perhaps she was playing a joke on him!

Certainly his efforts to discover her motives had been less than successful. Not only was he still unsure of them, but her obvious distress had made him feel the veriest cad!

But the possibility that Miranda might be looking on him in a new light was ludicrous, laughable. They had grown up together as brother and sister. If she hadn't married Sinclair all those years ago . . .

But he had been away, had joined the war effort to fight the little Corsican. He recalled her tears when he had said good-bye; he had felt such a flood of emotion. Perhaps if he had spoken then, she would have waited.

But her father had been anxious for her to wed and had arranged for her marriage a few months later.

His own father's death had brought him back to England only two years later. Miranda was newly widowed, and he had paid her a condolence visit. She had wept in his arms, but there had been nothing else, no hint of desire. For heaven's sake, she was his friend—albeit a very dear friend!

Adam scowled as he rode out of London, his thoughts much too serious to be contained within city streets. He tried to envision life with Miranda as his wife. He had never thought about the fact that her brown hair was long and glossy, had never considered what it might feel like to press his lips to hers. . . .

Yet there had been that one kiss at Christmas, under the mistletoe, when she and Aunt Sophie had come to Marsden Manor after Sinclair had died. She was wearing half-mourning by then, and her lavender gown brought out the green in her eyes; he had found her more attractive than ever, had felt that he was discovering their friendship all over again.

So, under the mistletoe, he had caught her unawares, spinning her about in his arms and holding her captive while he gave her a thorough kiss. Her lips, slightly parted in surprise, had yielded sweetly to his. He had felt a quickening of his senses and had set her away from him quickly, laughing to mask the awkwardness, the rush of emotions. Her wide-eyed gaze had worried him, he remembered. He had feared his impetuous kiss had frightened her.

So he had never repeated the act, had never even kissed her cheek. The flash of emotion he had seen in her eyes on that day—could it have been passion?

Adam shook his head. Could he have been so foolish for the past seven years? But no, she had merely been shocked by his action, by the heat of his kiss. He wondered if she remembered that kiss.

Had she yielded to Sinclair in the same manner? Had she been pretending he was Sinclair? That would explain much. And if Miranda now looked on him in a romantic sense, surely he would have seen some indication, something in her manner, or her eyes.

With a smile, Adam brought to mind those speaking green eyes. Most of the time, he knew what Miranda was thinking before she even spoke. Attending balls and routs, words were usually unnecessary between them when they observed some amusing incident; a mere glance was all it took to communicate.

But this morning, when those wonderful eyes had filled with tears, he had wanted to take her into his arms to comfort her.

Comfort? Was that all he wanted to offer Miranda? This question led to an even more difficult one: What did Miranda want of him?

Adam scowled again. This round-robin line of reasoning, never reaching a conclusion, was intolerable. When there was a problem, he solved it, just as he had the one between the Yardleys and his steward. The Earl of Marsden was a man of action!

Perhaps the dilemma he now faced was not going to be solved so easily, he admitted reluctantly. Part of the problem, as he saw it, was that there might not really be a problem.

"Bah! Devil take it!" he exclaimed, looking around and realizing he was now in the country, well out of London.

Adam loosened the reins, letting Shady Deal have his head. The sunshine, mixed with the pleasure of being on horseback, soon lifted Adam's mood, and he returned to town later with new resolve and new plans.

Miranda tried to wallow in her own troubles, but her obstinate nature betrayed her, forcing her to climb out of her bed, out of despair, and face facts. If she wanted Adam to consider her as a possible bride, she would have to learn to flirt with him. Such was not in her nature, but with grim determination, she resolved to learn.

She pulled out the next Valentine card and read it before giving it to her footman, who would find an urchin to deliver it for a farthing. It was sentimental drivel, perhaps, but it wouldn't do to allow someone else to steal her idea, intriguing Adam with daily cards until his mother's ball. He might receive two each day, but there was surely no harm in keeping him guessing. He would have to realize they weren't both sent by Lady Redmonton!

That evening, she dragged Aunt Sophie to the ball given by Lady Redmonton. She had sent her regrets earlier, but now she had a purpose for attending the forward widow's ball.

Miranda's newest ball gown, which had at one time possessed two rows of ruching around the neckline, had been transformed into a daring statement. Looking at her image doubtfully, Miranda hoped the message did not ensnare other unwanted attention in her net.

"How fine you look tonight," said Aunt Sophie.

"You do not think this gown too daring?" asked Miranda, glancing briefly at her aunt before returning to her self-study.

"Certainly not! You will have three times the covering of most of the young women! I have long said your mode of dress was too puritanical!"

"Hardly puritanical, Aunt. Conservative perhaps," said Miranda.

"But what has made you change your style for this evening? I seem to recall some extra ruching on that gown when you ordered it from Madame Celeste."

"Really, Aunt, we do not have time to discuss fashion now. We will be late!" said Miranda, allowing her maid to settle an ermine-lined satin cloak on her shoulders.

Lady Redmonton, as the mother of the three-year-old Lord Redmonton, lived in an extravagant town house in Regent's Street. Her entertainments were always lavish, bordering on ostentatious. This evening, her theme was spring, and the room was swathed in yellow silk with green palms and hundreds of yellow flowers—roses, daffodils, and tulips—gracing the tables on the edges of the ballroom.

As Aunt Sophie and Miranda surveyed the assembly in the ballroom, the elder lady raised one brow and muttered, "Must have emptied every hothouse in a one-hundred-mile radius of London. I shall probably sneeze all night!"

"No, you will not," said Miranda firmly, hiding her smile behind her fan. "I have things to accomplish tonight."

"Aha! I thought as much. And here comes your quarry, unless I am much mistaken."

"Sh!" whispered Miranda, lowering her fan and smiling brightly at Adam.

He looked her up and down, his dark eyes lighting appreciatively. Taking her hand and bowing, he said, "Well worth the wait, my dear." He released her hand and gallantly performed the same office for Aunt Sophie.

"Prettily said, Marsden," commented the spinster, favoring him with one of her rare smiles. With a wave of her hand, she asked, "Has our hostess put in an appearance yet? I am all agog to see her getup; I wager she is wearing the brightest yellow gown here!"

"Not at all," said Adam, suppressing his amusement but winking at Miranda. "She is wearing pink. I would imagine, before the guests arrived, the effect was all she could wish. A single pink rose amid a sea of yellow. Now, of course, she is only one of many roses, my ladies included."

"If you do not temper your compliments, Marsden, we will suspect you have turned Irish on us and kissed the blarney!" said Aunt Sophie, rapping his arm with her lorgnette playfully.

Miranda gaped and barely managed to restrain her laughter at Adam's surprised countenance. Aunt Sophie never, ever flirted, but there was little doubt that she was doing just that at the moment.

Miranda hid her gurgle of laughter by saying gaily, "There is certainly a crush of people for February."

"Indeed, I made just such a comment, and two people said they had come to town expressly for this ball and my mother's next week."

"Next week? Is it really so soon?"

"Only five days now," said Adam, smiling tenderly as a blush covered her features. If only he could be certain he wouldn't damage their friendship forever, he would take her in his arms then and there and put her mind to rest. A flash of impatience crossed his features; how he hated artifice!

"Come along, ladies," he said, offering an arm to each of them. "What would you like to do first, Aunt Sophie, watch the dancing or cards?"

"I think I'll watch the dancing for a while. I see your mother over there, if you'll be so kind as to escort me to her."

"Only if you assure me that I cannot persuade you to take a turn around the dance floor with me."

She trilled a girlish laugh and waggled a finger at him. "You are being a naughty boy tonight!"

Adam leaned close to her ear and whispered something, sending Aunt Sophie into the whoops.

"Naughty, I say!"

After Miranda had greeted the countess and seen her aunt settled, she accepted Adam's invitation for the next dance, a waltz. They had danced together hundreds of times, even performed the waltz on a dozen or more occasions, but this time it was different. Adam felt his palms growing moist, and he was glad he wore gloves. He placed one hand at her waist and clasped her hand in his, sweeping them onto the floor for the energetic steps of the waltz.

Miranda felt her smile grow fixed and wished she had not removed the protective ruching from her gown. What would he think of her! She, who had never worn a daring gown in her life!

"You look beautiful tonight," said Adam, his words eliminating Miranda's doubts instantaneously, and she smiled.

"Thank you, Adam," she replied. "It is a new gown."

"And a beautiful one," he said, allowing his eyes to linger on the swell of her breasts a moment before returning his gaze to her face. "Something about green on you, Miranda. A man could forget himself completely."

Her smile widened and she relaxed, giving herself up to the pleasure of being in his embrace; their movements were so closely attuned, she had no need to concentrate on the steps. In silence, they progressed around the floor, each lost in his own thoughts. Miranda couldn't recall a time when she had felt more at home; Adam reflected that he had never realized how beautiful his friend really was, or how much he enjoyed the feel of her in his arms. She fit there so perfectly.

But the music came to an end, and they were forced back to reality, a reality that included Lady Redmonton. Their promenade was interrupted by her appearance at Adam's side.

"My dear Marsden, I hope you will come to my rescue. There is a tradesman in the kitchens who refuses to leave without payment! Have you ever heard of such impudence?"

Adam, angry to have his time with Miranda cut short, asked curtly, "Do you already owe the man money?"

"No, of course not! Really, Marsden, if you could just speak to him! You understand how it is, a widow often is the victim of such impudent tradesmen!"

"Go on, Adam," said Miranda. "I will see how your mother and Aunt Sophie are faring."

"If you're certain . . . Very well, my lady, lead on."

When they arrived in the kitchens, there was no irate tradesman waiting, no one but surprised kitchen staff, who looked decidedly relieved when their mistress turned to leave.

"I am so sorry," purred Lady Redmonton as they returned to the ballroom. "I suppose the threat of my bringing a real man to deal with him sent him scurrying off."

"So it seems," agreed Adam dryly, scanning the room for Miranda.

"Only listen, they are playing another waltz!" she exclaimed.

"So they are," said Adam, who had already danced one time with Lady Redmonton upon his arrival.

Dancing twice with the same lady would bring his intentions to the attention of the assembly. Two dances was not quite improper, especially since Lady Redmonton was a widow, but he didn't want his name linked with hers permanently! Gazing out across the dancers

already on the floor, Adam discovered Miranda on the
arm of another friend, the handsome Lord Picton. He
felt a stirring of some undefined emotion and turned
impulsively to the willowy widow at his side.

"Would you care to take the floor with me, my lady?"

"I would be delighted, Marsden!" she cooed, taking
possession of his arm as though the rest was soon to
follow.

From the way Lady Redmonton pressed closer to
him as they waltzed, though she offered a laughing
apology for the crush of the dance floor, Adam realized she would willingly share the rest with him, marriage or not. But the idea of a liaison, even a fleeting
one, with the widow held no appeal at all to him. What
he had once found attractive in the woman, he could
not now recall, but his gaze fell on Miranda as she
swept past in Picton's embrace, and the muscle in his
jaw tightened imperceptibly.

"You are so commanding," Lady Redmonton whispered, leaning against his chest with great daring.

His eyes following Miranda's progress, Adam failed
to answer; taking this as encouragement, Lady Redmonton leaned her head on his shoulder. This action
brought him to attention, and Adam set her away from
him, finishing their waltz in a more circumspect fashion.

But the damage was done. Miranda, peering through
the swirling bodies, caught sight of their closeness, and
her temper flared. How dare he! Paying her compliments one moment and practically bedding Lady Redmonton in public the next! She had thought better of
Adam! Perhaps she had been mistaken in other matters as well!

But as Miranda kept up a polite conversation with
Picton about his children, she watched Adam and the
widow promenading most properly. Except, of course,
that Letitia Redmonton had no shame and was pressing against Adam's arm possessively.

"I think we are too far away to catch them up," drawled Lord Picton.

"I'm sure I don't know what you mean, my lord."

"I mean Marsden and Lady Redmonton, of course. You have been watching them throughout our waltz. You realize she plans to have him; they're even betting on it in the clubs," he confided.

"Really?" said Miranda, trying her best to infuse complete indifference into that one word. But she fooled no one, not even herself.

"Yes, really," replied Lord Picton with a smile. "My wife always said that you should make a push for him yourself."

"Really?" she asked again, meeting his merry eyes before lowering her gaze. "I doubt Adam would agree."

"Then the man's a fool, Mrs. Sinclair. I would court you myself if I didn't suspect you and Marsden . . . but I am being impertinent. Come, I'll return you to your aunt. Or would you prefer something to drink? I must admit I could stand a glass of something before squiring Lord Tellson's wife about the floor for the boulanger in a few moments."

Miranda shot him a quizzical glance, and he grinned, explaining, "Politics can make a man do quite strange things."

"Then let us find some champagne, by all means," laughed Miranda, accepting his arm as he led her away.

"I must admit I miss my wife inordinately at this sort of affair," said Lord Picton.

"Sarah always loved balls and parties," commented Miranda, smiling sympathetically.

"Yes. It has been three years, and I still miss her. But at least I have the children. I really do appreciate the interest you have taken in them, Mrs. Sinclair."

"But they are delightful!" she exclaimed. "Besides, I want to become friends with my little namesake.

Manda is a delightful little girl, so smart for six years old."

"Yes, I need to find a governess for her while I am in London. It's just that I don't quite know how to go about it. I have no one to ask either. My sister has only boys, and besides, her idea of discipline is much too stringent for me!"

"Oh, no, with a sensitive child like Manda, you need someone kind and lively," said Miranda. "If you wish, I could ask one of my other friends who has daughters how she found her governess."

"That would be wonderful. And," he added hesitantly, "I hate to ask, but could you possibly help me interview some of the candidates?"

"Certainly, though you must know I have no experience with children."

"But you did have a governess, didn't you?"

"Certainly. Miss Broom was a wonderful teacher!"

"There, you see, you do have experience," he said, smiling down at her. "At least you know what needs to be taught and what qualities to look for in a governess, and I know Sarah would approve of you helping choose Manda's teacher."

"Very well, I would be delighted to be of service," said Miranda, bowing her head slightly at the mention of her old friend. How she missed her! Sarah would have been able to advise her about Adam.

"But come, we mustn't spend the entire evening talking about my children. Tell me more about you. What have you been doing with yourself lately?" he asked politely.

"Since I visited you and Sarah almost four years ago, my life is virtually unchanged," said Miranda with a self-deprecating laugh.

"Perhaps and perhaps not," said the handsome lord, cocking his head toward the doorway to the supper room where they chatted. Adam scowled at them as he closed on them quickly.

"I wondered what had happened to you, Miranda," said Adam.

"We have just been discussing governesses and lessons," said Miranda, adding airily, "The last time I looked, you were well occupied elsewhere."

"Looks can be deceiving," said Adam dryly. "How are you, Picton?"

"Well. And you?"

"Couldn't be better. How is the session going?"

"It's a tricky time, Marsden, as you know. I'm concerned about these reform issues, especially this suspension of the Habeas Corpus Act."

"Who isn't? I daresay even speaking of the reform issues is enough to warrant a visit to gaol," said Adam. "I voted against it, but the Cabinet was too powerful."

"Nothing good will come of it, I am certain. But we shouldn't mix politics with such delightful company as Mrs. Sinclair. Have you come to take her away for a dance?" asked Picton.

Adam knew he shouldn't; he had danced only five times that evening, twice with Lady Redmonton and once with Miranda. Another dance might call his honor into question; to single out two ladies in one evening was certainly not good form. But she was waiting, watching him.

"If she would honor me," he said, returning the smile that instantly sprang to her lips.

"I would love to, Adam," forgiving him in that instant for his attentions to their hostess.

This set was a quadrille, an unexceptional dance that left each couple spending almost as much time apart as they did together. Miranda and Adam made up one quarter of a square, and each time they met, their conversation was light and pleasant.

Supper was to be served after the quadrille, and Miranda had the pleasure of knowing she would have Adam by her side.

When they were seated with plates filled from a

sumptuous buffet, Miranda asked, "Did you receive any more Valentines today?"

"Yes, as a matter of fact I did."

"How many?"

"Only the one," replied Adam, his dark eyes dancing with mischief.

Miranda dropped her gaze, pretending a great interest in her food, and so missed the opportunity to read his intentions. Looking up from her plate briefly, she asked, "Well, are you not going to tell me what it said?"

"It was a little different from the last one, sweeter and not as, er, warm," he said. "I am less sure that it is Lady Redmonton."

"Oh?"

"Perhaps that is not correct," he added thoughtfully, trying to gauge her reaction. "Perhaps it would be more accurate to say I hope it is not Lady Redmonton."

Miranda felt a flood of relief wash over her and favored him with a sunny smile just as the lady in question was conjured up, appearing at Adam's elbow and bending close to his ear, whispering some confidence.

Looking up, Lady Redmonton gave Miranda a syrupy smile that did not reach her eyes. "You don't mind if I steal dear Marsden for a few minutes, do you?"

So saying, she turned and walked away, pausing when she realized Adam was not on her heels. Shooting him a seductive, damsel-in-distress look, she saw him shake his head and rise.

"Sorry, Mir, but she has no one else to ask."

"That's all right, Adam. I don't mind," said Miranda, managing to school her features to polite coolness.

Miranda turned to her left and joined the conversation of several other acquaintances without another look at Adam's retreating figure.

She didn't see him again until the second set after supper. Where he had been, and where their hostess

had been, Miranda didn't wish to guess. Speculation
on the subject only led her to dejection and anger.
Odd, she thought, that until she had decided she was
in love with Adam, she had had no problem with lack
of confidence.

But there he was, on the other side of the ballroom
with Lady Redmonton, who was looking very self-satis-
fied indeed.

Miranda turned expectantly to the gentleman on
her right, the brother of one of her friends. She raised
her brows, and he immediately asked for her hand for
the cotillion forming.

Miranda suffered through the dance, trying not to
watch Adam, who was watching her. Unfortunately, his
head was often bent to listen to Lady Redmonton, who
remained firmly entrenched by his side.

How, she wondered, could he profess to be glad his
secret admirer was not Lady Redmonton when he so
obviously enjoyed her company? Didn't he realize that
engaging her in conversation for this dance, their third
of the evening, was tantamount to asking for her hand
in marriage?

The thought, once formed, would not go away, and
Miranda felt a curious nausea growing in the pit of
her stomach. She smiled and nodded, saying the odd
word to her partner as she became physically ill over
the thought of Adam wedding Lady Redmonton. As
soon as the music ended, Miranda excused herself and
fled.

The ladies' withdrawing room was full, and she
backed away, almost desperate for a few minutes of
solitude to regain her composure. Every room on this
floor of the narrow house was in use; she toyed with
the idea of joining her aunt in the card room, but she
had no desire to play or to spoil Aunt Sophie's enjoyment. Looking across the ballroom, she saw the tall
glass doors leading to the balcony.

Moving along the edge of the room, she gained her

objective and slipped out the doors into the cold, starry night. She pulled her thin shawl closer, but the cold soon penetrated the fabric, leaving her shivering and her teeth chattering. From inside, she heard the strains of yet another waltz. *Probably he is dancing with her,* she thought dismally.

"Miranda? What the devil are you doing outside? You'll catch your death of cold!" exclaimed Adam.

"I . . . I'm n . . . ot co . . . ld," she said.

"Rubbish," he replied gruffly, taking his gloved hands and rubbing her bare arms vigorously.

His touch sent more chills up and down her spine, and Miranda began to shiver uncontrollably. Adam threw his arms around her, pulling her into his warm embrace. She sighed and rested her head against his chest. It felt so right to be in his arms like this, she thought, her breath catching on a chill that made her body shudder.

"We must go back inside," Adam growled.

"No, I cannot bear it another minute," she managed to say, her voice muffled by his chest.

"Why, Miranda? Why can you not bear it?" he demanded, his tone rough with impatience and a growing desire to hear her voice her need for him.

But Miranda only shook her head.

Behind him, Adam heard the doors open. Immediately he took her hands, placing one on his shoulder and holding the other as he began to dance. Whispering, he said, "We are being observed. Better they think we are waltzing than sharing a clandestine embrace."

The strains of the waltz mingled with the cold air, warming her from within, and she stopped shivering. The voices from the ballroom faded, and Miranda clung to Adam, their bodies almost touching as they progressed around the narrow stone terrace.

This is our third dance, a warning voice kept whispering in her mind, *our third dance.* As the first inner voice whispered, *caution,* another louder voice answered with a line from Mr. Shakespeare's *Romeo and Juliet: ". . . not for the world. In truth, dear Montague, I am too fond."*

When the music stopped, Adam looked down at her, his expression unreadable in the shadows. Dropping his hands, he bowed formally and said distinctly, for all to hear, "Our third dance, Mrs. Sinclair. I fear now we will have to announce our betrothal."

Miranda staggered away from his words, her movement taking her into the pool of light from the candles inside. Several faces peered out the door, watching the spectacle with great interest.

"No!" she cried, wheeling and stumbling through the crowd, forcing herself to slow her gait and walk with her head held high as she sought her aunt and dragged her from the card room.

"What is it, child?" Aunt Sophie demanded.

"May I be of service," asked Lord Picton, rising from his place at the card table.

Though Miranda shook her head, he followed them from the room, calling for their cloaks and carriage.

"Thank you, my lord," murmured Miranda, her expression strained but composed.

"Please allow me to escort you home, ladies," said Picton.

"That won't be necessary," said Miranda with a slight smile that threatened to overset her poise. "You have been most kind, but we will be fine now."

The trio started down the front steps. There was Adam, regarding Miranda with cool detachment for a moment before he glared at Lord Picton and shouldered his way in to help both ladies into their vehicle.

When she was seated, Miranda leaned toward the opening and said coldly, "Come along, Lord Picton."

Masking his surprise, he pushed past the earl and climbed inside the carriage, shutting the door as he took the seat facing the ladies.

Adam placed one foot on the step, pulling himself

level with the window and leaning close, saying, "We will speak of this later, Miranda."

As the carriage rolled down the street, Miranda muttered, "The devil we will!"

Her audience exchanged surprised looks but said not a word.

Cowardice did not exist for Miranda, and she faced the morning callers with intrepid bravado the next day. There appeared to be a legion of them, word having spread rapidly through the Ton about the unusual parting of the Earl of Marsden and his boon companion, Mrs. Sinclair. Not only the ladies arrived, but their gentlemen as well, bent on discovering the latest gossip so they would know how to place their wagers at the club. Speculation had been rampant that Marsden would take Lady Redmonton, either for wife or mistress, but this latest development brought new possibilities to bear.

Miranda smiled and chatted; Aunt Sophie sent to Gunter's for more delicacies to feed their gathering of rumormongers. Lord Picton arrived at two o'clock and managed to oust the persistent grande dame on Miranda's right.

As he accepted a cup of tea, he whispered, "Would you like to cause even more of a stir? Excuse yourself, and go for a drive with me."

"I dare not," said Miranda.

"Why?" he asked bluntly, surveying the room full of people, chirping like hungry birds, waiting for some crumb of gossip to fall. "At least a drive with me would confound them."

Miranda smiled and nodded, replying, "Let me tell Aunt Sophie where I am going."

With her announcement, a hush fell over the visitors; as the door closed on her, she heard the buzz begin again, louder and more persistent this time.

Miranda breathed a deep sigh of relief when they reached the park. A poke bonnet on her head and bundled up in a mannish greatcoat that the cold could not penetrate, Miranda's eyes were bright with pleasure as the two horses trotted rapidly along the road.

A few moments later, Lord Picton slowed his cattle and turned his attention from the road to smile down at her.

"Isn't this much better?" he asked.

"Yes, much! Thank you for rescuing me, my lord," she said.

"You could call me Picton, you know. Or even Gerald, when we are alone like this," he offered.

"I could," said Miranda, blushing in confusion.

"We should become better acquainted, Miranda," he said. "Do you mind if I call you Miranda? Only when no one is about to hear, of course."

"I suppose not. I wouldn't wish to give anyone the wrong idea," she added, giving him a speaking look.

He returned his attention to his horses, nodding slowly as he said, "Ah, sits the wind in that corner. I should have guessed. I thought perhaps . . ."

She slipped one gloved hand from her fur muff and laid it on his arm, saying, "I *am* sorry. I do hope I have not given you the impression . . ."

"No, no, my dear Mrs. Sinclair, think nothing of it," he replied, transferring the reins to one hand and covering her hand with his briefly.

"Good afternoon!" came a hearty greeting, causing the two occupants of the carriage to spring apart guiltily as Picton reined in his pair.

Adam glared at them both before adding conversationally, "Cold day for a drive."

"Or a ride," replied Miranda tartly, looking pointedly to the cloud of frosted air issuing from his restless gelding's nose and mouth.

"Good afternoon, Marsden," said Picton, slipping an arm around Miranda's shoulder and pulling her close. " 'Fraid we can't stop; wouldn't do to let the horses cool down."

Adam missed Miranda's shocked expression as he scowled at Lord Picton, snarling, "Then good afternoon to you." With a nod, he cantered away, leaving Miranda gasping for air.

"What did you do that for?" she demanded, rounding on her escort and jerking away from him.

Picton grinned. "Won't hurt for that thick-headed simpleton to feel a little jealousy himself."

"Really! Of all the childish . . ." Miranda's ire cooled rapidly as she recalled Adam's outraged reaction to seeing Lord Picton's arm around her in that possessive manner. A slight smile formed on her lips, and she looked over to find Picton grinning at her.

"Well, perhaps a little jealousy," she said.

"That's the spirit!" he replied, picking up the reins and continuing their drive.

When Miranda finally arrived home, after sharing a cup of tea at Gunter's, the salon was clear of the curious and the meddlers. Miranda heaved a sigh of relief, but her ordeal was not over.

Aunt Sophie eyed her narrowly and demanded, "I haven't said a word about what went on last night, Miranda. Indeed, I have avoided all reference to it, but I have heard enough this afternoon to have developed a great curiosity. It is all well and good to fall in love with Marsden, even to marry him, but somehow you have managed to ruin your good name in the space of a single evening."

"Please, Aunt, I don't want to think about it. Besides, some other scandal will soon take the fancy of the Polite World, and we may be at peace again."

"But I heard he asked you to marry him!" exclaimed Aunt Sophie. "Isn't that what you want?"

"I will answer you with a question, Aunt. If a man

approached you, even the man you loved, and said, and I quote, 'I fear now we will be forced to announce our betrothal,' how would you answer him?"

"But Miranda, surely you can sort that out later. I'm certain Marsden didn't mean it the way it sounded."

"Nevertheless, how would you respond?"

Aunt Sophie's gray head bowed for a moment before she looked Miranda straight in the eye and said, "I answered no the first time. Given a second chance, I would turn back the clock and answer yes."

Miranda gasped; she knew her aunt's single state had been at the center of some scandal years before she was born. Her grandfather had sometimes alluded to it, whenever he was displeased with his sister, but she had never guessed their situations would be so similar.

After a moment, Miranda shook her head, saying, "Perhaps, Aunt, but I cannot say yes to such a proposal." She rose and walked slowly to the door.

Her aunt's chilling comment followed her from the room. "I only hope you and your pride do not regret your decision, my dear girl."

Only four days remained before St. Valentine's Day and Lady Marsden's celebrated masquerade. Miranda spent them alone and miserable. The visitors continued to arrive for two more days before they finally gave up all hope of learning anything from the reticent Sophie Grantham. As for Miranda, she refused all visitors after that first day.

She had little to say to Aunt Sophie, but she continued to send the cards to Adam each day. Somewhere in her heart, hope lived on that he would look on her with love in his eyes. Her mind scoffed; nevertheless, she sent the card each day, both intriguing her old friend and annoying him.

As for Adam, he was fed up with her games. He had decided to wed her; wasn't that what she wanted?

Wasn't that the purpose behind all those silly Valentine cards that continued to arrive with annoying regularity? Surely she didn't expect romance from him. They were friends, for heaven's sake!

But after two days without seeing Miranda, Adam reluctantly admitted to himself that he missed her. She played such a large role in his life.

He re-read those cards, chuckling at the poetry, at her choice of quotations. Mostly he found himself bereft without Miranda's sunny presence. He began to wonder if there was anything he could do to win her.

So far, the only thing that seemed to work was jealousy. He would not try to make her jealous with Lady Redmonton again. That had proven disastrous. No, not Lady Redmonton, but a new plan began to form in his mind.

Miranda had no idea that he had guessed the Valentine cards were from her. If she did, he felt certain she would not have continued to send them. With luck, he should be able to turn this to his advantage.

After the third day, Miranda relented and sent Adam a note requesting that he visit her at eleven o'clock in the morning, the day before his mother's ball. He arrived promptly and was ushered into the warm salon by Newsome. Miranda was expecting him, a tray with hot coffee and some of his favorite biscuits on the table in front of her.

"Good morning, my dear," Adam said, crossing the room in three long strides and joining her on the sofa. He lifted her hand to his lips and waited for her to make the next move.

She was looking wretched indeed, despite the elegant gown of soft yellow wool crepe. It could not mask the circles under her eyes or the lack of animation in her movements.

"Good morning, Adam. I trust you are well," came her stilted reply.

"Yes, very well. And you?"

"I'm fine," replied Miranda. "Would you care for a cup of coffee?" She stole a glance at him, her eyes searching his face for a split second before they came to rest again on his neatly tied cravat.

"Yes, please. Dreadful weather we have been having," he said, grimacing. Since when had the weather, that staple of polite conversation, seemed the only safe topic between them?

"Absolutely awful. I suppose your mother is worried that it will prevent people from attending her ball tomorrow night."

"Never fear. It would take more than a little rain or snow to keep our guests away. Would you like for me to escort you and your aunt?" he asked, and Miranda smiled for the first time.

"Certainly not! You only want to sneak a peek at my costume!" she replied tartly, some of her old fire igniting again.

"The better to keep an eye on you, my dear," he said, returning her smile. "No, no, I just know there has been much unrest in the streets of late. I would hate for you to run into trouble."

"I have been reading about that in the newspapers. All those petitions; do you think they will do any good?"

"I'm not sure. They have certainly given those in Parliament something to think about," he said, cursing the constrained conversation they were having. "But you see why I would feel better if I called to escort you, Miranda."

"You are very kind, Adam, but I shall be quite safe with Aunt Sophie. She could take on an entire mob and never have a hair out of place."

"She is formidable. Where is she this morning?"

"She is closeted with the housekeeper," said Mi-

randa. "I particularly wanted to see you alone, Adam."
He waited for her to continue.

"I thought I should clear up any misunderstanding
about the other night," she said quietly.

"The other night?" he inquired obliquely.

"Yes. We cannot pretend it didn't happen."

"What? The waltz? The embrace? The proposal?"

"That takes care of it all," said Miranda, giving him
a fleeting smile before she continued torturing the
hapless linen napkin she held, pleating it, twisting it,
knotting it. "You see, Adam, I didn't want you to think
you had to offer for me. I mean, we are friends. We
wouldn't want to lose that, would we?"

"No, Miranda, we certainly wouldn't," said Adam,
stilling her hands by placing his larger one on top of
hers. "If there is one thing I can say for certain, it is
that I value our friendship too much to allow this to
come between us. I do wonder, however, why you
turned me down."

Miranda's pride had been wounded grievously, but
she couldn't tell Adam that. To do so would be to
inflict further wounds on it. So she crossed her fingers
in her skirt and said solemnly, "If I should marry
again, Adam, this time I would want it to be for love.
You may call me silly if you wish, but I will not wed
without love."

"I thought you married Sinclair for love," he said
quietly.

"No, though I grew fond of him in time. And, setting that reason aside," she added, her eyes twinkling
in her old, friendly manner, "I would never marry a
lout who cannot even give a girl a proper proposal! 'I
fear,' indeed!"

Adam had the grace to grin at this. "It was rather
poorly done, wasn't it? But you must make allowances
for me; it is my first, remember."

"It was not just that, Adam. Don't you think our
friendship places us beyond social conventions? I

mean, everyone has come to accept that we are just friends, haven't they? Why should we wed simply because we were together for three dances?"

"Perhaps you are right. It does seem a pretty poor reason to wed," agreed Adam.

"I didn't hear you offering for Lady Redmonton, and I know you spent three dances with her," sniffed Miranda.

"Hardly!"

"What a whisker, Adam! Everyone knows you did!"

"I most certainly did not. Two I will admit to, but I never danced a third time with her!"

"Yes, you did, just before I went outside onto the balcony," she said, her eyes flashing angrily.

Adam shook his head, scowling at her . . . just like old times. Finally, he snapped his fingers and said, "I know what it was. I went to the card room to try to shake her off. It didn't work very well; she followed me and watched me like a hawk while I took my mother's place for a hand of piquet."

"Really?" asked Miranda eagerly, her smile breaking forth again.

"Yes, really. Look, Mir, I have no wish to be wed to Lady Redmonton. It wouldn't matter how many times I danced with her! You know what's she's like. A fellow couldn't rest wondering what she was up to next!"

Miranda raised a brow as he added softly, "Besides, I don't love her."

Snow fell throughout the night before the St. Valentine's masquerade, blanketing the streets and turning London into a beautiful, pristine wonderland. Commerce remained brisk, but no one who could avoid it ventured forth, preferring to gaze upon the scene from the warmth of the fireside.

In the afternoon, the skies cleared, and the sun bathed the city in bright crystals. The temperature remained well below the freezing mark and the white blanket, except for a few slushy ruts in the roads, remained pure, a fitting backdrop for the countess of Marsden's ball.

With the house full of out-of-town guests and relatives, Adam found it difficult to seize a few moments alone to read the card that arrived in the morning mail. Shutting the door to his study with a sigh of relief, he tore open the envelope eagerly. Perhaps Miranda would finally confess that she was his not-so-secret admirer. But the card was much the same, containing a snippet of poetry and a promise that all would be revealed that night. He would know her, it said, by her costume, and continued on with a detailed description.

A plan began to form in Adam's mind. It was almost too diabolical, he thought, grinning. But the result would be perfect! If the purpose behind Miranda's cards had been to win his love, then it was only proper that his plan would teach her a well-deserved lesson. If, on the other hand, the cards were part of some practical joke, then the plan would show he had not been fooled.

It was too clever! he thought, pocketing Miranda's card and striding out the door, calling for one of his visiting cousins.

Aunt Sophie's only concession to the masquerade was a half-mask which did little to hide her identity. But as she tartly told her niece, no one cared what an old lady wore.

Miranda perched on the seat in front of her dressing table while her maid styled her hair, sweeping it into a mound of curls on top of her head and allowing a few tendrils to frame her mistress's face. Annie studied the effect with an artist's eye, tut-tutting as she tweaked it here and there before pronouncing it perfect.

"You'll be the belle of the ball, ma'am," said the older woman fondly.

Miranda smiled, saying, "I believe you are prejudiced, Annie, but I accept your compliment gladly. Could you tie this ribbon around my neck?"

The maid took the red velvet choker, shaking her head in wonder. "I don't know where Madame Celeste found a heart-shaped diamond," she said.

"I think she had it especially cut, but it is glass, not a diamond."

"It sure sparkles like one, ma'am. It's just perfect with the silver embroidery on your skirt."

"I think it will do," said Miranda, rising and allowing the maid to help her step into her costume.

She waited patiently while her maid fastened the tiny row of buttons up the back, not daring to look in the glass until this task was complete.

"There you are, ma'am," said the maid, stepping away so her mistress could get the full effect of her image in the cheval glass.

Miranda smiled, her green eyes sparkling. "It is perfect!"

"Indeed it is," said Annie, stepping forward and smoothing a panel of the organdy overskirt.

Miranda touched the double curves of the neckline; her hand trailed down the scarlet-colored velvet to the pointed *V* at the waistline.

"It really does look like a heart," she murmured.

The full skirt, bolstered by layers of petticoats, fell almost to the floor, leaving her red velvet slippers peeking out saucily.

"Don't forget these, ma'am," said Annie, handing Miranda the short white satin gloves and her red-velvet half-mask.

"Thank you, Annie," said Miranda, smiling despite her nervousness.

"Are you ready, Mir . . . ?" called Aunt Sophie from the doorway.

"Yes, I'm ready," she said.

"You look absolutely beautiful!" said the old lady impulsively. Then, in more characteristic tones, she added, "If Marsden doesn't notice you tonight, he really is a dunderhead!"

"Aunt Sophie!" exclaimed Miranda, laughing.

When they arrived at the front door, Newsome handed an envelope to Miranda, saying, "This just arrived for you, ma'am."

"Thank you," she replied, taking the letter and moving toward the candle sconce on the wall.

Dear Miranda,

I look forward to seeing you tonight. I have wonderful news!

Marsden

"Who is it from?" asked her aunt impatiently.

"It's just a note from Marsden. It seems he has some wonderful news to impart." She gave a nervous laugh as the butler helped her with her black satin cloak.

"Dunderhead," muttered her aunt, though Miranda chose not to respond.

The lights shining from the Marsden town house turned the street below into a sparkling fairyland; even Aunt Sophie smiled and commented on the beauty of the scene. After several minutes, it was their turn to descend and hurry into the warmth of the house.

The aromas of cinnamon and apples dominated the hall as they greeted their hostess. Of Marsden, there was no sign.

"Where is the boy?" asked Aunt Sophie of her friend.

"I have no idea. From what he has told me, I understand he plans to slip into the ballroom with no one the wiser. He even refused to tell me what his costume was to be," laughed the countess. "How he hoped to keep it secret from all the relatives we have staying here, I don't know. You look charming, Miranda, my dear."

"Thank you," she replied. "I suppose it is no use trying to keep my identity a secret when Aunt Sophie is so obviously Aunt Sophie."

"Oh, get along with you, child, and enjoy yourself," said her unrepentant aunt.

"I will!" vowed Miranda, tripping down the three steps and disappearing into the crowd of masqued revelers.

She quickly realized finding Adam was going to prove more difficult than she had at first supposed. She wished suddenly that she had not quarreled with him. Then she could have had a hand in helping him choose a costume.

A French musketeer swept off his plumed hat, greeting her with a grand bow and blocking her way.

"Zee preetty lady, she vants to dance *avec* me?" he asked, his accent somewhere between French and German.

Miranda laughed and shook her head, saying, "A charming invitation, *mon ami,* but perhaps later, yes?"

"I shall look forward to it," he said in more sensible tones.

Bent on finding Adam, Miranda received several more invitations as she circulated through the room, some proper and some more scandalous. It never ceased to amaze her how a costume and mask, neither of which was sufficient to hide the identity of the wearer completely, induced people to leave their manners—and for some, their morals—at home!

She looked up to see the proper Lord Ravenwood stealing a kiss from a young shepherdess who squealed and slapped at his straying hands playfully. Unless she was much mistaken, the shepherdess was none other than Miss Allgood, who would never, under normal circumstances, have encouraged such behavior.

"What makes you frown so, my lady? Do you need some dragon slain? Your wish is my command," said a knight in full armor, clanking as he tried to bow. His visor slammed shut, and he gave a muffled curse as he struggled to open it.

"Lord Picton?" asked Miranda in wonder, laughing when he nodded, and his visor snapped closed again.

"Here, let me help," said Miranda, reaching up and tugging at the offending headgear. "There! I daresay it won't last, but at least you can breathe for the moment."

"Thank you, fair damsel," he intoned, managing a smile and a nod before the visor closed yet again. "Argh! I've got to get this dashed thing off," he said, tugging at the helmet.

Miranda reached up to help, and he placed it on the empty tray of a passing footman before turning back to Miranda.

"I apologize for my language, Mrs. Sinclair. This seemed like a wonderful idea when little Manda suggested it, but I can readily see that it is less than conducive to dancing," he said, re-tying the half-mask he had been wearing under the helmet.

"No, I fear you will clank something dreadful," she said, smiling up at him. "But then again, I doubt anyone would notice. I believe there are more people here than last year!"

"It is a sad crush," he agreed. "Would you care for some refreshments? I can offer you that and a little rational conversation at least."

"Well, I . . ." Miranda hesitated, scanning the crowd again.

"We could sit over there on that dais where some of the chaperones have taken up residence. From that vantage point, you can see everything . . . and everyone," he added.

"You are too kind," replied Miranda, accepting his arm. "I don't suppose you have seen him?" she asked, knowing names were unnecessary.

"No, or rather, I did not recognize him if I did. What type of costume is he wearing?" asked Lord Picton.

"I'm afraid I don't know."

"Will he recognize you?" asked Lord Picton, trying to hail a passing footman with a snap of his gloved fingers. "Deuced inconvenient, this," he grumbled.

Miranda chuckled and motioned to the footman, who presented them with a tray of glasses. Miranda took two, waiting for Lord Picton to divest himself of his gloves before handing him one.

"Well, will he?" he asked after sipping the golden liquid.

"I don't know. My costume is hardly concealing, but it is difficult enough in this crowd to find anyone, costumed or not. I'm certain we will run into one another," she added casually. She could not tell Lord Picton that she had described her costume to Adam in great detail in a Valentine's card.

"Of course," he replied. "Tell me, have you been to see the wild animals at the Exeter Change?"

"No, I haven't. Are you planning to take the children?"

"Yes. I was wondering if you might like to join us."

"I would love to," said Miranda, beaming at him from behind her mask. "I believe they would also enjoy a visit to Astley's Amphitheatre. It has clowns and acrobats, as well as daring equestrians."

"That's a marvelous idea; I will be certain to give you credit for it," he said.

"You are too kind," said Miranda with a laugh. "I must admit I enjoy Astley's as much as a child, but I dare not go without an excuse, you know. Only think of the gossip that might engender. There goes the simpleton Sinclair, they would say."

Very much in charity with each other, they settled on a date and time for the children's outing.

The next set began to form, and Lord Picton said, "Perhaps you would care to dance with someone else. Do not feel you have to sit and bear me company all evening."

"But I am enjoying myself," she protested. "Besides, no one has asked me to dance, aside from a very inebriated Greek god and a musketeer, neither of whom I see at the moment."

"Good, then I shan't feel so badly keeping you here to entertain me."

"Nor I, you," she replied, her ready smile fading as she gazed across the ballroom and caught sight of someone gowned in a similar costume, all red and white.

Her twin was in the arms of a tall, dark-haired man; they were laughing and appeared to be enjoying themselves immensely. The gentleman was dressed rather like a Robin Hood, except that the colors were all wrong. Cupid! she decided. He was supposed to be Cupid! At least, she guessed he was Cupid; he wore flesh-colored tights with a red tunic and cap. On his back was a tiny bow and a quiver full of gold arrows.

Just then, he threw back his head and laughed at something his beautiful partner said.

"Adam," murmured Miranda, half-rising before Lord Picton's hand restrained her.

"Wait," he said quietly, cocking his head toward the interested chaperones nearby. "Wait until they are closer. This is the waltz; they'll come by soon, and then you can see if it is really him."

Miranda had no doubt that the outrageously dressed Cupid was Adam, but the girl in his arms she had never seen before. And how had she come by a gown so similar to her own? Had Madame Celeste . . . no, the astute couturier would not have done so. She knew why Miranda wanted the gown, knew she was to wear it to the countess's masquerade ball. She would never have produced another gown so similar for someone else!

Then how?

"Pray, excuse me," said Miranda, hurrying away before Lord Picton could voice a protest or urge caution. She scurried off to the ladies' withdrawing room to put her chaotic thoughts into some sort of order. But how? she wondered.

Miranda felt as if she were being swallowed up by a whirlpool, being pulled lower and lower into the depths of hell. How could such a calamity have happened?

There was Adam, thinking he held in his arms the lady who had written all those love notes, all those carefully chosen words and quotations. She would have to tell him, confess to him, that it was she all along, that the woman he held in his arms was an impostor!

When she walked out, Lord Picton was waiting at the door; he had shed his breast plate and wore a mail tunic, making his movements much easier.

"Miranda, come this way."

She followed him blindly down a hall and into the library at the back of the house. Pulling her inside, he held a finger to his lips and surveyed the room before speaking.

"I saw them go down this hall and into the next room. I don't know what this is all about exactly, but they appeared to be on very intimate terms. I thought you should know that before you barge in on them."

Miranda pursed her lips, anger and determination lighting her eyes as she said, "Thank you, Gerald. I can take it from here."

She turned on her heel and walked the short distance to Adam's study. She knew the house almost as well as she knew her own. She also knew that there was nothing in Adam's study to attract a female except Adam himself.

She threw open the door and gasped.

"Miranda! There You are!" said Adam, stepping away from the woman in his embrace.

"Adam! How could you?"

It was his turn to be indignant, and he played it to the hilt, saying arrogantly, "How could I? A better question is, why shouldn't I, my sweet Valentine?"

Miranda gasped again, her eyes growing wide. "You knew!"

"Of course I knew!" he declared.

"You knew all along!" she said, fear and uncertainty warring with an overwhelming flood of discomfiture.

"Well, almost all along," he admitted, taking a step toward her.

She held out a hand to stay him, and he grinned. Turning, he motioned the other woman forward. "Miranda, I don't think you've met my cousin Adelaide. She agreed to help me teach you a lesson."

Miranda put her fist to her mouth to keep from crying out. He had known all along; how he must have laughed at her! Shaking her head, she backed away, turning and running down the hall before Adam could think to stop her.

"Miranda!" he called, his voice a mixture of amusement and exasperation. "Hasn't there been enough playacting between us?" he added, stepping into the hall.

"Where is she?" asked his cousin, peering over his shoulder.

"Miranda!" he called, his voice taut with anger. "Devil take her!" he declared, striding down the hall and throwing open every door, peering inside for a moment before continuing his search.

"Miranda, please, you will make yourself ill," said Lord Picton helplessly, patting at his metal tunic for another handkerchief.

"I . . . I am fine," she declared with less of a sob. Taking a deep breath, she dabbed at the few remaining tears with the sodden cloth. "Do you think you could take me home, Gerald?"

"I would be honored. I'll just go and find your aunt."

"N-no, please. I will leave word for her that I am already gone. She would be bound to tell me how I have bungled this entire affair, and I don't want to listen to her lectures at the moment," she said, giving him a watery smile.

"Of course, and you shan't. Come along. We can reach the front of the house without going through the ballroom."

"Good. I don't think I could bear . . ." She did not finish; only tears lay in that direction of thought. "It was clever of you to hide us as you did, Gerald. I don't know what I would have done if you hadn't been here."

Lord Picton placed a protective arm around her shoulders as they made their way out of the library and through the darkened halls. Miranda waited in the shadows until Lord Picton motioned her forward several minutes later.

"My coach is at the door," he said quietly, slipping his arm around her again.

"Just where the deuce do you think you are going?" asked Adam, his tone quiet and dangerous. "I'll thank you to take your hand off my betrothed," he added, glaring at Picton.

"The lady wants to go home, and I take leave to tell you, Marsden, that she has said nothing to me about being your anything."

A small crowd of masqueraders began to gather as Adam crossed the marble floor; only inches from Lord Picton's nose, he growled, "Let her go."

"Adam, you are being childish!" whispered Miranda. He didn't reply, but one hand snaked out and pulled her to his side. Lord Picton held the other arm, threatening to make Miranda the rope in an angry tug-of-war.

"Marsden, don't be a fool. Miranda is leaving with me."

"Devil take you! She's staying with me!" Adam wrenched Miranda out of Picton's grasp and shoved her behind him.

Pivoting, he let fly a blow that sent Picton reeling. Lord Picton picked himself up and charged headfirst at the earl, who stepped to one side like a Spanish bullfighter. Too late did Miranda realize her danger as Lord Picton's head hit her stomach, sending them both sprawling on the floor.

"Miranda!" shouted Adam, flying to her side and helping her sit up. "Are you all right?" he demanded, frantically feeling her limbs.

"Answer me! speak to me!"

"I . . ."

"Miranda, can you ever forgive me?"

"I . . ."

"Please, please, say you will marry me! Promise me!"

"I . . ."

"She's got the wind knocked out of her, Marsden," said Lord Picton, climbing unsteadily to his feet, blood running down his chin from his swollen lip.

"Oh, Mir, I've been such a fool! Please say you'll forgive me! You know how I feel about you, my love. You must forgive me!"

"I . . . lo . . . love . . ." She rested a moment, trying to catch her breath so she could complete her sentence, but her eyes spoke for her, and Adam's anxiety began to slip away. He smiled down at her tenderly.

"You," she managed, fighting for air all over again when he covered her lips with his, catching her up in a passionate embrace.

"Huzzah! Huzzah!" cheered the masqueraders, none louder than Aunt Sophie and Lady Marsden.

Adam raised his head, his face wreathed in smiles. "Then you will marry me, my love?"

"Yes, Adam, I will marry you, on one condition."

"And what is that?"

"That you will never dance the waltz with anyone else."

"Never?"

"Never."

"Why not, my love?"

"Because seeing you holding another female in your arms makes me do the most idiotic things!"

"I love you, Miranda!" he shouted, much to the delight of their audience.

"And I love you," she replied, giving herself up to a real kiss, one that still left her gasping for air.

THE VALENTINE BRIDE

by

Catherine Blair

CHAPTER ONE

"Is it considered against tradition for the bride-groom's man to see the bride before the wedding?" Margaret called out with a laugh as she descended the stairs. "You're here very early! The wedding is not for four more hours! I was just putting the orange blossoms on my veil. Of course they are silk, as I could never find the real thing in February." She gave another bright, nervous laugh. "I can't believe that by this evening I will be Mrs. Captain Spencer Weldon, the Valentine bride. I think that Valentine's Day is the most romantic day in the year to be marr—"

She caught her breath. Her fiancé's friend had looked up and smiled, but it was the tense smile of someone who is determined not to look upset.

"Good heavens, what is wrong? Has something happened?" She took the last steps in a bound and grabbed his sleeve. "Is it Spencer?"

Austin gently detached her, patted her hand, and indicated the presence of the butler with a subtle tilt of his head. "We'll talk in the drawing room." A strange tone in his voice made her insides twist painfully with fear.

Margaret followed him upstairs and shut the drawing room door. The room seemed very hot, despite the modesty of the coal fire on the grate. She felt suddenly as though she were stifling. "What is going on?" she demanded. She repressed a shudder as he carefully took her hands. She had never seen him look so grim.

"This is very hard for me," he began, with an expression of anguish.

She involuntarily dug her nails into his palm. "Tell me," she growled.

"Spencer, he . . ." Austin dropped her hands and turned from her. His voice trailed away helplessly.

"Dead?" she cried out wildly.

"I wish."

"What!?"

"He's crying off, Margaret."

The room was instantly still. The cheerful snap of the fire on the grate and the sounds of the household moving about in other rooms as they prepared for the wedding seemed suddenly very loud. She felt a desperate urge to fling open a window to relieve the terrible closeness of the room, but she could not move.

Austin wheeled around to face her. "Did you hear me?"

She vaguely registered that his expression was one of utter agony. "Yes," she heard her own voice reply at last. He caught up both of her hands again and led her to the couch. The straw-colored silk of the upholstery was cool, but she did not feel better.

"I have made a hash of it," he exclaimed in frustration. "I should have told you more carefully. Do you feel faint? I will get you a glass of sherry. You will not topple over if I get up, will you?" He stood cautiously, assessed her stability, and went to pour her a generous drink from the decanter on the side table.

Spencer was crying off.

Austin pressed the glass into her hand and sat down again beside her. The worried furrow between his brows grew deeper in the silence.

"Why?" she asked finally.

Austin raked a hand through his chestnut hair and

then pressed his fingers to his tightly closed eyes. "I don't know," he said at last. "He just . . . He just asked me to tell you."

"Where is he?"

"He's gone up to Longford. He has family there." He brought the glass to her lips and forced her to drink some of the sherry.

She waved him away with a distracted gesture. "Yes, of course. His mother and her cousin, I believe," she said faintly. The sherry burned all the way down to her painfully knotted stomach. She swallowed again to try to force down the lump of hysteria rising inexorably in her throat.

"I would have hauled him here by the scruff of the neck to say it to you himself, but he was gone by the time I got there. I'm sorry. You should not have had to hear it from anyone but him."

Austin was ineffectually patting the limp twist of her fingers. With a jerk of impatience, she stilled his hand between her own. "Didn't you see him?" she demanded.

"He sent around a note this morning. It is for you. It was accompanied by another letter addressed to me, asking that I come to speak with you. He asked me to explain, but I can't." His hazel eyes were tense with misery. "His note only said that he would not be able to . . ."—he searched for a delicate term—". . . to follow through with the wedding plans and that he had left town. I'm sorry," he said in a gentle voice that she hated for its edge of pity. He forced another large gulp of sherry upon her before he reluctantly leaned back and drew a folded sheet of foolscap from his waistcoat pocket.

She felt a wash of uncomfortable prickles when she saw the bold slash of Spencer's handwriting. The reality of the situation dawned on her for the first time. Snatching the paper from Austin's hand, she turned from him while she poured over the few lines. "He has discovered that his passion was not of a lasting nature. He believes that it would be cruel to marry me when he no longer feels love for me," she said in a hollow voice.

Austin tentatively put his hand on her shoulder. "Margaret, if I'd known what a bounder he was, I never would have introduced you to each other."

She whirled to face him. "It can't be true. Something must have happened! He was forced to write this! It can't be true! We must do something! If the letter was sent around this morning, he cannot be too far away. If we hurry, we can catch him!" She leapt to her feet and took a few steps toward the door. "There has been some mistake!"

Austin looked miserable. "Sit down," he said in a low voice. She continued to stand stubbornly in the middle of the room, but he continued. "We both know it is true. I've known Spencer Weldon since we were at Trinity together. I loved him like a brother, though I always knew he was flighty. We both know that he didn't deal well with uncomfortable situations. But I never thought he would cry off like this. I blame myself."

"I am not an 'uncomfortable situation'!" She was indignant.

"I didn't mean that."

"There must be some mistake," she said again, fervently. "He would not do this to me. I know he wouldn't."

He got up and retrieved her from where she stood in a daze, and she allowed him to lead her like a child to her former seat on the couch. Her feet felt disconnected from her body, and there was a numbness radiating out from somewhere deep inside her.

"What will I do?" she asked at last. "The wedding is in a few hours. He will change his mind and come back. Surely he will be back by the time we are due at chapel. He loved the Trinity chapel, you know. He made special arrangements that we should be married there." She was babbling.

"Have some more sherry. No? Would you prefer tea? Shall I ring for tea?" Austin could not meet her eyes.

Her voice rose to a desperate pitch. "He'll change his mind, don't you think? He is only nervous. That must be it. Just wedding jitters." She looked at him pleadingly.

He passed his hand over his forehead, but the furrows remained. "No," he said at last, looking solemnly into her face. "He'll regret it, Margaret, but he won't marry you."

"Are you certain?" She felt her throat closing.

His eyes remained locked with hers. "Yes."

She stared at him for another long moment. At last she blinked several times and rubbed a shaking hand across her brow. "Thank you for coming to tell me." She was surprised to hear how normal she sounded. "I think I need to discuss this with my mother."

He pressed her hand between his own. "You don't need to do that. I will explain everything to her. Tell me what I can do for you. You don't know how miserable I am to be the one to bring you this news."

"Thank you for telling Mama." She smiled faintly. "I don't think I want to talk about it. I don't think I want anything, just to be alone." She cleared her throat, willing the explosion of tears to wait until he had gone. "You . . . you're certain?" she asked one last time in a tiny voice. She saw his expression of sympathy and turned her face away. She knew he was right. No cataclysmic disaster had forced Spencer's desertion. He simply didn't want to marry her.

They sat in silence for a moment. "I tell you what, Meggie, let's go out. I can't leave you here after dropping the news in your lap like that." Austin slapped his thighs and forced a laugh. "We'll go out for a drive, and I'll buy you an ice."

"In February?" she asked tiredly.

"Hot nuts then, a sweet bun, whatever you like." He stood up and made a pretense of joviality.

"Do you think that I am a child who can be distracted from my misery by the promise of sweets?"

"Don't rip up at me," he said with a defeated smile, pulling her to her feet. "I just want to get you out of the house." He strode across the carpet to pull the bell cord.

"No. I can't. I want to be alone," she insisted through clenched teeth.

"Have Miss Fitzpatrick's maid help her change her gown for a driving costume," he ordered the butler. "You have a quarter of an hour before I come upstairs after you. I will tell your mother we have gone." He led her out into the hallway.

"Stop it, Austin. I don't wish to go. Please understand. I just want to be by myself for a while."

"That's the last thing you should be right now. A quarter of an hour," he said firmly, giving her a gentle shove.

He watched her walk up the stairs, her drooping shoulders the only indication that her life had been irrevocably destroyed. She was not a very tall woman, but now she looked positively childlike and frail. Her golden brown hair was dressed in an elaborate style for the wedding, but he saw as she reached the landing that she was beginning to pull the pins from it. She jerked them out and let them fall to the floor with a motion that reminded him of a clockwork windup toy. He suddenly felt very worried for her.

Any other woman would have fallen into hysterics. He almost wished she had. Then he could have summoned the doctor to take over. No, Margaret was made of sterner stuff than that. He had known her since she was in pinafores, and she was never one to succumb to emotional fits. She would survive. It was Captain

Spencer Weldon's survival he would like to jeopardize. . . .

He paced the hallway, impatiently slapping his driving gloves against the leg of his pantaloons as he waited for the butler to return with Margaret's mother.

"Oh, Austin, how lovely it is to see you." Mrs. Fitzpatrick rustled down the stairs in a stiff, heavily flounced gown of green silk. "How is your mother? I declare, the house is at sixes and sevens today with the wedding this afternoon. Do you think this gown is all right? It just came from the dressmaker's, and I am not at all sure.

"Have you seen the bridegroom? Perhaps you are bringing a message from him. I don't know what Margaret and Captain Weldon were thinking; getting married on Valentine's Day. I'm sure they had the notion that it would be very romantic, but when you consider that we have only had a few months to plan the wedding, it is enough to try even my patience!"

The lace of her cap trembled in indignation as she continued. "It is almost as bad as eloping—this kind of hurly-burly, rushed affair. Who knows what people are saying! It looks a bit suspicious for them to marry so indecently soon after meeting. I can't say that I like these whirlwind courtships. It isn't at all the thing. Hardly any time to post the banns or get up a proper trousseau. Mr. Fitzpatrick should have insisted on them waiting. Mary and Anne will have decent engagements, I can assure you of that. I won't have this kind of marry-in-haste for my other daughters. I myself blame Sir Walter Scott and those romantic novels of his. Chivalry and romance," she said scornfully. "Really it's quite enough when—"

"Mrs. Fitzpatrick!" Austin interrupted violently. "I must insist that you listen to me."

She turned to stare at him in surprise. Austin was struck with the irrelevant notion that Margaret had inherited her mother's remarkable Wedgwood blue eyes. He drew the woman into the salon he had occupied with Margaret and closed the door quietly.

"There will be no wedding this afternoon. Captain Weldon has cried off."

Mrs. Fitzpatrick staggered and grabbed the back of a chair for support. "What? But Margaret . . ."

"I have told her already. She is devastated, of course, but I am sure that with our support . . ."

"Today? He cried off today?" Her voice rose. "When I have over one hundred people coming to the wedding breakfast after the ceremony? How am I going to tell those people that the wedding will not take place? The scandal! Margaret will be the talk of the town! What will people say?"

Her voice had risen to an almost unbearable pitch, but Austin willed himself not to flinch. He hoped that Margaret could not hear her mother's hysterical reaction from upstairs. He realized how imperative it was that he get her out of the house.

"Oh, dear God, who knows what they will surmise!" Mrs. Fitzpatrick wailed. "I must tell Margaret's father. He will call Captain Weldon out for this!" She struck the back of the chair with emphasis. "Crying off on the day of the wedding! Who ever heard of such a thing!" She gasped at a sudden thought. "And then the captain will kill him! I shall be left a widow with three girls to support, and we shall be thrown out into the street to starve! We shall be the ridicule of all our friends, and I shall have to live with the girls in some horrid lodging house in the Coombe, begging the landlady not to throw us out, just because the rent is three months late. We shall be forced to eat nothing but stews, or whatever it is that those dreadful poor people eat. Oh, my nerves! This shall very likely kill me!"

"The captain has left Dublin," Austin said grimly. "Perhaps we had best leave it at that. I suggest that you hold the wedding breakfast anyway and explain that the captain has had an emergency that prevents the wedding from taking place today. There is no need to put it about just yet that the match has been called off."

"Do you think the captain will change his mind?" Mrs. Fitzpatrick asked, suddenly hopeful.

"I think it best if we assume he will not. I have not had any indication that he will change his mind."

"You saw him and yet you let him get away? Austin Bourke, I am surprised at you. How positively infamous! I should have thought that we could have counted on you to take care of such things. He should have been hauled down to the chapel by force if necessary. Letting him cry off, indeed! Unheard of! What with you a family friend, and Margaret with no brothers to protect her from—"

"Captain Weldon only sent a note to me," Austin cut her off deftly. "He was long gone by the time I received it. Let me impress upon you how delicate a situation this is. For the sake of Margaret's reputation, I think that it is imperative that you hold the party anyway and brush this off as a trifling postponement. I am sure that you will contrive to manage beautifully, despite this terrible inconvenience." He accompanied this with a low bow, knowing that flattery would assure her compliance.

The small woman drew herself up to her full height and sniffed. "Well, I would think he could give us more notice! How incredibly rude." Her blue eyes were blazing. "Well, I must say, my opinion of the captain is quite destroyed." Her brows drew together. "Margaret must be devastated. She is so very romantic."

"I was hoping to take her for a drive. I know you will excuse her from the party. It would obviously be too much to expect her to attend, considering the circumstances."

"Of course," Mrs. Fitzpatrick agreed weakly. "But

what will people say, seeing her driving about with you on her wedding day? I will not have my daughter's name bandied about. We'll send her over to my sister in England. Yes. She will go away for a while. That will let the scandal die down." She nodded vigorously. "I shall write the necessary letter this instant! Poor creature, but she may very well be better off in London, you know. She could have made a very eligible match there during her Season last spring if she had only applied herself a little more. Three offers she turned down, you know! And not from half-pay officers! Yes, London will do nicely. I know you will excuse me, Austin, but I have so very much to do, now that this complication has arisen." She made as though to leave the room.

"Indeed. But let me say that I think it might be unwise to send Margaret off to London, or anywhere at this point. It will simply confirm any rumors the tattlemongers put out. I would suggest that she remain here and act as though there were nothing wrong. I am sure that you will manage to convey the notion that this is simply an inconvenient delay. The news of the betrothal ending can wait until later."

"Yes, yes. Perhaps you are correct. I should hate for any breath of scandal to damage her reputation. I shall tell her papa that very thing. Oh, dear. He will be very angry indeed. Perhaps you had better tell him, Austin. You do these things so very well. I quite see why Captain Weldon chose you to be his groomsman."

"I am afraid that I am unable to. With your permission I would like to take Margaret out of the house as soon as possible. Please convey to Mr. Fitzpatrick my regrets that this has occurred. I am sure that you will be able to manage everything." He had been pacing the length of the drawing room carpet but now turned to face Margaret's mother. "I am aware that I introduced Captain Weldon to Margaret and so bear part of the blame. I am very sincerely sorry for my role in this most regrettable event."

"Indeed I should think you would be sorry! But then," she softened, "I am sure you must have been as sadly deceived as we were as to Captain Weldon's character." She gave a heavy sigh. "Well," she said with a martyr's resign, "Mr. Fitzpatrick will be very angry. Perhaps it is best if we do give the breakfast. All that lobster going to waste! He would have an apoplectic fit." She closed her eyes at the grim mental picture. A moment later, her eyes popped open again. "You are taking Margaret out? Without a chaperone? You must take Mrs. Ash along. I am sure that she can be spared from Mary and Anne for the day. She is perhaps not the most *sensible* female, but of course you must have someone to play duenna. Although, it is not as though you two weren't practically raised together. Like a brother and sister." Her brows rose a little. "We quite thought the two of you might make a match of it until the captain came along. He quite swept her off her feet." Her expression suddenly grew speculative. "But now . . ."

"I would not dream of courting Margaret when she has just suffered this blow. It would be terribly unfair of me."

"It might console her," Mrs. Fitzpatrick protested.

"No, indeed, madam. Margaret loves Spencer and has never felt anything more than friendship for me. I will play the role I have always played: the good brother." He bowed politely and turned away from Margaret's mother so that she would not see his bitter expression.

CHAPTER TWO

"This is madness." Margaret scowled into her lap. "Everyone is staring at me. What a stupid idea. Do take me home." Just as she looked up pleadingly at Austin, a woman in a blue straw bonnet positively rife with yellow grosgrain ribbons caught her eye and waved enthusiastically.

"Why it's Miss Fitzpatrick! The Valentine bride!" Mrs. Donovan exclaimed delightedly. "What in heaven's name are you doing out driving on the morning of your wedding? You should be at home getting ready—merciful heavens!" she gasped, looking at the watch pinned to her yellow-ribboned bosom. "The time! You must . . ."

"I'm afraid the wedding has been postponed," Austin cut in smoothly. "The captain had a death in the family."

"Oh, dear." Mrs. Donovan's brows rose a full inch. "Please convey my condolences." After a few other disjointed apologies, she hurried down Sackville Street.

"She has doubtless gone to inform the rest of the Town Biddies," Margaret muttered bitterly. She shoved her arms up to the elbow into her white swansdown muff and sat up straighter in the curricle seat.

Mrs. Ash craned to look over her shoulder in the confined space where she rode bodikin between Margaret and Austin. "I should say that she is. She has just met Lady Olivia Metworth and appears quite animated in her conversation. Why, yes, I do believe she is pointing at us. How very mortifying, to be sure."

"Do turn around, Twitter," Margaret begged, using their old schoolroom name for the chattery governess-turned-companion. "The old quizzes shall see you staring."

"Why, Mr. Bourke, Miss Fitzpatrick!" a woman cried from her carriage. "Why aren't you—"

"We're eloping, Lady Ballingary; do excuse us." Austin tipped his hat cheerfully to the gaping woman and drove on.

"The captain came down with the measles quite suddenly."

"The captain was shot by a band of marauding Turks."

"The dean of St. Patrick's, who was to marry them, ran off with Lady Cork and Orrery."

"Miss Fitzpatrick has run amok. I'm conveying her to the lunatic asylum."

"*Do* take me to the lunatic asylum, if you please," Margaret said with narrowed eyes as the curricle left yet another stunned acquaintance in its wake.

Austin smiled triumphantly at this scrap of humor, dry as it was. He evidently felt he was doing a marvelous job of cheering her up. "No, indeed," he replied brightly. "We are going to the Gillmont Hotel. They are going to make us up a picnic luncheon."

"What a marvelous idea!" Mrs. Ash exclaimed, "It is just the thing when the daffodils are out, and this month has been so unseasonably warm. I declare, one really does want a picnic when one has been cooped up all winter long. It will perk up those megrims of yours, Margaret."

"I don't want a picnic luncheon. I want to go home." Margaret shot Austin a baleful glance to discourage any illusions he harbored as to her mood. "Hello, Mrs. Coit. No, it's been . . . it's been called off, actually," she stammered against the tide of questions pouring forth from a woman in a barouch that was stopped beside them in the Sackville Street traffic.

"It turns out the captain is already married to a girl in Lisdoonvarna. Who would have thought?" Austin clicked his tongue to his teeth and shook his head sadly before starting the horses again. Margaret could hear Mrs. Coit's confused sputterings as they drove away.

"It might be true, you know," Mrs. Ash said thoughtfully. "Perhaps he was estranged from her for years and only just remembered her." She looked bewildered when both Austin and Margaret shot her similar looks of slightly bemused impatience.

"Here we are," Austin said, after several moments of driving in ominous silence. "Do you wish to come in with me, or shall I send Will in to procure something for us?" He indicated with a jerk of his head the young tiger who rode at the back of the carriage.

Mrs. Ash thought for a moment. "I think that I should like to stay, myself. It is so difficult to get in and out of a curricle. Not that it is not a fine piece of equipage. Why, I never thought I should ride in such a smart carriage. My father would be shocked indeed to know I had ridden in a curricle. He'd likely say—"

Margaret cut short her cheerful monologue with an exclamation of horror. "Here comes Mrs. Murphy and her daughters. Do let's go inside." She vaulted from the carriage and pulled him into the hotel. "What can you be thinking to drag me out in public like this! It's humiliating!" she hissed.

Ignoring her outburst, Austin spoke softly with the

concierge about the possibility of the hotel providing a packed luncheon from their dining room. When they were left alone, he turned to her and guided her to one of the graceful chairs that lined the wall of the lobby. "I am sorry to have made you suffer, but I did not know of another way. There was no hope that the . . . ah . . . change in plans—"

"Jilt," she supplied brutally.

"Thank you, yes. There was no hope that the jilt would go unnoticed. However, it is now unlikely that society will ever quite know what has happened."

Margaret looked up at him for a long moment. "Thank you," she said at last in a low voice. "I understand now. You are very kind."

He shrugged and smiled at the concierge, who was making his way back toward them. "You know I'll take care of you, my dear," he said lightly, before turning his attention to the procurement of lunch.

For several moments Margaret sat silently with a small crease forming between her brows. "I don't understand why this has happened," she said to Austin in a small voice at last. "Oh, dear, I must have repeated that seven hundred times in the last two hours." She sighed heavily. "Do you think . . ." she began hesitantly. "Do you think he will perhaps change his mind . . . someday?" She saw her knuckles whiten on the edge of the seat and forced her fingers to loosen.

"I already told you what I think about that," Austin replied gently.

"He will not marry me," she repeated hoarsely. She felt the hysteria rise within her again. In another moment she was going to disgrace herself by having a screaming, crying fit in the lobby of the Gillmont Hotel. She stared around its dark wood interior, blinking hard. How humiliating to have to go about in public when she had only had the news this morning. It was too much to expect her to maintain any dignity. She looked up in surprise when a handkerchief dropped into her lap. Austin gave her a rueful smile and continued to pace the length of the carpet.

"I'm sorry, Margaret. I hate putting you through this. You know it is best, though," he said softly as he passed her on one of his revolutions.

"Why did this happen to me?" she demanded in a savage whisper. "For two months my whole life has been wrapped around him. He was so perfect for me. At Christmas, when you introduced us, I thought my heart would stop. When our eyes met, I knew, right then, that he was the man I would spend the rest of my life with. It was real. It was true love, I know it." She looked at him defiantly, but he was examining his watch with sudden interest.

"Two months is not so very long to know someone," he replied carefully.

She knew she was only torturing herself with this conversation, but she continued. "It was long enough. I knew right away that he was the one I would be with forever. And now it is over before it has even begun."

"Better than it ending after it had begun," Austin said with infuriating logic.

She suddenly felt as though she couldn't breathe. How just like Austin to be so sensible about the whole thing. The man did not have an ounce of feeling. "You are probably glad this happened. Now you can say you told me so," she spat out.

He turned quickly to look at her, then returned his attention to the carpet. "No. I don't believe I told you anything. I would never wish you unhappiness, and I genuinely thought that you and Spencer would be happy together."

"I shall never be happy now," she announced, not feeling the least bit mollified by his kindness. How infuriating for him to be so placid when she would so dearly love to scream at him like a fishwife. She contented herself with narrowing her eyes at him and then preserving a frigid silence as he paid for the enormous hamper of food that had been brought up.

"Are we quite ready for this ridiculous expedition?" she asked acerbically as he handed her back into the curricle.

"Oh, no, indeed. We still must procure linens, flowers, candles, jugged hares, quail eggs in aspic, and, of course, several footmen to wait on us."

"Good heavens!" Mrs. Ash exclaimed. "Why ever should we need all of those things? I should think that a nice meat pie and a bottle of Madeira would be all that we really need. Indeed, a cold joint or a jelly might be nice, but I don't know at all how we should manage jugged hares."

"You are joking," Margaret accused him.

He looked at her blankly for a moment. "Yes"—he cracked a thin smile—"I'm joking. One more stop, then we are on to St. Stephen's Green. My dear Mrs. Ash, could I possibly prevail upon you to let Margaret sit beside me? It might distress you to have us arguing over you."

"I assure you, Austin, I have no desire to even speak to you," Margaret replied regally.

He ignored her and continued to Mrs. Ash: "As you can see, she is in a towering rage, and I am in for a blistering dressing down for being the most unsympathetic, intolerable, and insensitive brute who ever walked the face of the earth."

"Oh, dear!" that woman murmured faintly. She hastily changed seats with Margaret as Austin walked around to the other side of the carriage and climbed in.

As Austin had already labeled himself with most of the epithets Margaret had been considering, they drove on in silence for several minutes. He shot her a look of absolute contrition so comical that she could not help but give an unwilling laugh.

"Don't tell me I have escaped without a scold?"

Margaret sighed and twisted her hands in her lap. "Don't be cross with me, Austin. I know I'm being impossible. I just—I just can't seem to decide how to feel. One moment I think I shall die for love of that man and the next I should like to strangle him with my bare hands."

"Would one wear gloves, generally?" he asked mildly.

"Do stop your horrid teasing. I know you are trying to cheer me up, and you are very kind to take such an interest in me and take me out, but you must know that I am not going to be very good company. I do wish you had let me stay at home. I am cross, and I think I should be allowed to be so for a good long while, considering what has happened."

"Be as cross as you wish." He gave a cheerful shrug. "Now," he said briskly, "on to the dry goods merchant."

"Why?"

"We must have something to sit on," he replied. "And I cannot have you catching your death in that very fashionable, but tissue-thin pelisse. It is mild this year, but not so mild as that. Why, Mrs. Ash would never allow me to treat you so shabbily."

"No, indeed," Mrs. Ash agreed. "It is a fine pelisse, isn't it? I told Margaret that the garnet velvet trimmings were just the thing for that shade of gray. 'It suits your eyes my dear,' that's what I said. I meant the gray, not the garnet, of course. She would look very peculiar to be sure with garnet-colored eyes. Not very nice indeed. Of course her eyes are not gray either, but the gray wool does make them look as if they might be so. Indeed, I—"

"Please, Twitter! Do stop talking about me as though I was not here!" Margaret begged. She caught Austin concealing a lopsided smile.

"I only meant to say—Well! In any case, you are good to think of everything, Mr. Bourke. The blankets will serve very well, I am sure. How nice it will be to dine *al fresco* today. It is just as perfect as it could be."

"It is nice," Margaret agreed, looking about her as though for the first time.

"I have always thought this time of year the most magical." Mrs. Ash sighed with a pleasure Margaret could not help but resent slightly. "Right on the cusp of winter and spring," the governess continued blissfully. "There is still that sharp feeling in the air, but you can tell that spring is just teasing you, ready to pop out at any second. Such anticipation!"

She nodded vaguely. Her insides were beginning to ache again. "What a beautiful wedding day this would have been."

"It depends on who one is marrying," Austin replied darkly.

Margaret pounced upon him with claws unsheathed. "Don't you dare turn turncoat! How dare you speak ill of him? Spencer is your closest friend. You should be grateful and honored to be the groomsman. That is, you were to be." She turned her face from him as her throat closed up painfully.

"Spencer *was* my friend," he corrected. "After this trick he has pulled, I no longer count him as such."

She continued to looked away, but she could feel his gaze intently on her. "And I have always been your friend," he said solemnly. He urged the horses onward, though they were already moving as fast as the crowded streets would allow. She noticed that the muscle in his jaw was rigid with repressed emotion, but she was too angry to stop the flow of words that seemed the only thing that kept her from suffocating.

"How can you insinuate that I am better off without Spencer, when not but two months—indeed, two days ago—you were telling me how happy you were for us both."

"Margaret . . . conduct . . . open carriage!" Mrs.

Ash gasped out, clinging to the side of the curricle as
it feathered the corner at Henry Street.

Austin negotiated the space between a delivery
wagon and a large traveling coach before he replied.
"That was before I knew him to be capable of this."
His voice was infuriatingly calm.

"Spencer can do anything he likes. It is my fault he
found he does not love me. I will not allow someone
who claims to be his friend to malign him in this manner." She drew herself up and clenched her teeth,
fairly shaking with rage.

Mrs. Ash gasped and murmured, "Margaret,
please!" several times in a horrified undertone, but
she did not dare enter into the conversation. She
sagged visibly in relief when they pulled up in front
of the dry goods shop.

"I told you there should be a squall, Mrs. Ash. Now,
Will, run in and buy several good-sized blankets. Then
we can continue our quarrel without the least inhibi-
tion, knowing that you are hanging on our every
word." Austin placidly tossed a handful of coins to his
tiger. He turned to Margaret. "First, Captain Weldon
is no longer my friend, as I have told you. Second,
anyone who does not love you is an idiot."

Margaret made a noise that might have been a snort.
"You have known me far too long to expect me to
believe such ridiculous flattery."

"I think I will go and help your tiger make the selection," Mrs. Ash said loudly. "Don't you think you
should come with me, Margaret?" She gave her charge
a pleading look.

"No, I will stay here," she replied stiffly. They
watched in silence as the governess fled the scene.
"Spencer is not an idiot," Margaret continued indignantly, once they were alone in the curricle.

Austin shrugged carelessly and did not reply.

His very negligence tempted her to push the rather
one-sided argument into forbidden territory. "You

were always jealous of him." She wished instantly she could unsay such cruel words.

He appeared unaffected. The brief flare of anger she had seen was now replaced by bland affability. "Who could not be? He was quite the paradigm of everything perfect," He peered into the window of the dry goods shop to assess the progress of the transactions within.

"There is no need to be sarcastic," she snapped. "I know you were . . . were fond of me, and you were jealous of Spencer, and now you are probably pleased as punch that he has jilted me."

"You know that isn't true, Margaret," he said in a low voice.

"You are probably hoping that I will fall right into your arms if you are kind to me, now that this has happened." She felt the knot in her stomach rising up to choke her, but she could not control her rage. "Well, you can nip that thought in the bud. If I cannot have Spencer, I will have no one!"

"I don't believe I suffer any illusions as to your feelings toward me or the captain." His voice was still calm, but she knew from its edge that she had gone too far.

"I hate all men, especially encroaching, pushy, bullying ones like you." Her voice had risen to an unseemly volume and her breath was coming in strange pants.

"I am sure you will feel better after you have had some tea. We are very nearly ready for our luncheon."

"Stop being so damn solicitous!" she hissed. "Take me home. This outing is stupid, and I am convinced you did it on purpose just to humiliate me."

"You are getting hysterical. Please try to calm yourself."

"I will not be calm! I am going to have screaming hysterics, and I very much would like to be alone at home when I am doing so." Her fists were clenched in her lap, shaking.

"Oh, just see the things we have found for the picnic." Mrs. Ash emerged from the store spouting rather forced cheer. Margaret could see her eyes darting between herself and Austin to assess how things lay between them. "We have found a large tarpaulin to lay on the ground so that the damp doesn't come through the blanket. Isn't this a nice color? I declare it is a good deal too fine to go sitting on in the park, but I allowed your tiger to talk me into it, Mr. Bourke."

"You have excellent taste, Will," Austin said dryly. The tiger looked highly affronted and mounted the back of the curricle with a disdainful flourish.

Mrs. Ash continued to enumerate their purchases as she mounted the step into the carriage until she saw Margaret's face. Her animation suddenly evaporated. "Why, my dear! You're white as paper! Mr. Bourke—" She turned on him, prepared to take him severely to task.

"No, it isn't his fault." Margaret forced out the words. "I am quite in control of myself now."

"Now, don't go and faint in full view of society! Your mama would be shocked! Dear me, this has been too much for you. I should never have allowed Mr. Bourke to take you out of the house. I told your mama that you would not be able to stand it. I told her to send for the doctor, not send you out driving! Take us home this instant!" Mrs. Ash shot Austin a baleful glance.

"No, no, I am quite recovered." With a savage swipe, Margaret dried the angry tears that threatened to spill out. "I think that we should go on to the park as we planned. I have no desire to go back home to face the sympathy of my family." She looked down the length of the Liffey as they crossed Essex Bridge and drew a deep, stabilizing breath.

"Are you certain? We could always go round to your

Aunt Dalton's house. She could call Dr. Heyton. It would not do for you to have a spasm in the park."

Margaret insisted that they continue, glancing at Austin to see if he was even willing to escort them. He appeared completely absorbed with maneuvering the horses through the traffic, and she could not see his face.

"Please drive us to the park, Austin," she begged.

He did not reply, but obediently guided the curricle to St. Stephen's Green. It was cool in the shade, but somehow restfully quiet after the bustle of Grafton Street. She felt some of the tension leave her body, and she took several deep breaths. There was still a pain under her rib cage, but she no longer felt as though she was suffocating. She looked tentatively at Austin. It was difficult to tell what he was thinking. The trees cast a dappled shade down the streets that bordered the square, and the shadows moving across his face made interpretation impossible. She felt very ashamed. What in Heaven's name had made her say such cruel things to the one person she could depend on to support her? It made no sense.

When they reached a clutch of trees set on the green, Austin tossed the reins to the tiger and leapt out of the curricle. "Take them back to the stables on Dame Street. There's a bit of a wind and I don't want them standing. Come straight back, for we'll need you to help with the food." Will set up a protest that he was not a butler, but Austin silenced him with a playful cuff. "I meant help eating it, you beggar."

He turned back to his guests and held out a hand to help Margaret down. His smile had faded and his upturned face was impassive. She retained his hand for a moment, trying to convey her misery and plead for his patience. How could she face losing Spencer and then Austin, too? The idea gripped her by the throat, and she felt again as though she would strangle. No. It would not happen. Austin would not be turned away by a few words spoken in anger. He was too faithful a friend for that. A small, recalcitrant voice in her head pointed out that Spencer was the one who had proved himself faithless, but she shook those unloving thoughts immediately from her mind.

CHAPTER THREE

Margaret waited for Austin to gather up their purchases and then fell into step beside him as he carried them toward the site he evidently intended for the picnic. "I . . . I didn't actually mean those things I said," she began sheepishly, wrinkling her nose in distaste.

"I know."

"You're a great gun to do this for me, and even though I'm not enjoying it, it is very kind of you. Well, that didn't sound very nice either. I mean, I know I'm not good company today, and even considering the circumstances, it was still awfully rude of me to rip up at you. Especially about . . . well, I just . . . I . . . could we just forget I said anything? Do say you'll forgive me." She gave him a pathetic smile.

"Of course." He picked a spot in the sunshine that was shielded from the road by the trees and laid the tarpaulin on the ground to protect them from its dampness.

"You have picked the most perfect spot on the green," Mrs. Ash pronounced, obviously back in charity with Austin. "We picnicked here last summer, do you remember? Such a lovely day. There was croquet on the lawn and we thought that your young cousin Corneileus got sick from tainted oysters, but it turned out not to be so." She sighed happily and began unpacking the hamper. "He had only eaten too many green apples the day before."

"You will never guess what the concierge managed to procure for you, Margaret." Austin smiled. "Roly-poly pudding."

"What? Really? I have not had that since Mrs. Bartworth left us. Roly-poly pudding . . ." she said nostalgically. "She was such a marvelous cook. The Frenchman Mama employs now would never consider making anything so gauche as a pudding. Except at Christmas, perhaps. How did you ever get it at the Gillmont Hotel?"

"It seems that you are not the only one with a preternatural fondness for the stuff." He laughed. "I hear they also make an irresistible pigeon pie, though I have never tried it myself."

"I love a good pigeon pie. There is nothing I love so much if it is not a good pigeon pie. Except for perhaps lark pie. Yes, indeed, if the crust is made properly." Mrs. Ash began a rambling treatise on "Pies I Have Known."

Margaret sat down with a sigh. "I'm afraid I am not very hungry."

"Dear me. How will I ever consume all this Devonshire cream all by myself?" Austin looked anxiously into an earthenware jug, then grinned at her.

"You wicked man. How dare you remember all my weaknesses? Mama says its disgusting to eat it straight, but I can't seem to help myself." She smiled at him. "You've certainly put yourself out for me."

"Only for today. Tomorrow I shall be as unbearable as usual," he replied lightly. "There is your cream. Not only is it straight, but you must eat it from a jar. Your mother would have fits." He handed it to her.

Her smile faded. "How did she take the news?"

"She was upset, but only because she was concerned for you." His eyes roved across the park to where a nursemaid chased after her charge, who chased after a dog.

Margaret gave a sharp laugh. "What fustian. She probably started shrieking 'What are we going to do with three stone of lobster, if there's to be no wedding?' "

"Something like that."

The nursemaid caught up the child in her arms and it instantly set up a bereft wail. The dog, yapping in protest, made little darting rushes at the nursemaid's heels.

"Well?" said Margaret, after they had watched the saga played out before them. "What will she do with them?"

Austin looked bewildered. "What?"

"Mama versus the lobsters."

"Ah, yes. Well, the lobsters will be eaten, I would imagine. She is holding the party anyway."

He stayed her surprised and slightly hurt look with a gesture. "It was the only thing to do, Meggie. I told her to do it. It will make things look like less of a calamity. She is going to simply say that Captain Weldon was called away."

Margaret nodded but could not speak. Her throat was getting that aching, tight feeling that she knew preceded tears. How terrible to suddenly become such a complete watering pot. No, she would not cry in front of him. Not when he was trying so hard to please her. She picked disinterestedly at a piece of cheese and blinked very hard.

"Your mother was considering sending you to London," he began, loading a plate from the Gillmont Hotel with food. He paused with the spoon suspended. "Would you prefer to skip everything else and go straight to the roly-poly pudding?"

"No, I will be a good girl and save it until last. Why would she send me off to London? To avoid the scandal, I suppose." She took the plate from him and dutifully made an effort to eat.

"I have attempted to dissuade her. I think that it would only look . . . well, it would look as though we were trying to cover something up."

"I suppose you are right," she conceded with a disinterested shrug. "I would like to leave Dublin, but I am not overfond of London. I went for my Season, and everyone seemed to think I was pathetically provincial. It was very irritating."

"And so noisy!" Mrs. Ash put in. She tucked a blanket more securely around her knees and began a second piece of pigeon pie. "No, I don't think that London would do at all. I quite dread the day when Mary makes her come out, for I shall be obliged to go there again to chaperone her."

"Come now, we had a grand time when I was there," Austin exclaimed. "What a pity I could not have stayed longer. But there was too much to be done at my mother's house. But you cannot deny we had good fun at Astley's Amphitheater and at Newmarket. And I know you enjoyed Vauxhall, Mrs. Ash, though you pretended to be quite severe regarding the conduct of the parties enjoying themselves there."

"Indeed, I did enjoy it. Such a lovely ham they served. Beautiful ham. We had several very nice outings while you were there, Mr. Bourke. It was indeed a pity that you were called back to Windrose House."

"Yes, we did have a good time." Margaret smiled nostalgically as she took a large spoonful of the Devonshire cream. "Ah, that is nice," she commented, indicating the jar. "It was good of you to remember that I like it. We did have a good time when you were there, but it was deadly dull once you left."

"Well, I did not want to be forced to call out some of your more foolish conquests. That Wilding fellow was dashed bold!"

She laughed. "My conquests, indeed. You know I was

not considered anything out of the common way. I certainly should not have accepted an offer from any of the ludicrous jackanapes who did hang about. The ones who were not fortune hunters were unbearably mush-headed. Did I tell you I received a poem from Heckels? Comparing my neck to an alabaster column or some such rot."

"Impudent cur!" Austin exclaimed in exaggerated shock.

"When I asked him if my neck was Doric or Ionic, he said with the greatest of pomp that my neck had nothing to do with a door and he hadn't meant the compliment with the least bit of sarcasm. I think he was thinking of 'ironic.' But in any case, it was I who was speaking sarcastically. The man had no humor in him at all."

"I thought it was a rather nice poem," Mrs. Ash interjected. "As least I did until Anne and Mary wrote the parody of it, comparing Cook's neck with a turkey's. It was quite impertinent, and I daresay your mother would have turned me off without a character if she had discovered they wrote such a thing. Though I don't see how it could be my fault. In fact, I am not sure how they got hold of the original poem if you did not send it to them, Margaret."

"I suppose I might have," she admitted with a vague gesture. "But in any case, that is why I did not care for London. Too full of coxcombs, and it did not suit Twitter's constitution. I wish Mama would ship me off to Greece instead."

"Oh, dear. That would not do at all. Greece is full of Greeks!"

Margaret bit her lip to keep from smiling. She heard Austin choke back his laughter and then attempt to mask it with a highly artificial cough. "So it is," she said mildly, not wishing to hurt the dear woman's feelings.

"Well, where would you go if you had the choice?" Austin asked her when he had recovered.

Margaret settled down into a lying position on her elbow and helped herself to a tiny portion of the rolypoly pudding. It was very sweet of Austin to get it for her, but her appetite was entirely gone. "That is a difficult question," she said after a moment of thinking. "I should like to see Cork."

"Margaret, must you sprawl in the grass like that? I daresay your mama would not find it at all ladylike."

"Yes," she said simply. "I must."

"Cork?" Austin gave his portion of wild-goose in wine sauce a derisive poke. "What about the Continent? What about India? China? America?"

"Oh, yes!" she exclaimed eagerly. "Let's go there."

"Which one?"

"Oh, all of them." She flung her arm out in an encompassing gesture. "I would like to see the world. I mean the real world—not this one."

"This one is not real?" His left eyebrow quirked along with the left side of his mouth. Margaret had always liked that expression.

"Yes." She frowned thoughtfully. "It is real enough, but I always think of the real world as something more exotic than Ireland. I want to go somewhere where they wear turbans, or feathers, or nothing at all. I want to hear music from strange instruments and live in a house made of leaves and eat curried monkey meat or some such disgusting thing."

"Indeed." He wrinkled his nose. "I believe that that is a well-known Cork delicacy." He lay down on his back beside her. "I had no idea you had such a wild desire to travel."

"Oh, I do." She pulled up a blade of grass and twisted it around her finger. "I wish I could have gone on the Grand Tour with you. What was it like?"

"Oh, you know . . . grand."

She threw a handful of grass at him. "Don't be difficult, you horrid creature."

"I have told you about the trip a thousand times." He brushed the grass off his face and into his hair.

"But you know I love to hear about it. It is like a bedtime story to me. Perhaps I should go to Venice or some such place and end up being frightfully disappointed, because now I have everything all set out in my mind." She rolled onto her back beside him. She shot a glance toward Mrs. Ash to see how this would be received, but the woman had settled with her back against a tree, tucked a blanket up to her chin, and fallen asleep. A half-finished piece of pie was sliding slowly off her knees.

Austin was staring up at the canopy of leaves fluttering in the wind above them. "I don't think you would be disappointed wherever you should choose to go," he said. "Do you remember the plans we used to make for all our travels when we were children? You would build a tent in the nursery, and I would come up and tell you tales of my travels."

"Yes, but now I realize that you had never been farther than boarding school in County Louth."

"I may have misrepresented the extent of my wanderings, yes."

"But your description of the wandering tribes of the Sahara was so vivid," she said sarcastically. They lay in companionable silence for a few moments, looking through the leaves at the layers of clouds floating past each other in the sky. "Do you know where Spencer wanted to take me for our honeymoon?" she asked suddenly, turning onto her elbow again. "Longford."

"Nice place," he replied noncommittally. "To see his family, I suppose?"

"To spend a week with his mother. Now I am certain that Mrs. Weldon is a very nice woman, but it is not my idea of a honeymoon. I wanted to go to Italy or perhaps even Egypt, but I knew, of course, that we could not afford it on his officer's pay. Not when he had such a fondness for sporting carriages and gambling parlors. Mama and Papa were very kind, and they never opposed the match because he hadn't any money, but I always felt a little sad that I would never see Italy."

"Well, now you can," Austin said briskly.

"I suppose. Now that I am going to be an old maid. I intend to be quite an eccentric and travel everywhere I like. I could go to Constantinople or Malta, like Lady Elgin and Lady Stanhope." She rolled her eyes in self-mockery. "But you could come with me. That would be nice. Perhaps you and Kit and I could go."

"My sister is now married to Lord Evans and a child is due in May." He laughed. "She is quite big as a barn and very unlikely to wish to go to Constantinople."

"Oh, yes, I had forgotten that she had gotten married. How stupid of me. And how very inconvenient. I don't suppose she would want to go anywhere once the baby has come." She absently began picking the blades of grass out of his hair. It was nice, the way the cinnamon-colored curls sprang back when she combed through them.

Austin frowned and sat up, shaking the rest of the grass from himself impatiently. "Most likely not. Are you cold?"

Margaret sat up and looked around her, feeling slightly as though she had come out of a dream. Mrs. Ash had slipped farther down the tree trunk and was emitting faint snores. The familiar knot of pain wound up again beneath her ribs. "Yes," she said, chaffing her fingers. "February isn't exactly the ideal time for picnicking."

"Let's go for a quick walk around the park to get our blood moving again."

"I shall wake Twitter and tell her. She would be in quite a panic if she were to wake up and find us gone."

She leaned over and shook the woman's ankle gently. "Twitter dear, we are going for a walk. Just around the perimeter of the park. There is no need to bestir yourself in the least."

Mrs. Ash sat bolt upright. "Yes, yes, I was listening. We were talking of Lord Heckels's poetry. What a very well-bred man, not at all like an alabaster turkey."

Margaret could not help but laugh. "Austin is going to take me for a walk," she repeated.

"Yes. Lovely idea. Do take your muff, and dear me, your bonnet is on quite cockeyed. That is what comes of lying in the grass like some gypsy girl. Let me straighten it for you. Now, don't get out of my sight, mind. Your mama would be annoyed if anyone saw you walking without an escort. Even if it is only Mr. Bourke."

Margaret thought she saw Austin freeze as he was pulling on his gloves, but when she looked, he was brushing grass from his coat with an expression of utter unconcern.

"There. Now I am presentable," he said placidly. "Let us start at once. I find that I am always coldest after a meal."

"That is because all of your blood goes to your stomach to help you digest. Or so Spencer used to say."

"Well, I suppose he would know." Austin shrugged.

"Why do you say that?" she asked, allowing him to pull her to her feet.

"His father was a medical man." He adjusted her pelisse around her as though she were a child, settled her garnet-trimmed bonnet straight upon her head, and then pulled her into a very brisk walk across the lawn.

"Was he?" she said, thoughtfully. "I didn't know." She pondered this for a few moments. "I don't suppose I knew Spencer very well at all."

Austin did not reply, but picked up a stick to throw

to the mongrel who had previously been playing with the child.

"He just swept me off my feet, I suppose," she continued, almost to herself. "He has such a way with words that he makes . . . made me feel like I was the only person in the world. But I suppose he could charm the leaves off the trees. I feel like a true idiot to have allowed myself to fall in love with a red coat and pretty manners, like some schoolgirl." It felt strange to be angry with Spencer, but she realized that he was a much more appropriate target than Austin. Austin, who had allowed her to be swept away by Spencer's charm right from under his nose. But what would she have had him do?

The stick he had thrown was much larger than the dog itself, but the animal dragged it back across the lawn, comically wrestling with the awkward length of it. He growled playfully and refused to relinquish it. Austin crouched over and played tug-of-war with the stick for a few moments, then let it go. The shaggy creature staggered off triumphantly with its prize.

"Do you think he ever loved me?" she asked suddenly.

Austin stood up but didn't look at her. "Yes. I know he did. He just couldn't sustain it. It was his way. I knew it, but I thought that this time was different. I thought he would stay in love this time."

"That isn't very flattering." She frowned and walked beside him in silence for a long time. She turned and waved to Mrs. Ash, just to make sure the woman could see them. "I think," she said at last, "that I was also fickle." She darted a tentative glance at him. He turned to her and then looked away with a dismissive shrug.

"You knew how I felt about you, Margaret," he said in a low voice at last. "But I wanted you to be happy. That was the important thing."

The dog reappeared and dropped the stick expectantly at Austin's feet.

"Throw it!" demanded a little boy wearing a blue coat with four rows of enormous gilt buttons who was sitting with his nursemaid on a nearby bench. He had evidently been watching the interaction between Austin and the dog with an envious fascination. He shrieked with glee when Austin complied. The dog bounded after the stick. "I want to throw it next! I want to throw it next!" He slid off the seat and ran to watch the dog worrying the stick several yards away.

"Come back here, Robbie. Don't bother those people." His nurse attempted to pull him away. The boy promptly squatted onto his haunches and leaned back, preventing her from moving him without physically dragging him.

"He isn't bothering us," Margaret laughed. "But it isn't our dog. I don't know if he is friendly or not. I would hate for the boy to be bitten."

The animal was now making comical darts at Austin, taunting him with the stick it smugly dragged by one end. Two other children, a brother and a sister, towed their frazzled-looking nursemaid over to watch the antics of the little black and white cur.

"Give me the stick! I want to throw it!" Robbie demanded imperiously. His four-year-old face was set with determination.

"The dog is playing with it now," Margaret explained.

Austin pretended to lunge toward the animal, and it retreated, obviously delighted with the game. At a safe distance, it gave a triumphant yip, and the stick dropped to the ground. The children screamed with laughter. Egged on by an appreciative audience, the dog barked again, then dragged the stick back to Austin and begged him to repeat the performance.

"Throw it far! Throw it far!" the small mob clamored excitedly. Margaret looked around to see that several other children of various ages had joined them. Austin gave the stick a heave that sent it spinning end over end across the lawn, and they cheered.

"I wanted to throw it!" Robbie shouted, his chubby face going livid. Margaret braced herself for the inevitable screaming scene.

"How about we throw you?" Austin pretended that he was going to grab the boy and throw him after the dog.

"Nooooooo!" The child squealed and ran a few steps, looking back over his shoulder to assure that he would be chased.

Margaret doubled over with helpless laughter as the entire crowd of children ran after Austin as he pursued Robbie. This, of course, led to an impromptu game of tag.

"Nursie is a safe base!" a little girl screamed, her red sausage curls flying wildly as she flung herself into her nursemaid's arms.

"All nursies are safe bases!" an older boy announced. "But you can only stay to the count of three."

"And the pretty lady!" A boy, inches from being tagged by Austin wrapped his arms around Margaret's leg.

Austin grinned. "No, the pretty lady is *it!*" He gave her an ungentlemanly prod in the arm and ran, the flock of shouting children behind him.

The nursery maids, in their identical gray-and-white uniforms, gave her a collective look of sympathy. She dropped her fur muff onto the grass, flung her bonnet on top of it, and ran after the children.

CHAPTER FOUR

The game ended, as most do, with someone falling down and crying. Margaret picked up the unfortunate one, dusted him off, and by the time he was returned to his nurse, he was ready to announce solemnly that it was a very good game and would she please come play it with him again tomorrow.

"Perhaps I will." Margaret laughed, watching with regret as the nursery maids mobilized themselves to the task of sorting out children and assessing the damage done to skin and clothing.

The dog, who had raced about after the children in a wild and inscrutable game of his own, now flung himself panting onto the grass.

"I'm afraid you look positively hoydenish," Austin said as he returned to her, attempting vainly to tidy his cravat. He looked boyish with his hair wildly askew and his cheeks ruddy from running. He looked just as he had when he was fourteen after a game of football with the neighborhood lads.

"I'm certain that I do." She ineffectually smoothed her hair and pressed her cold hands against cheeks she knew were as flushed as his. "Oh, do stop it. You're only making the matter worse." She pushed his hands away impatiently and carefully uncrumpled the linen at his neck. The exercise must have been more vigor-

ous than she had thought. Her heart was still beating
quite fast from it as she stood beneath his chin with
her wrists resting lightly on his collarbone. He looked
down at her, his hazel eyes laughing as he gave an
exasperated sigh.

"My valet will have my hide. He spent a good three-
quarters of an hour on that this morning."

She realized after a moment that she had not replied
and was only staring up at him. She saw his eyes go
blank as he stepped slightly back with a deliberately
neutral expression.

Muttering something indistinguishable, Margaret
stepped away from him and turned to retrieve her
muff and bonnet. Her wool pelisse now felt unbearably
warm, so she dragged it off. How dare her body betray
her with that sudden, unexpected wash of desire?
Could she actually feel attracted to another man only
a few hours after Spencer's betrayal? And to Austin, of
all people!

It had been obvious last Christmas that he cared
deeply for her. He had always been kind, but somehow
his feelings had changed from those of a friend to
those of . . . of more than a friend. She was glad her
face was red from the game, as several extremely un-
maidenly thoughts unexpectedly darted through her
mind.

But when his dashing friend Captain Weldon had
appeared at the Coits' Christmas ball, any thought of
familiar, comfortable Austin had melted from her
mind like snow. As she picked up the muff and dusted
it off, the dog made a little dash at it, yipping and
growling furiously.

"It's not another dog, you silly creature!" she chided
it, happy to have some distraction from the tall man
standing behind her. She demonstrated by shaking the
muff, but the dog continued to bark.

"Poor thing. He is jealous. Give that to me, and you

must go and pet him to show him that you still love him best," Austin said with forced joviality.

"Good heavens! The animal's filthy!" she exclaimed with a laugh as she reached down to gingerly rub the mongrel's head. "Aren't you filthy, you naughty thing. Who do you belong to?" she asked the dog in a caressing voice. "Who let's you run around harassing children in the park?"

The shaggy black-and-white animal rolled delightedly onto his back, his mouth agape with pleasure. He appeared to have entirely forgotten the existence of the encroaching muff.

"There, now I have paid attention to you, little mangy monster. Go off and find someone else to play with while we go and pack up our lunch." She pulled his ears fondly and then stood up to tie her bonnet back onto her head.

"Let's pack up the luncheon things and drive out to Sandymount Strand. I hear there is a point-to-point on. Brendan Coit is running that gray of his in it." Austin spoke in such a normal voice that she decided that the momentary awkwardness she had felt between them had been entirely her imagination.

"That sounds nice." They walked together toward where they had abandoned the remains of their luncheon. The dog rolled to his feet and cheerfully followed them. "Coit's always had dreams of raising a Newmarket winner. Is this the gray sired by Chieftain? I hope he has refrained from overtraining this one. Last year the bay he ran was near touched in the wind." She chattered on, hoping to tease him out of the distant politeness he had withdrawn into.

A sudden motion caught her eye. "Oh, dear, that dog is following us," she said. "We shouldn't have paid so much attention to him. Oh!" she gave a sudden shriek of dismay and pounced on the animal, who had streaked ahead of them and was now happily gobbling up the last of the roly-poly pudding. "You terrible creature! My pudding. You had to eat that. I might have shared the Devonshire cream, but not the lovely pudding." She wrestled him away from the plate he was licking, laughing so hard she could barely restrain him when he transferred his affection to her face.

"Oh, dear!" Mrs. Ash exclaimed. "What is that dog doing here? Get it away, Mr. Bourke! He is eating up all the food! Shoo! Get away! Oh, don't let it near you, Margaret! It is most likely diseased!" She flapped her blanket at the dog, who continued to lavish affection on Margaret.

Austin dropped to his knees and began putting what was left of their luncheon into the hamper. "I never would have thought you would have such an ill-mannered dog," he said mockingly. He shook his head sadly as the animal's loving maul knocked her entirely over.

"My dog?" she protested indignantly.

"I think he's yours now."

"Oh, no. I have no need for a dog. Besides, Mama would have a fit. Especially when he is such a very ugly creature." She ruffled his dusty fur and then turned to help Austin and Mrs. Ash with the dishes.

"With your permission, Twitter, we would like to drive out to Sandymount Strand this afternoon. Don't you think that the seaside would be just the thing? It is such a very fine day."

"Oh, dear. Your Mama will not know where we have gone. But I suppose she is busy with her guests. She would most likely not wish to be bothered. After all, she did say that I was to see that you were amused and did not fall into the megrims. But it is always so windy by the seaside. And of course there would not be seabathing this time of year. Though as we have not brought our seabathing costumes, we should not have been able to go anyway. And of course it would not have been at all the thing for Mr. Bourke to accompany us."

"We are not going seabathing. We are going to see a point-to-point."

"A horse race? Are you certain it is appropriate? Will ladies be there?"

"Of course," Margaret replied. "Papa has taken me out there many times. It is everything proper. Besides, I shall have you to lend me countenance." She gave her companion a saucy grin. Mrs. Ash reluctantly agreed, but bewailed for several minutes the likelihood of losing her position without a character.

"For heaven knows I don't like to deny you girls anything. Your mama says I am far too lenient with you."

"We use you grievously," Margaret agreed fondly.

"Then it is settled," Austin said briskly. "I sent the curricle home. I didn't want to keep the horses standing, or force Will to walk them up and down the street for some indeterminate amount of time. My home is only a little ways from here on Dame Street. When that tiger of mine deigns to return from whatever personal errand he has disappeared on, I will have him order up the phaeton." He smiled wickedly at Mrs. Ash. "I would never be so chuckle-headed as to order the curricle. Mrs. Ash would make me ride on the dickey with Will while she drove it out to Sandymount herself."

"Oh, good heavens!" that woman exclaimed. "I don't even know how to drive a donkey, never mind those fine bays of yours, Mr. Bourke. It would be a fine thing, me driving a curricle. But you are teasing me. Of course, if you wish to order the phaeton it would be infinitely more comfortable. I don't mind riding bodikin for a short time in a curricle, but you must agree, it was not a carriage desired for more than two. But I should hate to inconvenience you. If you would rather use your curricle, I am sure that it is a fine piece of equipment. I should never insist on the phaeton!"

"Miss Fitzpatrick, your duenna is a termagant."
Austin bowed ironically.

"Oh, dear! I didn't mean—"

"Oh, do stop torturing her, Austin," Margaret said
absently, a furrow forming between her brows. She
caught the concerned look Austin threw her.

"Ah! There is the miscreant," he said cheerfully as
Will ambled across the lawn, gravely eating a large slice
of bread and cheese. An apple in each of his pockets
made his breeches stand out on each side like panniers.

Inquiry revealed that Will had gone to the corner
of the park to mock the inferior positions of several
tigers who attended gentlemen possessing less splendid
cattle than those of his own master. He cast a regretful
look at the empty roly-poly pudding plate and then
trotted off on his errand.

"Margaret, will you take a turn around the park with
me while we wait for the carriage? Would you mind
waiting here for the carriage, Mrs. Ash? I should hate
for my groom to miss us when he drives up."

Margaret was about to protest that they had just
come from a walk around the park when she saw that
Austin was trying to silently convey a wish to speak
with her alone.

"You are certainly one for walking, Mr. Bourke! I
daresay that is how you keep so fit. You may walk as
much as you like." A decided twinkle appeared in her
eye. "But this time you will refrain from playing tag.
I am not such an old woman that I cannot see when
you are behaving like a pair of bear cubs. I am certain
that I do not mind, but I think that Mrs. Fitzpatrick
might have different ideas about propriety. I should
hate for her to scold me."

"You are awake on all suits." Austin acknowledged
this hit with a slight bow. "We shall only take a very
sedate walk this time, I assure you." He drew Margaret

We'd Like to Invite You to Subscribe to Zebra's Regency Romance Book Club and Give You a Gift of 4 Free Books as Your Introduction! *(Worth $19.96!)*

If you're a Regency lover, imagine the joy of getting 4 FREE Zebra Regency Romances and then the chance to have the lovely stories delivered to your home each month at the lowest prices available! Well, that's our offer to you and here's how you benefit by becoming a Zebra Home Subscription Service subscriber:

- 4 FREE Introductory Regency Romances are delivered to your doorst
- 4 BRAND NEW Regencies are then delivered each month (usually befor they're available in bookstores)
- Subscribers save almost $4.00 every month
- Home delivery is always FREE
- You also receive a FREE monthly newsletter, *Zebra/ Pinnacle Roman News* which features author profiles, contests, subscriber benefits, bo previews and more
- No risks or obligations...in other words you can cancel whenever you wish with no questions asked

Join the thousands of readers who enjoy the savings and convenience offered to Regency Romance subscribers. After your initial introductory shipment, you receive 4 brand-new Zebra Regency Romances each month to examine for 10 days. Then, if you decide to keep the books, you'll pay the preferred subscriber's price of just $4.00 per title. That's only $16.00 for all 4 books and there's never an extra charge for shipping and handling.

It's a no-lose proposition, so return the FREE BOOK CERTIFICATE today!

Say Yes to 4 Free Books!
Complete and return the order card to receive this $19.96 value, ABSOLUTELY FREE!

(If the certificate is missing below, write to:)
Zebra Home Subscription Service, Inc.,
120 Brighton Road, P.O. Box 5214, Clifton, New Jersey 07015-5214
or call TOLL-FREE 1-888-345-BOOK

FREE BOOK CERTIFICATE

YES! Please rush me 4 Zebra Regency Romances without cost or obligation. I understand that each month thereafter I will be able to preview 4 brand-new Regency Romances FREE for 10 days. Then, if I should decide to keep them, I will pay the money-saving preferred subscriber's price of just $16.00 for all 4...that's a savings of almost $4 off the publisher's price with no additional charge for shipping and handling. I may return any shipment within 10 days and owe nothing, and I may cancel this subscription at any time. My 4 FREE books will be mine to keep in any case.

Name _____

Address _____ Apt. _____

City _____ State _____ Zip _____

Telephone ( ) _____

Signature _____

(If under 18, parent or guardian must sign.)

RN010A

Terms and prices subject to change. Orders subject to acceptance by Zebra Home Subscription Service, Inc. Offer valid in U.S. only.

away, smiling as he saw the dog trailing faithfully behind her.

"Why the long face?" he asked at last, after Margaret realized she had unleashed another heavy sigh.

She lifted her shoulders and let them fall. "I don't know. I suppose I started thinking again."

His brows drew together. "Now that means I am not doing my job. You are not allowed to think today."

She tried to laugh with limited success. "I'm just confused. I think I will be all right, and then I realize that I am having a good time, and it seems all wrong. And then it all comes rushing back to me that Spencer isn't going to marry me."

"I imagine you will continue to feel this way for a while. And then you will realize that you think of him a little less. And then you will start to enjoy things a little more and perhaps feel a little guilty for that. And then one day, poof, you will realize that you hardly ever think of him at all, and perhaps you don't remember his face very distinctly, and maybe, just maybe you could possibly be a little better off without him."

She heaved another sigh. "Can't I just skip to that part?"

He looked at her, his face suddenly solemn. "If I could go through it for you, you know I would."

She felt an inexplicable rush of tenderness toward him. "I wouldn't put you through this." She gave him a pathetic rendition of a smile. "Yes, yes," she continued mockingly. "And when I am nearly recovered, he will return to say it has all been a mistake."

"No, he won't," Austin countered darkly. "If he ever sets foot in Dublin again, I will call him out." His mouth had compressed into a thin, deadly line. "Which arguably should have been done anyway." He paused, seeing her shake her head violently. His next words were low and serious. "Promise me that you will never take him back after this."

She was silent for a long moment, pretending to settle the skirts of her pearl-colored lutestring gown against the cool wind that had sprung up. The dress, with its deep border of garnet embroidery, was meant to be her going-away gown for when she left on her honeymoon with Spencer. She decided not to wear it again. "I wouldn't," she said at last. "I'm not likely to get the opportunity to take him back, but I wouldn't. How could I ever believe him if he were to say that he loved me, when he said it only yesterday." She looked up at him in bewildered pain. "Was it yesterday?"

"I don't know, Meggie," he said softly.

"Yesterday," she repeated vaguely. "And today he doesn't." She looked straight ahead, glad that the narrow poke of her bonnet was enough to hide her face.

Austin took her hand and pressed it between his own. She felt the warmth of his hand come through their gloves and suddenly longed to strip them off to feel his bare hands with her own. She needed real contact. In an instant she had flung her arms around his neck and was crying uncontrollably into his mangled cravat.

She felt his arms tighten in surprise around her. "Margaret, Margaret . . . you know it isn't that simple. He did care for you. He must have. I . . . I don't know why this has happened to you." He patted her tentatively on the shoulder. "Please stop. I don't know what to do when you cry."

She knew he didn't want this. She could feel his resistance as she clung to him, but she couldn't force herself to release him. "I'm sorry." Dragging out the handkerchief he had given her in the hotel, she tried to staunch the tears, but they were already out of control. Austin stood still and let her sob against him for a long time. Even when she had stopped, she stood for ages, just breathing rhythmically against his chest. If only everything could stop now. She could stay here forever in the circle of his arms, drawing strength from the comforting smell of his coat as the wind fluttered her dress around them both.

She stepped back at last, snuffling and somewhat disoriented. The top of her head felt bare, and she noticed with surprise that her bonnet was hanging by its ribbons down her back. The sun was still shining, in blatant disregard for her feelings. "I'm sorry," she said again, her voice hoarse.

"It's all right," he tried to laugh. "That's what I'm for."

She tied her bonnet back on, very aware that her face must be very blotchy from the tempest. "I shouldn't have," she croaked. She suppressed the surprising and mutinous idea that if his role had been reversed with Austin's, Spencer would not have been so understanding. He disliked scenes, and tears confused and irritated him. He was a man of charm and passion, but not really the best man in an emotional crisis. But how wicked of her to even think such a thing.

"There now," Austin broke the awkward silence that threatened. "Your dog has become very anxious about you." He pointed to where the shaggy mongrel lay in the grass, regarding her with patient brown eyes. The instant they looked at him, he sprang up and began tearing around in excited circles.

"He's not my dog," she insisted.

"Perhaps we should name him."

"No. Honestly, Austin, I can't take him home." She shoved her handkerchief into the pocket inside her muff and wished she could breathe through her nose again without snorting. How extremely undignified.

"But he's so very fond of you," Austin persisted.

"He's the only one," she muttered.

"Ah now, don't say that," he chided gently.

She smiled. "Of course I don't mean it. You have been very kind. More than kind. Very wonderful. And you even let me cry on you, when I know you hated it." Austin made a small noise of protest in his throat, but she continued. "And I quite ruined your cravat."

"I'm sure if you make a formal apology to my valet . . ." He twitched the linen at his neck carelessly. "Now, as for your dog . . . how about something pertaining to Valentine's Day?"

"Like Cupid or Sweetheart?" She grimaced. "Austin, I never want to remember today. If I called the creature Valentine or some such thing, I would always remember the circumstances of how I found him. Not that I intend to keep the animal," she amended.

The dog left off harassing a flock of rock doves and bounded after them as Margaret and Austin continued around the perimeter of the park.

"How about Blackie?"

"That's very ordinary."

"Killer? Tiger? Gentleman Jackson? The Fancy? How about Molyneaux?"

"I will not name the poor cur after some boxer," she asserted stoutly. "Actually, I don't care. It can be your dog. You can name him whatever you want." She knew he was trying to cheer her up with this silly conversation. It was pointless, but it was kind of him to try.

"Cuchulainn? Brian Boro? Bran?" he continued.

"He isn't quite fearsome enough for such epic names."

"Fluffy?"

She rolled her eyes.

"Mister Fluffy Bunny? I quite like that. What do you think?"

"Mister Mangy more like." She cast a glance backward to see the creature blithely following them, stopping occasionally to pay attention to the needs of his resident fleas.

"How about Roly-Poly Pudding? It is his preferred dessert, after all."

Margaret could not help but laugh. "Oh, it would

be a good name, but really, I don't want to get attached to him. He probably belongs to someone or will run off just when I am thinking of him as my own." She patted the creature's dusty head and smirked in derision at herself. "It must be difficult being such a highly symbolic dog."

"Now don't become a watering pot on me again, my dear," Austin cautioned. "Or I shall have to distract you by trying to think of even stupider names for your dog."

She leaned her head affectionately against his sleeve as they walked. "Oh, don't. I won't cry. I just need some time to be sad."

"That is allowed." He nodded gravely. "I am sure I plague you more than any brother ever could."

She wondered briefly if he could ever again think of her as something more than a sister. Surely last Christmas it had seemed . . . but now things were different. "Of course you do. That is what keeps me sane." It was positively wicked of her to even think of Austin when she was in love with his closest friend. "How lucky your sister Kitty is!"

"I am not certain she always would have agreed. I don't believe she ever forgave me for hiding behind the couch while she received her first proposal. How I taunted her for that! She had been practicing what she would say for weeks, and then she completely fell apart when the moment came."

"I wish I had been there!"

"You were barely out of leading strings at the time."

"That's impossible. I am only four years younger than you." She gave a dry half laugh. "Well, you had better look behind the couch when you are proposing to some young miss. You know how very much I would like to hear you doing the pretty to whatever little widgeon you choose."

"Very unlikely," he grunted.

Margaret wondered if he meant that it was unlikely

she would be present at the event or unlikely that he would propose with finesse to this unknown creature who had caught his fancy. It was probably eating too much roly-poly pudding that gave her a tiny pain in her stomach.

"There is the phaeton," Austin said suddenly. "I should make Twitter drive, just to tease her."

"As if you would ever let anyone but yourself handle your horses."

"I didn't say I would. I said I should," he laughed. "Mrs. Ash," he called out, "I am afraid that you will have to hold the dog on your lap."

"What?" The poor woman looked at the filthy animal with an expression of complete repulsion.

"Margaret has become very fond of the creature, and since it is obviously a stray, we have decided to take him with us. But you will have to hold him on your lap so that he doesn't jump out of the carriage. It won't take over an hour to get to Sandymount."

"Oh, dear. Well, if you insist. I am not at all sure that Mrs. Fitzpatrick will be pleased." She gave a nervous laugh. "Are you quite certain? After all, he might not like the carriage. I would not like to be bitten." She regarded the dog with the greatest misgivings. "He is quite dirty."

"Most of that will probably rub off. I'd mind your gown if I were you. It's the fleas that will have to be scrubbed away," he said cheerfully, giving Margaret a subtle wink.

"Poor Twitter, you know he is teasing you. The creature will most likely not want to get into the carriage anyway. We will leave him in the park. Surely here he will have children to play with and plenty of pudding." She shook her finger at the dog in mock remonstration, fondled its ears for a moment, and then allowed Austin to hand her into the phaeton. She gave a surprised yelp when the dog bounded up after her without a moment's hesitation. "Oh, dear. You really are persistent. You nearly knocked me off my feet. Could we really take him with us, Austin? What if he already has an owner? It would be cruel to steal someone else's dog."

"Of course he will come. He belongs to you." He helped Mrs. Ash into the phaeton and then got up on the perch. Will jumped onto the dickey and the entourage swept away, leaving the groom who had driven the carriage over to St. Stephen's Green to carry home the remains of the luncheon and shake his head over the strange starts of Quality.

CHAPTER FIVE

The dog, now officially christened Roly-Poly Pudding, stuck his head over the side of the phaeton and barked. His greeting was answered by a chorus of yelps from a pack of highly bred hunting dogs who were romping about on the bluff of sea grass at the edge of the strand.

"I see that everyone's gathered at the other end. They are running several races today. Coit's gray runs in the fourth. It should be nearly ready to start." Austin guided the horses over to where a large crowd of people had formed. Most were local farmers, fishermen, and innkeepers, but a number of gentlemen had ridden out from town to see the race. There were a few female faces among the crowd, and one conspicuous carriage full of ladies.

"Why, hello, Miss Fitzpatrick!" one of the women called out. "How very delighted I am to see you!"

The young lady wore a bonnet so highly festooned with feathers that it was difficult to see her face, but there was no mistaking her voice. Margaret cringed.

"Sorry, Meggie. I didn't know," Austin murmured as he opened the door of the phaeton and handed her down. Roly-Poly had the bad manners to leap out the door the moment it was opened. As the dog pushed past her, she nearly lost her balance, but Austin steadied her with a firm hand on her waist. She smiled gratefully up at him when she was safely on the ground. "Thank you. That would have been humiliating on top of everything." She read his eyes. "It doesn't matter. I would have to face her at some point." She watched in amusement as the faithless Roly-Poly raced around in frenetic circles with the other dogs.

"Do come over and sit by me, dear Miss Fitzpatrick. We shall have a nice comfortable coze, just you and me." Miss Chloe Waring pushed one of her younger sisters into the back-facing seat to make room in their stately landau.

Margaret shot Austin a look of silent agony and then turned a pleasant face to Miss Waring. "How nice to see you. I hope that you are well. You remember Mr. Bourke, and of course Mrs. Ash."

"Indeed, I am very well." She simpered coquettishly at Austin and ignored Mrs. Ash completely. "It is you I am worried about. My dear, I heard the news!" Her voice dropped to a volume that was still absolutely audible but held deep imprecations of scandal, "How terrible for you!"

"The wedding has only been postponed. There is no need to stop the printing presses at the *Times,* Miss Waring," Austin said lightly. "I saw the captain just this morning, and he was absolutely distraught. Terrible emergency in his family. You know how delicate his mother's health has always been. There was nothing to do but postpone the event. It would not be at all fitting to continue with the wedding if his mother was not able to attend."

Margaret threw him a grateful look, which he pretended not to see. Indeed, she had never even met Mrs. Weldon, and Spencer had assured her that she would be much happier if she could be spared the trouble of coming to Dublin for the wedding and

would be happy to receive her new daughter-in-law
when they arrived in Longford for their honeymoon.

She reluctantly allowed Austin to hand her into the
landau and civilly greeted the clutch of Warings who
cheeped out their greetings in exact imitation of their
older sister. They were all eyeing her as though she
were an exotic animal at the Tower Zoo in London.

"Is that her?" asked the youngest in a reverent tone
of horror. She evidently was under the misapprehen-
sion that cupping her hand to her sister's ear rendered
her words entirely private.

"I am surprised to see you here, Miss Waring," Margaret said coolly, "I had no idea you were interested
in horse racing."

"Oh, good heavens, I'm not. I am here because
Mayo's horse is running. You know Lord Mayo, my
fiance." She smugly indicated an elderly gentleman
mounted on a magnificent black hunter. Margaret
bowed politely and smiled her sympathy toward him.
It was well known that the match was made between
Mayo's title and the Waring banking fortune.

"Will Mayo ride?" she asked.

Miss Waring gave her a look of disdain. "Himself? I
should think not. A groom will, of course." She
slapped the hand of the youngest Waring, who was
biting her cuticle, and then smoothed her own tan
Limerick gloves with careful precision.

Margaret critically eyed the horses who were gathering for the next race. "I think that if I raised racing
horses, I should like to be the one to ride them in
races. Not the large racing meets, of course, but infor-
mal ones, such as these."

"Really, Miss Fitzpatrick? How very shocking!" Miss
Waring's hand flew to her mouth in exaggerated
shock. "But you always were so . . . original in your
ideas."

"I meant if I were a man," Margaret explained
haughtily through clenched teeth.

"Of course," Miss Waring agreed condescendingly. "I am sure you hardly know what you are saying. You look dreadfully pulled, my dear. But who could blame you, after what has happened. I am surprised that your mama let you go driving. I should be just prostrate if my wedding were"—she paused infinitesimally—"postponed."

Margaret responded with a tight smile. How infuriating to have to put up with Chloe Waring's thinly veiled mockery! Of course, the girl would lose no time in telling the town that she had seen the poor, jilted Margaret Fitzpatrick at the point-to-point and she looked just dreadful, poor creature. Margaret had made her come-out in London the same year as Chloe but had never been able to like her much. Now she would have liked nothing better than to slap her pretty, smirking face.

"Did I see a dog arrive with you?" Miss Waring asked.

"Well, yes. I seem to have acquired him just today."

"You cannot possibly mean that mangy black-and-white creature! He looks like a stray!"

"Yes. His name is Roly-Poly Pudding."

The Warings gave a collective shriek of laughter. "What a very odd name for a dog, to be sure!" Chloe eyed the dog with disapproval.

"And he isn't very roly-poly at all," added one of her sisters. "In fact, he's all skin and bones."

Margaret watched fondly as the animal raced happily around with the other dogs. "I shall fatten him up."

Miss Waring's smile was brightly innocent. "What kind of dog is he?"

"Oh, purebred mongrel, I believe." The creature looked rather comically out of place among the pack of hunting dogs. "But the other dogs don't seem to mind at all. How very democratic they are," she laughed.

"Indeed. I am sure you are so very kindhearted to

bring home a stray dog. I am sure you bring home street urchins as well. How lucky you are to have a mama who does not think these things ill-bred." She gave a little titter. "My mama would be shocked, indeed, if I were to bring home diseased animals. But she is very particular. Perhaps you do not have to be so careful of being labeled eccentric, as you are to be married so soon."

Margaret was spared the necessity of a retort when Brendan Coit turned his mount from where he had been talking with Austin and approached the carriage full of the Waring ladies. After greeting Chloe and her sisters, he turned to Margaret. "How do you do, Miss Fitzpatrick?" he said so solicitously that she knew that he had heard the whole story.

"How do you do, Mr. Coit? I hope your gray is in fine form today." She frankly admired the deep-chested animal with its small, intelligent head and well-formed shoulders.

"Isn't he the sweetest goer you ever saw? Did you see him run at Punchestown? Sired by Chieftain, you know. I do hope you are going to lay your wagers in my favor."

"Of course I will. But I am afraid you might be up to some strong competition from the O'Conner bay. I saw him run the Merrion Strand point-to-point last month. How is Fomorii in sand?"

Coit patted the gray's neck proudly. "I never saw such an animal for a soft run." He grinned confidently, lifted his hat to her, and then turned the horse to join the group of contestants.

"What a shocking flirt. Small wonder Captain Weldon jilted her."

Margaret heard the words faintly behind her and set her jaw.

Squire Mannix was reading out the list of entrants for the fourth race of the day. "All right, gentlemen," he concluded, "I am sure you all know the rules because they couldn't be more simple. We'll start the race at the north end of the strand when I fire my pistol. The finish is between that big boulder and the land. My boy Reginald will stand on the boulder with a towel so you can all see him, and he will be the judge of any close finishes." The squire pulled out his pocket watch, gave a decided grunt, and then mounted his cob to lead the contestants out to the starting point.

The rest of the crowd moved in a disorganized train toward the finishing point. The bookmakers with their leather money pouches and books of yellow betting stubs began scribbling the odds on their slate boards, keeping a close eye on the competition and calling out to the crowd that they offered best payout on a winner.

"I put ten pounds down for you for Coit's gray to win," Austin announced, striding alongside the Warings' carriage as it made its slow way toward the finishing point.

"And how much did you put down for yourself?" Margaret asked, wishing she could escape from the landau. She took the yellow ticket he handed her and tucked it inside her glove.

"A pony."

"Twenty-five pounds?" she gasped faintly.

"Well, the odds started out in favor of the gray." He shrugged sheepishly. "But now it is nearly even with Michael Kelly's bay. Have you seen it, Margaret? A great monster of an animal. You know everything out of the Kelly stables is top-notch. It will be close."

"Are you betting, Miss Fitzpatrick?" Miss Waring's pale brows rose nearly into the brim of her be-feathered bonnet. "How very dashing, to be sure. I am not at all sure that my mama would approve if I were to gamble on a common horse race. Especially one that isn't even on a downs." The younger Misses Waring echoed this sentiment eagerly.

"But you do gamble at faro, do you not? I fail to see the difference."

Chloe Waring gave a trill of laughter. "It is entirely different. A lady might have a gentleman lay a bet for her at Ascot or Newmarket or some such genteel gathering, but really! A point-to-point! My mama would have the vapors, to be sure."

"Then we must certainly be glad that she isn't here," Margaret replied coolly.

The nest of younger ladies all chirped their agreement, but Chloe scowled. "Well," she said brittlely, "I am certain that some gentlemen would consider it very unladylike, but as long as Captain Weldon doesn't mind. . . ." She smiled sweetly. "And you, Mr. Bourke—I shall be very cross with you if you forget that you are engaged to dance the first waltz with me at Lady Sligo's masquerade next week." She shook her finger at him with an expression of arch coquetry.

Margaret looked at Austin in surprise, but his face was impassive. "Of course I would not forget," he replied.

She realized she had been waiting for him to deny it, but he was smiling and bowing over Chloe Waring's hand like the veriest of fools. Austin and Chloe? The thought was insupportable. Of course he had a right to dance with whoever he wanted, but how could he admire someone with such a cruel streak behind her lovely china doll face? Besides, Austin had always claimed *her* for the first waltz. At least until Captain Weldon had come along.

"Shall I place a bet for you, Miss Waring?" Lord Mayo asked, looking over his shoulder from where he was taking a betting ticket from a bookmaker.

Miss Waring shuddered dramatically. "No, indeed!"

"I am sure Miss Fitzpatrick will agree with you when she has lost ten pounds," Austin laughed good-naturedly.

"Mr. Bourke?" one of the younger Misses Waring

piped up. "Why don't gentlemen just pick a horse they *think* will win without putting any money on it, and then just wait to find out if they guessed correctly? That way they would not be in danger of losing any money," she concluded logically.

Both Margaret and Austin blinked at her in bemused disbelief. "I believe the excitement comes from actually risking the money, unfortunately," Austin said at last, his crooked smile the only evidence that he was having trouble keeping his mirth in check.

"Well, that's what I would do anyway," the young Miss Waring asserted firmly.

"Do you know, Austin, I don't believe I shall be able to see the race very well from here. Will you hand me out so that I can stand nearer the strand?" Margaret stretched out her hand pleadingly.

She took leave of the Warings and gave a mental sigh of relief as Austin handed her down from the carriage. "Of course, the child is quite right." Margaret laughed as they walked along the shallow bluff. She squinted out over the stark flatness of the strand. The hard blonde sand at low tide stretched out nearly as far as the eye could see. It was hard to believe that at high tide the water would have lapped nearly to the wheels of the carriages.

"It would make perfect sense to only bet mentally," she said. It would be unfair to censure Austin's admiration of Chloe Waring. After all, it was nothing to her. She only didn't want to see Austin hurt, since Miss Waring's engagement to Mayo was quite settled. "You are either a gambler or you are not. Young Miss Patience Waring is likely to never be in debt her entire life."

"I have no doubt that even a gaming hell flat would have trouble losing the Waring fortune," he returned. "Rich as Croesus, old Waring. But I would not trade places with Mayo for anything."

Margaret shot him a quick look. "You gave me the impression that you admired her very much."

Austin turned to her with a frank expression in his hazel eyes. "She is the most catty creature on the face of the earth, to be sure, but she is very beautiful. And she is a particularly good dancer. Furthermore, she is engaged to Mayo, and therefore I can enjoy a good waltz without fear of any need to come up to scratch for it."

Margaret was conscious of a very unpleasant sensation underneath her ribs. "How convenient," she murmured neutrally.

"Are you jealous? It hardly suits you."

She gave him a wide smile. "Not in the least," she lied. "I only want for you to be happy, and I should be sorry if Mayo had stepped in ahead of you." At least that was true.

"Not at all," he laughed pleasantly.

The entire subject was making her feel depressed again, so she pushed it from her mind. After all, Austin's romantic entanglements were of supreme indifference to her, so long as they did not jeopardize his friendship with her.

The wind from the sea was sharp and pungent. Margaret inhaled it deeply as she held her bonnet to her head with one hand. The sea birds wheeling overhead took turns folding their wings to plunge down and pluck small crabs from the shallow pools that decorated the wide strand like mirrors. A Martello Tower, built to keep watch for an invading French fleet, stood solemnly at the south end of the beach. It seemed a slightly ominous reminder of reality compared to the frivolity of the point-to-point.

She shaded her eyes and looked across the beach to where the contestants had gathered at the starting point. "You are right, Kelly's bay looks like a good goer. You can tell how big he is even from here. It may well be goodbye ten pounds. But I shall have confidence in Coit." They watched in silence as the riders prepared for the starting gun. The wind blunted its sharp crack, but they could see the animals bound into motion.

The crowd let out a roar of approval and surged to the edge of the shallow bluff, where they could see the small figures of the horses moving as a fluid clump, the sounds of their hoofbeats too far away to be heard. After their initial shout, the crowd fell quiet as they concentrated fully on the race that seemed to be taking place in miniature and in silence at the end of the strand.

"Kelly's ahead!" Mayo shouted, and the crowd sprang back to life. In an instant everyone else was shouting and squinting and demanding that Mayo, the only one who had had the foresight to bring opera glasses, give a report. "Kelly followed by the O'Conner filly! Third is between Merrion's roan and the Coit gray! The gray is third! Only half a length behind the filly!"

Margaret clutched Austin's arm and gave a delighted whoop. The horses were coming closer. Faintly she could hear their disembodied hoofbeats roaring across the hard-packed sand. The riders lay nearly flat over their horses' manes, urging them on with shrill cries. Far down the strand lay a scattering of hats, lost in the first instants of the race. Squire Mannix came loping down the beach, far behind the riders.

"Kelly and Coit! Kelly is first by a neck with Coit gaining!"

The riders were barely a quarter of a mile away when Margaret felt something brush by her skirt. The pack of dogs had seen the horses and were now racing across the strand barking wildly.

"Get the dogs off the course!" Mayo shouted. Michael Kelly's younger brother gave an urgent whistle and the pack of hunting dogs stopped on their haunches and turned around, their tongues rolling delightedly. The black-and-white mongrel continued running directly toward the galloping horses.

"Stop!" Margaret screamed, entirely aware that the dog would not mind her. She ran after him, her gray halfboots sinking helplessly into the strip of soft sand. Her feet could not keep up with her, and she fell to her knees in the sharp, salty grass that grew at the edge of the beach. There was no way she could catch him. She knew the horses would instinctually attempt to avoid trampling him, but riders could be killed if the animals fell or threw them.

The crowd gave a collective gasp of horror as the riders veered away, sawing at the bits and colliding violently with each other as they tried to control their mounts. The big bay shied and balked, throwing the unfortunate Mr. Kelly over his head and into the shallow water of a large puddle.

The younger Kelly began a long string of rather ingeniously cognated curses.

"Get the dog off the course! Who let that animal out there?" Lord Mayo roared.

Austin was the first to recover. He ran out on the strand and caught the reins of the frightened bay. Kelly stood up, far more furious than hurt, and the rest of the riders dismounted to assess any injuries to their mounts.

"Is everyone all right?" Margaret gasped, running up to where Brendan Coit was inspecting the gray's legs.

"He's fine." Coit looked around him. "Everyone else appears all right. But the damned race is a complete bollocks. Excuse my language, Miss Fitzpatrick. Neck and neck! Damn! Who let that dog on the course?"

"I'm sorry, Mr. Coit."

"It's mine, Brendan," Austin announced grimly, coming up to where they stood. "I found it just today and as you can see, it is entirely untrained. I will take responsibility for any injuries to the riders or their mounts."

Margaret looked up in surprise. "No, Mr. Coit, the dog is mine."

"Bourke!" Mayo bellowed. "You should know better than to bring some untrained mongrel out here. Get that animal out before I shoot him."

"No, milord, it is my fault. The dog is mine," Margaret insisted.

"I don't care whose dog it is! Get the cur off the course!" young Kelly shouted. The crowd roared their approval.

Margaret swept the dog into her arms and staggered up toward the bluff. A furious debate had begun regarding the outcome of the race and the paying out of bets. As she approached them, they gave a collective cry of disapproval. The dog wriggled in fright and nearly slipped out of her grasp. She felt a hand at her waist, and Austin put his arm around the dog, stabilizing it against her. He pushed them quickly through the crowd, which seemed near violence in its disgust at having the race ruined.

She got into the carriage with less grace than haste, and Austin whipped up the horses. Their retreat was hailed by the roar of the triumphant mob and Mrs. Ash's confused wailing.

"What has happened? Why are we leaving?"

"Did you not see?" Margaret demanded in shock.

"Oh, dear me. I couldn't see a thing. I had just gotten my network out of my reticule, and I was starting to work on that purse I am making for your mama. You remember she was saying that her black one was quite worn out! I wasn't paying the slightest attention to what was going on because, you see, I had nearly thought I had brought the wrong size net hook. I don't much care for horse races. Or horses, for that matter. I had a pony when I was quite young, but that is not quite the same thing, is it? But it turned out that I had the right hook after all." She brandished it awkwardly as they bounced around in the jolting phaeton.

"A fine chaperone you are," Austin said dryly from the box.

"What has happened? Must you drive quite so fast, Mr. Bourke? My bones are getting quite rattled apart back here!"

Margaret held the whimpering dog with one hand and the edge of the swaying phaeton with the other. "We were near being tarred and feathered back there! The stupid dog ran out on the course and ruined the race. We were drummed out of town!"

"What town?"

"Oh, Twitter! It is a figure of speech!"

Austin suddenly gave a loud, uninhibited laugh. "We shall have to go on the lam, of course."

Mrs. Ash gave a faint scream.

The ridiculousness of the situation suddenly dawned on Margaret and her sense of humor overwhelmed her awful sense of humiliation. "We will flee to the Continent! We will hide in caves until the next packet to India. I suspect we shall have to change our names as well," she agreed enthusiastically.

Mrs. Ash began a loud protest.

"It was becoming a lynch mob!" Margaret exclaimed delightedly. "Did you see poor young Kelly! I thought his head would burst! Thank goodness no one was hurt, but . . ."—she collapsed into helpless laughter against the squabs—"oh but they were so *angry!*" She gasped for breath. "And to think that we had to . . . had to *escape!*" She held the little dog closer to her and laughed until it hurt.

CHAPTER SIX

"Oh, dear, Margaret, you will make sure that you tell your mama that the whole affair was not my fault. I should so hate it if she was cross with me," Mrs. Ash said for the ninth time as she twisted her gloves in her lap.

"Of course, Twitter. I told you everything would be all right." Margaret leaned her head back tiredly and closed her eyes for a moment. When she opened them, she saw Roly-Poly Pudding lying with his dusty head on the seat of the carriage as he regarded her with worshipful eyes.

"She will be so displeased to hear that you made a scene."

"Well, it hardly signifies now. The damage is done." She suppressed a smile at the memory. "Please don't let it worry you."

Mrs. Ash continued to wring her hands. "We had better go home at once. I would hate for her to hear from someone else that you were forcibly ousted from a point-to-point meet. I noticed that Miss Waring and her sisters were there. Once her mama knows, the whole town is likely to hear it. I never met such a woman for tattle-mongering!"

Margaret could not keep from laughing this time. "Mama is hardly likely to hear. She and the horsey people don't really frequent the same circles. Even if Mrs. Waring does spread the story about, ten to one everyone will have forgotten the silly dog by the end of the next race."

"Well." Mrs. Ash was somewhat pacified. "Perhaps so. But you had better take us home just the same, Mr. Bourke. It will be getting on toward twilight in another hour or so. Dear me, the sun does set early this time of year. The day has just flown by."

"Indeed," her charge said dryly. "It has certainly been memorable. However, I am not very certain I would like to repeat it any time soon. But please Twitter, don't say we must go home just yet."

"What would you prefer to do?" Austin asked from the box.

"Can't we just drive on forever? I'm not ready to go back to dealing with my life yet."

Mrs. Ash tried to nudge the dog's head farther from her own skirts. "Oh, dear, no. That wouldn't do at all. We would all be caught at nightfall somewhere, and that wouldn't be at all the thing. Besides, driving is so very tedious, even with you at the ribbons, Mr. Bourke. I would doubtless get carriage sickness if we were to go driving on forever. And we should have to stay at an inn, which is never very pleasant, for they never manage to air the sheets very well. We are now on the outskirts of town, and it would be quite ridiculous for us to drive into the country until dark when we have nowhere to go. And you never know about highwaymen. Good heavens! Can you imagine? Do take us home."

Austin obediently turned the horses' heads toward the house on Merrion Square. As they drew closer to home, Margaret felt an uncomfortable anxiety rise unexpectedly within her. Her house stood at the side of the square, nearly every window illuminated. It was obvious that the wedding breakfast, or rather the jilting breakfast, was still going on. It was not uncommon for these things to go on into the evening. Light, music, and conversation burst out of the door as several of the guests departed with jovial thanks and gushing pronouncements of eternal friendship. As Austin helped her out of the carriage, she gripped his arm with a sudden urgency.

"I don't want to go in. I shall go mad if I have to face my very sympathetic parents and their friends. Please don't make me go in."

"I shall not make you do anything," he said, his straight dark brows rising with surprise.

"Margaret!" Mrs. Ash called from the top step. "Aren't you coming in? I daresay your mama is wondering what became of us. We have been gone nearly the whole day. I do hope she isn't angry about the scene at the point-to-point. Perhaps you had better take the dog to the stable before you come in. You will explain that it wasn't my fault you disgraced yourself, won't you?"

"Actually, I think that I will take Margaret for a little walk. She does not feel comfortable coming home with the party still continuing. Do tell Mrs. Fitzpatrick that I will bring Margaret home before dark."

Mrs. Ash's mouth fell open. "Oh, no, that would not be at all correct. I know that you are a family friend, but Miss Fitzpatrick should have a chaperone."

"In these circumstances, I feel sure that she will understand. Margaret and I are like brother and sister. There is no impropriety at all. Will, walk the horses back to Dame Street if you please. I will come home on foot later." He took Margaret's arm and began to lead her down the street.

"Mr. Bourke! You can't just walk off. I shall tell Mrs. Fitzpatrick. Wait! I shall accompany you! It isn't proper, Mr. Bourke!" Mrs. Ash flapped her hands in agitation and darted halfway down the steps.

Margaret pulled Austin into a run and they dashed

around the corner with the dog barking excitedly behind them.

"Is she following?" she gasped.

"No. Why did you run off like that? You act as though you were escaping bedlam."

She laughed, but there was little joy in it. "I feel like I am. I just don't want to go back."

"This morning you didn't want to go out," he reminded her.

"Oh, do humor me. Take me for a walk. I don't care where. I just need to be alone."

"Hmph."

"No, I didn't mean that you don't count. It is just . . . Well, I can think with you around, and Twitter . . . Well, you know how she is."

"I do. And I do understand, if you can believe it."

She smiled gratefully up at him. They walked for a moment in companionable silence. "You know, Austin," she said in a low voice, "I don't think of you as a brother." They walked past St. Stephen's Green. It was dark and still now, nothing like this afternoon, but she was warmed with the memory of their picnic. She thought of how he had held her while she cried, and felt an uncomfortably pleasant sensation tickle through her. Maybe it was only the bittersweet memory of Spencer.

"Indeed?" He did not seem particularly interested in discussing the subject.

"No. I don't." She kept her eyes on the pavement in front of her. "I just wanted you to know that."

Austin remained silent.

Grafton Street was crowded as usual. The length of it was a morass of carriages, drays, peddler's carts, and pedestrians. Margaret sighed happily, but Austin could sense that it was mostly show.

"See, I feel much better now. I feel much more . . .

anonymous. If I were at home, I should feel that everyone was staring at me and feeling sorry for me." She politely declined the offer of an itinerant artist to cut her silhouette and pulled Austin over to listen to some musicians who were set up in the doorway of a pub.

Austin noticed that when she wasn't concentrating, a furrow formed between her brows and her mouth drooped. She was trying to be cheerful, but the strain was beginning to tell. Oh, when she forgot herself she could produce that genuine laugh he longed to hear, but then she would remember Spencer and the little line between her finely arched brows would reappear.

He was angry with himself for being angry. After all, on the December night when he had seen Margaret's dazzled face glowing from the attention of his friend, he had sworn to himself that he would play the role of the supportive family friend. She would never know, in her little bubble of happiness, how much she had hurt him. Even hearing the praises of Captain Weldon sung day and night had left him unaffected.

Now he felt his jaw ache from clenching when he thought of how little the captain had valued his prize. But it was not Weldon's fickle heart that made him long for a good cathartic spar at the boxing salon. It was his own. How easy it would be to take advantage of Margaret's grief. He knew he could twist his position from that of chief consoler and faithful, kindly brother figure into that of suitor. She herself had implied that her feelings were not solely sisterly. *It would be better for her in the end,* an inner voice tempted him. *You will take care of her better and bring her more happiness than Weldon ever could. What does it matter the means that you used to get her?*

He watched her as she looked around behind her, making sure the silly dog had followed her. His resolve had very nearly crumbled when she had thrown herself into his arms in the park this afternoon. Hadn't she nearly looked as though she wanted to be kissed when she looked up at him, tearstained and pleading? Even now she had forced him to take her out un-chaperoned, a bold move, even considering his posi-tion as family friend. He clenched his hands at his sides and took a deep breath. No, Margaret would never have cause to blame him for seducing her in her present state of emotional turmoil. She tucked her hand into his elbow and looked up at him with those trusting blue-gray eyes.

"It was very kind of you to try to take the blame for Roly's conduct at the race."

"Well, I could hardly let you shoulder it, when you had only acquired the unmanageable creature a few hours before. I took the blame only with the intention of holding it over your head, so that you will train the animal to behave. Otherwise, I will take him away from you and claim that you were a hoydenish bad influence on him."

"As if you would ever be so cruel." She regarded him and then the dog fondly. "But it was kind of you. And of course I will teach him to have beautiful man-ners." She suddenly lay her other hand on his arm. "Austin, you know I don't have a penny with me. Do you think that you could buy us a bun?"

"Of course." He smiled, wishing she would not stand so close.

"Would you like one?" she asked, as an afterthought.

"Who did you mean by 'us' if not me? Was it the royal 'we'?"

"No, silly! Myself and Roly," she replied pertly. "He has not had a bite to eat since that pudding, you know."

Austin handed over a few coins to the bun man and received three hot rolls. They steamed in the cool of the evening air. He turned to make sure Margaret had put on her pelisse before her precipitous flight from the house. She had forgotten that ridiculous muff, but at least she wore gloves. "I am sure you will spoil the creature until it is indeed roly-poly," he said as he passed the buns to her.

"I intend to. I am quite resigned to keeping him. I think I will enjoy having something of my very own." The furrow appeared, but she hid it as she bent down to offer the animal a bit of the bun. "You do love me, my little darling, don't you?" she crooned as the greedy dog swallowed the offering without a single chew.

"For the love of Murphy, Margaret. You sound like old Lady Doyle talking to her seven pugs," he teased.

"Yes. I mean to be every bit as eccentric, too. I shall be an old, rich spinster who talks to her dog."

Austin did not argue, and he wondered if he imagined the faint expression of irritation that crossed her face when he did not disagree. She fed the rest of the bun and most of her own to the dog and then stood up.

"I feel the need to buy myself an extremely extravagant present," she announced suddenly.

"That sounds like a fine idea."

"Not that I am feeling sorry for myself," she added sharply.

"The notion had not occurred to me."

She examined the goods in several shop windows before she spoke again. "It's tomorrow that worries me," she said at last, abandoning all pretense of levity.

He looked at her in mild surprise. "Why?"

"Well, today I survived only because I was so shocked that I could hardly feel anything, and because you were so kind and distracted me." She smiled weakly. "But what about tomorrow? And all the days after that? How can I countenance all the spiteful comments from—"

"The Miss Warings of this world?" Austin supplied. "I am well aware of her faults, Margaret, so there is no need to pretend I am languishing in love for her, or that I have any interest in the chit whatsoever." He wondered if he was flattering himself by thinking that she looked vaguely relieved.

"Well, in any case," she continued with a faint blush, "even more than the spite, how will I ever survive all the sympathy and the kindness? It is different when you are kind, but when the whole world is just sickeningly nice because they feel sorry for you . . ." Her voice trailed off. She turned back to the milliner's window, her lips compressed.

"You'll survive."

"Maybe I *should* go to London. I don't care if it does kick up a scandal. It will be better than staying here."

"Perhaps. But I think it would look slightly melodramatic. Think it over. If you still wish to go, I will help you." He was beginning to wish that he had not let her drag him out here unescorted. As long as the mood between them was light and teasing, he was on familiar footing. Then he was the old Austin and she the old Margaret, and things were just as they had been when they were growing up. They could pretend that the tension of the last year did not exist. Tension that was his own fault, he reminded himself. If he had not fallen in love with her, things would have gone on comfortably. He had destroyed that pleasant, friendly relationship forever when he finally, after such a long concealment, had allowed his feelings for her to show. How foolish of him to think their friendship could easily turn to love.

CHAPTER SEVEN

Austin seemed entirely wrapped in his own thoughts. He was probably tired of taking care of her. It wasn't as if she had been very good company: crying on him one moment and then ripping up at him the next. Yes, maybe it would be best if she were to go to London. Then she wouldn't be confronted every day with the fact that she had lost her chance with him. She was dumbfounded with the realization. Spencer's jilt was humiliating and hurtful. But her real ache stemmed from the knowledge that her stupidity over Spencer had cost her Austin.

"Spencer always said he was going to take me to London. I told him of all the things we did when you were there during my Season, and he said he should have told you to skip all the deadly dull sights, and that when we went he would make sure we were invited to the really dashing parties." She wished she had not mentioned Spencer.

"But I thought we had a very nice time in London, and I liked all the sights that we saw. I never thought you were a dull dog just because you took Mama and me to see the Elgin marbles rather than the kinds of high-stakes gaming parties Spencer always preferred." She realized she was only making matters worse. Austin's mouth had tightened slightly, but his expression remained neutral. "I daresay Spencer's friends would have been a good deal too fashionable for me," she finished lamely.

They stopped at the window of a bookshop. "I am sorry that I have been so tedious. I am likely to continue to be so for a while at least. But you are right. I'll survive." She gave him a wan smile and shrugged helplessly, then pushed open the door to the bookshop.

"Are you looking for anything in particular?" he asked, after watching her stride up and down the aisles of books for several minutes.

"What? Oh, yes. Oh, no. I mean, I am not looking for anything."

She felt her cheeks go warm in confusion. What was wrong with her that her mind kept leaping back to comparisons between Austin and Spencer. It was pointless, since the damage was already done back at Christmas.

"Who let a dog in here?" the shopkeeper demanded.

"I'm sorry, sir. He is mine." she replied, scooping up the bewildered animal.

"Yours?" The shopkeeper eyed the scruffy bundle in surprise. He was obviously aware that the genteel tastes of gently bred ladies ran toward dogs of known parentage. Not to mention a semblance of hygiene. "Of course, miss. But please do not let it"—he gave the animal another scrutinizing look—"do not let it run around."

"Oh, dear. He wasn't very impressed with you, was he, Roly?"

"I should think not." Austin grinned. "You'll ruin your gown, holding him like that. He's full of burs and fleas, most likely."

"As though the gown hasn't already been abused with rescuing Roly from the mob at Sandymount Strand." She moved to a shelf of newly published books. "Look, here is something new by Maria Edgeworth. Do you remember *Castle Rackrent*? This one is *Belinda*. I wonder if it is set in Ireland, too." She tried to pick up the book with the dog in her arms but succeeded only in nearly knocking an entire stack of copies to the floor. Austin picked up one and looked through it.

"It looks like a society satire. It should appeal to you, little bluestocking that you are."

"Now you know I'm not. But I think I will get it."

"And how do you propose to pay for it? I thought you didn't have a penny with you."

She knew he was teasing her again, but she wished he didn't treat her quite so avuncularly. "I have credit here," she countered in an insulted tone.

He tucked the book under his arm. "No," he said with a smile, "I would like to buy it for you."

"You don't have to do that. I wanted to buy myself something."

He waved off her objections with a flippant gesture. "And don't start thinking I am doing it because I feel sorry for you either. I owe you a Christmas present, if you remember."

"Oh." She did remember that, at the time, he had said he had a present for her, but when she had happily announced her engagement to Spencer, it had never materialized. She felt a sudden urgent desire to know what that present was to have been. "Thank you, Austin," she said meekly as she followed him to the front of the store. He paid for the book and handed it to her with no ceremony. "Won't you write something in it?" She felt strangely as though she were poking a bruise.

"If you wish." He took the book back and asked the shopkeeper for a pen and inkwell.

"Did you see that we have a selection of love poetry for sale? Byron? Coleridge? Shakespeare sonnets? They are a very popular gift for Valentine's Day." The shopkeeper gave Austin a hinting look. "All ladies are soft on love poetry." His voice dropped lower, "It might advance your purpose a good deal with your sweetheart."

Margaret felt her cheeks go very hot. She turned and pretended to examine a book and then dropped it as though it was on fire when she discovered it was one of the very volumes of love sonnets the shopkeeper had suggested.

"Pen and ink are all I require," Austin replied coolly. He turned his back to her as he wrote something carefully in the flyleaf of the novel. He waved the entire volume back and forth several times to dry the ink and then presented it to her. *For the bluestocking Margaret Fitzpatrick from her old friend Austin Bourke.* What had she been hoping for? The pinch of disappointment was entirely overshadowed by an enormous feeling of foolishness. "Thank you," she said with a smile.

Margaret set Roly down once they were outside the shop, and he ran in circles around her legs, yapping in his delighted, ill-mannered way. They continued down the street, but she did not take Austin's arm this time. He watched her as she walked with her eyes on the ground and her bonnet entirely hiding her expression.

An errant pale brown lock had escaped from the back of her bonnet. It had lost the curl her maid had ruthlessly forced upon it that morning and hung nearly straight down the nape of her neck nearly to where her shoulder blades would be beneath her pelisse. For some reason he found it strangely erotic. It was only for a moment that he envisioned her with her fawn-colored hair about her shoulders, but the picture was not easily erased. God, how depraved he must be. He locked his fingers behind his back and scowled.

"Perhaps you should consider going to London after all."

She looked up, those Wedgwood blue eyes open in frank surprise. "Why? I thought you said to wait out the scandal."

He examined the knot of string that tied up the book parcel. "I was just thinking that you could do with a change of air."

She looked nonplussed. "Perhaps it would help. Would you come?"

"Me? Of course not. I have far too many obligations here." He pulled the knot savagely tight.

Her face fell. "I don't want to go if you won't go. I would not know anyone. You remember how I hated the place during my Season. I was bored to flinders, and there was not a single race meet suitable for a lady except Ascot, and that was a colossal disappointment."

He forced a smile. "You would not wish to go to dashing and fashionable parties?"

She gave him a disgusted look. "You know those things are not important to me. Spencer wanted me to cut a dash in real society; he thought Dublin vastly provincial compared to London, but I don't think I am suited to London society. I much prefer to remain here."

"Don't worry, then. We won't ship you off, if you would rather remain here."

"Thank you—Papa," she added with some asperity. "No, I think I had better remain here and just weather the smug little sympathy calls. Not that I do not have a good number of genuine friends," she amended. "But it has been hard since both Cordelia and Maria were married. I am happy that you are around." She was looking at the ground again, and he could only see the top of the chipped straw bonnet trimmed with ribbons of garnet velvet. And that lock of hair.

He focused his attention on a grubby child who was

warbling an unintelligible song in front of his father's upturned hat. He threw in a few coins, but the urchin paused for a moment, taken aback at his grim expression. The child's father gave him a nudge to continue.

At the bottom of Grafton Street were the grounds of Trinity College. Wordlessly they entered the gate. "I would have been married here today," she said softly, looking up at the chapel that made up one side of the courtyard.

"I know." He could not look at her. They watched the dog as he gleefully stormed a flock of birds that had been pecking innocently for crumbs between the cobbles of the square. They rose from the yard in a dark cloud, their wingbeats sounding like a rainstorm as they ascended. Roly trotted back to Margaret, a smug expression on his doggy face. Behind him the birds silently resettled.

"He went through a lot of trouble to arrange to have the wedding here. He said he liked the way the pews faced each other, rather than toward the front."

"I always liked that, too."

She looked up at him in surprise. "Yes, he said that you suggested the chapel. In fact . . ." Her brows drew together slightly. "I would bet that you were the one who made all the arrangements, weren't you? It wasn't him at all." He could not read her expression. Hurt? Realization? Alarm?

"I just wanted you to have something nice," he replied lamely. He crossed his arms and shoved his hands into his armpits as he walked in a tight, anxious circle in front of the church. She stood still, staring at the church in the fading light, completely oblivious to him. God, he wished Spencer had married her. At least then he could have ruthlessly amputated that tiny, painful bit of hope.

"You know, Austin," she began hesitantly, after a long silence, "I think that I am glad Spencer and I are not going to marry."

He raised his eyebrows questioningly but did not reply.

"Yes," she continued, "I am decidedly glad. He has proven that he is unreliable in the most dramatic of ways. I could not marry a man who was unreliable." She stopped and looked up at him, waiting for him to reply.

"Most people are not exactly what we would wish them to be." He shrugged noncommittally.

"Yes," she said slowly. "In fact, I think he may have been a bit of a snob." She looked a little sheepish. "I know you will think it is sour grapes for me to say that, since it didn't seem to bother me in the least for the last two months. Isn't that an awful thing to say?"

"I suppose it is honest."

"And he was quite tone deaf." The furrow between her brows reappeared.

"Indeed?"

"And we should have always had to economize. He tended to live beyond his means . . . a bit." Her lips trembled slightly.

"It might have been difficult."

She blinked very hard several times. "And I abhorred the way he blew his nose."

"Then you are well rid of him indeed." They paused as the bells of the churches across the city began to toll the hour. When she looked up at the sound, he could see two tears had slid out from under her lids.

"Yes," she said fervently, "I am very, very glad he did not marry me."

He half expected her to throw herself into his arms again, but when she did not, he pulled her to him anyway. He stood for a moment, his cheek resting against the crown of her bonnet and inhaled the sweet, grassy smell of the straw. He could feel her gasping deep, painful sobs against him. The stray lock of hair brushed against his hand and he pressed a silent, impassioned kiss on the top of her head.

She drew in a sharp breath, but he could not tell if she had felt it or was only trying to keep her grief from physically suffocating her. He kissed her forehead, pretending to himself that it was only to comfort her. He should be shot for taking such grievous advantage of her weakness. But somehow he found that he was pressing his lips tentatively against one of her brown eyebrows. She made a tiny noise in her throat that might have only been a sob. One of her arms crept from his back to curl around his neck and she rose onto her toes to bring her mouth to his.

CHAPTER EIGHT

She hadn't meant to do it. But she knew that he was going to let her go in a moment, and there would not be another chance. She kissed him slowly on the mouth, a languorous, sensual imitation of the chaste kisses she had allowed Spencer once or twice. Those brief experiences had left her feeling shyly affectionate, not dazed and panting. Her breath could not seem to keep up with her heart, which spun the blood through her limbs with a tingling lash.

Austin did not let her end it with one kiss; this time he was the one to close the space between them. He parted her lips with his own and kissed her deeply. She felt dangerously close to disgracing herself by fainting. Since when had people begun kissing like that? She heard a faint whimper and realized that she had made it.

As though he had belatedly realized who she was, he pulled violently from her. She staggered slightly without his arms supporting her. He backed fully two steps away and raked his hand through his hair several times, as though to brush from his mind what had just happened.

"I'm sorry. I'm sorry," he gasped. He took another horrified step away from her.

She pressed her fingers to her lips, wishing she could hold his kiss to them. "Austin, I—"

"Don't say it! I'm sorry! Forgive me!" He closed his eyes tightly. "I don't know what happened, but I am entirely at fault."

"Please don't—"

"It never happened," he interrupted again. "Please consider that it never happened. I know who you were thinking of."

He said this last bit in a low voice, and for a moment Margaret was not sure who he meant. "Spencer?"

"I have taken unconscionable liberties. Both he and you were my friends, and I have thrust myself between you in a way that was just as wrong as if you had been married."

"But he left me," she reminded him prosaically.

"I took advantage of your grief. Please don't let's speak of it anymore. I will take you home."

"But I wanted you to kiss me."

He stared at her for a moment with a look of suppressed fury. "I'll not be your second choice, Margaret," he said in a low voice. "You loved Spencer more than me, and I won't have you kissing me and pretending it's him."

The trembling in her arms and legs now felt as though it came more from the cold. The quick, early twilight of February had fallen gracelessly over the city.

"I'll take you home," he said again, sounding tired this time.

Margaret remained silent and allowed him to lead her back across the square. After giving the birds a warning charge, Roly cheerfully followed them out the gates and toward Nassau Street, blissfully unaware of the cataclysmic change in his new mistress's life. But, Margaret thought wryly, perhaps he assumed that every day in her life was as full of emotional outbursts, narrow escapes, and passionate embraces as today.

Austin had set a blistering pace, and she nearly had

to run to keep up with him. His jaw was set, and he did not look around when she nearly stumbled over Roly, who insisted on prancing about directly under her feet. Of course he had thought he was second choice. He could never believe that she loved him, when she had thrown him over so completely for Spencer not but two months before.

As they came around the corner into Merrion Square, she saw the curtain in the drawing room of her own house flutter, and a moment later Mrs. Ash ran wildly into the street.

"Merciful heavens! You are back!" she panted. "I had given you up for completely lost. It will be pitch dark in another ten minutes, and then what would Mrs. Fitzpatrick have said! I will lose my position over this, Margaret, you'll see I will. You wouldn't want to see your Twitter out on the street, would you, pet? Do go and tell your mama that it wasn't my fault and that you were being willful. She knows there is nothing to be done with you when you are being willful." She took Margaret by the arm and began pulling her forcibly up the steps.

"I can't go in just yet, Twitter. Just give me a few moments on the steps. I have something to say to Austin."

"It will keep," he replied brusquely. "We have nothing to discuss that cannot be said some other day."

"Do stop pulling on me, Twitter! Austin, wait!"

Several of the guests from the wedding breakfast met them on the way down, and the trio was forced to stop their bickering in order to bow and smile at the departing couple.

"Is the party still going on?" Margaret asked in amazement.

"They were the last to go. You know how Mr. Tottenham and his wife can never take the hint to leave. It was quite a success, the party. Your mama is in high

alt. That is the only reason she was not more upset at
your running off with Mr. Bourke."

"How nice to know that my wedding breakfast was
a success," she said dryly.

Austin bowed abruptly. "Thank you, ladies for a very
memorable day. I wish you good evening."

"Wait," Margaret begged. "Just one moment. Please."

His look was cold. "As you wish."

"Oh, dear," Mrs. Ash said in a stage whisper as they
entered the hallway. "What are we going to do with
that animal? Perhaps I should have O'Malley take him
to the stables?"

The butler looked at the dog with an expression of
extreme distaste.

"No. If you would, O'Malley, please take him to the
kitchen. I will deal with him in a moment." Margaret
gave him an irresistible smile.

With a look of supreme forbearance, O'Malley gestured to the dog and walked a little way down the hallway. Roly remained firmly lodged between Margaret's
skirts and Austin's trouser leg. "Here, doggie," the butler said weakly.

Margaret was struggling to suppress her laughter
when O'Malley's daughter Anya passed by at the end
of the hallway bearing a tray of leftover lobster patties.
Roly bounded delightedly down the hall. The subsequent squeal and crash suggested that he had obtained
his goal.

Everyone in the hallway turned to stare at Margaret
in horror. "Please come up to the drawing room," she
requested majestically, before the aftermath descended
upon her head.

The room was in shambles. The doors between the
two large drawing rooms had been opened up and the
rugs rolled up for dancing. Several large tables had
been set up in the second room, and these were still
covered with the remains of the wedding feast. Most
of the candles had been snuffed or were guttering.

Half-empty glasses stood on every available surface in both rooms. There was something very desolate about the entire scene. Three musicians were packing up their instruments and looked up tiredly as they entered.

Austin did not take the seat she offered, but stood in the middle of the room. She sat for a moment on the sofa, trying to think of what to say.

He began, his voice crisp with impatience. "I apologize again for my behavior at the church. If you cannot forgive me, I understand. I do not feel that there is any point in discussing the matter further."

"But I think you must have misunderstood," she began.

"I don't believe that I did. This is a painful conversation for me. I must ask that we not go on." He turned to the pianoforte and absently pushed all of the glasses to one side.

Several servants continued to clear the tables at the far end of the room. Margaret was aware that they must be listening very closely to this interesting conversation.

"Thank you for all that you did for me today," she began in a low voice.

"You have thanked me several times. I was happy to be of service to you." He bowed and made as though to end the conversation.

"I hope . . . I hope that you will continue to be my friend."

"Of course." Did she imagine some hesitation?

They were silent. Austin sighed in disgust. "Look, are you trying to wring a confession of love from me? Is that what you want? Do you want to know that you have held my heart from the moment you turned fifteen, and that I have loved you every minute since?" She had risen to her feet to stop him from speaking, and now he strode up to her and stood so close that their toes were touching. "Do you want to know how agonizing it was to watch you fall in love with my best friend?" he hissed. "Is that what you dragged me up here to tell you? Do you feel better, now that he has jilted you, to know that I am still here? That I will be your spare admirer until you find someone else to enchant?"

"Enough!" she exclaimed. A sudden bustle at the other end of the room told her that the two maids had been listening with rapt attention. She waited until they had scuttled out of the room. "Enough," she said again, quietly this time. She looked up at him for a moment. His face was inscrutable in the dim golden light from the sputtering candles. She turned away and walked a few steps. Her footsteps sounded loudly on the uncarpeted floor.

"Do you know why I was crying at the church?" she asked in a conversational tone.

"I can guess."

She turned back to him. "From relief. I did care for Spencer, but I allowed myself to romanticize him. Perhaps because he was someone new and so different from—"

"Different from me?" he supplied, his hazel eyes unreadably cold in the dim light.

"Yes. I suppose. I did not fully appreciate you, I know. But can you not see? I am relieved that Spencer had the sense to see that we did not suit and left me before we were doomed to a life of mutual disappointment."

"Then I congratulate you."

"That is all you have to say?" she demanded in a hurt voice.

"What would you have me say?"

"I just told you that I was happy that I am not marrying Spencer, and I hope you know I was certainly *not* thinking of him when I kissed you." Just saying the word made the blood warm her cheeks. "I feel like I have a second chance at finding real love!" She jerked her chin up defiantly. He said nothing. "Austin! I am telling you that I am . . . available. I love you, and you love me, and there is no impediment between us!" The man seemed unable to grasp the obvious.

"Are you waiting for me to throw myself to one knee and propose?" he asked calmly.

"Well, I think that you should kiss me again, at the very least," she said indignantly.

He smiled faintly, and she felt a sudden wave of relief. "Do you, indeed? What a very demanding creature you have become. Come and sit beside me."

She complied willingly, fighting a sudden feeling of shyness.

"No, I am not going to kiss you just yet, so you can stop looking so frightened." He laughed and put a finger to her mouth to stop her protests. "While it would seem neatly tied up, with Spencer conveniently out of the way and each of us proclaiming our love for each other, I think that we need to consider a few things."

Margaret leaned back against the sofa. "I know what you are going to say. You do not believe that I love you. You think that I am just confused by some kind of . . . of post-jilt emotional upheaval." She was rather pleased with the phrase.

He laughed softly. "Something like that."

"Oh, but Austin, given time, I can show you how very sincere I am. I am not saying that there will not be times in the next few months when I will not suffer from Spencer's leaving, but I know my heart now. You will see, in time."

He had captured a lock of hair that hung down her back and twined it around his fingers. "I think that we both need time." He caught her chin in his hand. "Fortunately we have both gotten a second chance." He smiled as he stroked the line of her jaw with his thumb. "It's Valentine's Day; maybe Cupid gave it to us."

"I think I am going to have to insist that you kiss me now," she breathed.

He leaned over and complied with a passion that left her entirely unable to respond when the upstairs maid burst into the room.

"Miss Fitzpatrick," she began in dire accents, "that mongrel you brought home has eaten up every last bit of the trifle Cook was saving for tomorrow. He said the creature is to be thrown out of the house immediately, no matter whether you are fond of it or not, being that it is his kitchen." She twisted her apron around her hands and assumed a slightly dramatic pose. "He says he will have someone drown it!"

Margaret reluctantly disentangled herself from Austin's arms and stood up. "Let us go and rescue our dog." She pulled him to his feet. "We must convince Cook that if Cupid has deemed us worthy of a second chance in love, he must be at least as generous and give poor Roly a second chance as well!"

THE RUBY HEART

by

Lynn Collum

CHAPTER ONE

A knock sounded at the Countess of Crossley's communicating door; then the earl, looking handsome in evening clothes, entered. Her ladyship's maid discreetly left the room, her mistress having no further need for her, but the servant took one last peek before she closed the door to see his lordship bend and place a kiss upon Lady Anne's neck.

Closing the door, the young girl thought, *It just ain't proper for a pair who are nigh on to bein' in their dotage to be carryin' on in such a manner.*

At the dressing table, Lady Anne smiled at her husband of twenty-seven years in the mirror as he rose from giving her a soft token of his affection. "You are very handsome this evening, Randall. Where are you off to?"

"Spending the evening with a few friends at Brooks. And you, dearest?"

"Lady Marlin invited me to dine and meet her girls, who will make their come-out during the Season. No doubt she is hoping to garner an invitation to my annual Valentine's party at Naunton."

The earl's brown eyes twinkled. "Ah! I forgot. Tomorrow is the first of February and the much coveted invitations will be posted."

Her ladyship turned and looked up at her husband,

a slight frown marring her still lovely face. "Forgot! Randall, have you not spoken with Justin yet? I still don't have the name of the lady to whom he will bestow the Crossley Ruby Heart. Will it be Lady Kate or Miss Norris?"

Lord Crossley was but teasing his wife, for this year's party was more significant than any in the last twenty-seven years. At five-and-twenty, Lord Justin Andrews, son and heir of the earl, was expected to bestow the exquisite ruby and diamond necklace on the future Countess of Crossley at the annual Valentine Ball, as had been the tradition for some two hundred years.

Tilting her chin up, the earl kissed his wife's pouting lips. "That is why I must depart a bit early, my dear. I plan to stop in South Audley Street to visit the young man in the hope he'll have the name of his final choice. I'll inform you in the morning to which lady you must address the all-important invitation."

With that the earl bid his wife a pleasant evening and departed for this night's entertainment. As promised, he made the trip to his son's rented rooms, but found to his disappointment that Lord Justin had already departed. The one bit of good news he learned from Justin's valet was that his son planned to return early from his revels.

Confident that he would run his son to ground before the cock crowed, Lord Crossley went to meet his particular friends at Brooks and spent a pleasant evening arguing politics with the more radical Whigs who formed his circle of acquaintances. Ever mindful of his promise to his lady wife, at midnight he rose, to the regret of the company, and departed once again for South Audley Street.

Upon knocking, the door was opened by Becket, Lord Justin's gentleman. "My lord, your son is returned and upstairs with Major Dandridge."

Crossley knew the major was a former comrade of his son and also rented rooms in the house. As the servant turned to lead the way up, the earl, seeing the tray of empty glasses sitting on a hall table, called, "There is no need for you to show me up, Becket. I never stand on ceremony with my son. You may go about your business."

"Very good, my lord. They are at the end of the hall in the major's rooms." With that the servant retrieved the tray and disappeared into the rear of the house.

The earl climbed the stairs and was about to pass the door of his son's rooms when the muted sounds of voices could be heard coming from behind the oak panel. Thinking that Justin had returned to his own room, the earl opened the door and stepped into the chamber that served as a sitting room. To his utter amazement his gaze fell upon two young men seated near the fire holding two giggling females in their laps with an unseemly expanse of feminine leg exposed. The women, whose gowns were heedlessly hiked up, had their limbs propped upon the chairs' arms.

When the door clicked shut, four pairs of eyes riveted on the visitor. One lanky young man with a boyish face hurriedly jumped up, dumping his companion on the floor with a hard thump.

"Father!" The single word held a great deal of trepidation.

The female on the floor shrieked in pain. "Are ye daft? Ye'll break a lady's arse bein' so careless."

The young man, seeming to remember his manners, helped the woman up, then shushed her as she continued to complain of her treatment.

"Stubble it, Nell," the young man growled.

The earl lifted his quizzing glass to inspect the scene with distaste. "Why, may I ask, are you in London, Adam?"

Mr. Adam Andrews, younger son of the earl, suddenly looked all of twelve instead of twenty as he shuffled his feet and shot a warning glance to his friend, Barkley. "Been sent down again, sir. Knew Justin wouldn't kick up a dust about it, so I came to him. He's next door, talking with the major."

There was nothing to belie the earl's anger save the tone of his voice as Crossley remarked, "I must speak with your brother on a matter of some importance. I will expect your guests to be gone when I return."

With that, his lordship exited the room and made his way to Major Dandridge's rooms and knocked. He discovered the two men near the fire, enjoying a brandy and reminiscing about life in Wellington's army. The major still held his commission, but Justin had sold out after Waterloo.

"Dandridge, your servant." The earl nodded at the young man with sun-bleached brown hair. "May I have a few words with my son in private, Major?"

The old friends and former compatriots exchanged a look, and the major nodded. "Use my room, sir. No need to run across the hall if you are only here for a moment."

The earl cocked an eyebrow at his son, but made no comment as the soldier departed to his other room. "If you and your friend are thinking to keep me from seeing Adam, you are too late, dear boy."

Lord Justin Andrews gestured to the chair near him as he gave a deep laugh. "I told Adam you would find him out, but you know I couldn't betray him, sir. Was there something important you wished to see me about?"

The earl settled in the leather chair, then eyed his son, who'd resumed his seat opposite. Justin bore a strong resemblance to his brother. But there was nothing of the boy in his handsome countenance or athletic build. Yet both young men owned dark hair and gray eyes like their mother. There the resemblance ended for Justin. While Anne was gentle and content with life, the earl thought his eldest son had always seemed to choose the opposite of what was expected of him. He'd wished a life in the army, much to his family's dismay, and now seemed little interested in finding a bride in the time-honored tradition of Andrews heirs.

"I believe you must remember that your mother is anxiously awaiting the name of a certain female."

Justin was well aware to what his father referred. Yet he hadn't gone to his mother with a name simply because he was so uncertain which lady he preferred to be his bride. Since returning from Brussels last September, he'd made an effort to fall in love, but it had proven damned hard work despite the flock of marriageable females thrown at his head. Now time had run out. He must chose or risk disappointing his entire family. Not wanting his father to know he was still so uncertain, he grinned. "Pray, have Mother invite both Lady Kate and Miss Norris to Crossley Court."

The earl's gaze dropped to the glowing coals in the grate. "Were you thinking to marry them both? Miss Norris your country wife and Lady Kate your London one, perhaps? Let me remind you that despite the excesses of the *haute ton,* two wives are still considered a crime by the Crown."

Justin sighed, then his gaze followed his father's to the fire. "I know, sir, but truth be told, I still don't know which lady will be the one I choose to give the ruby heart." And his own, he thought, for he'd long hoped to have the kind of loving marriage his parents had.

The two ladies under consideration had drawn his attention immediately upon his entry into Society during the little Season last autumn, but for completely different reasons. Lady Katherine Dailey was beautiful, lively, and amusing—up to any game—whereas Miss Belinda Norris was beautiful and elegantly reserved, with a quiet dignity that would suit a future countess.

Still, when he was away from them, he never gave either a moment's thought, and that disturbed him. Should he not burn with desire for the woman with whom he would spend his life? Had not all his friends become complete moonlings over the females they'd formed an attachment for? Yet here he was, completely unaffected by Lady Kate's sparkling blue eyes or Miss Norris's raven black curls.

Breaking the silence, the earl spoke kindly. "Have no fear, dear boy. Either lady would likely make an excellent wife, and if you do not love her as much as you would wish, know that it is very likely to come with time."

Justin looked at his father in surprise. "But I thought that you married for love, sir."

The earl rose to leave. "And so I did. But my love for your mother has only grown greater with time, my boy, as I am sure yours will, once you settle your attention upon one lady. As to the invitation, I shall tell your mother to invite both and no doubt you will know which is your choice by the night of the ball."

Justin profoundly hoped that was true.

The earl drew on his gloves. "Now, I intend to take that young cawker in the other room home before he can get into any more trouble. Shall you journey to Naunton with your mother next week?"

"If you wish it, sir."

"I do. I cannot leave until near the end of that week and cannot like her traveling unescorted."

"Then I shall happily be at her disposal." But Justin was anything but happy to have to make such an important decision when his heart was so untouched. Yet he knew that despite his uncertainty he would do his duty to his family as he had for his country.

The village of Naunton lay on the road between Cheltenham and Stow-on-the-Wold in the north Cotswold region of Gloucestershire. There was little of note in the small town save the sixteenth-century Church of St Andrew and the River Windrush, which flowed on the north side of the village. While the Earl of Crossley was the most elevated peer in the neighborhood, the locals considered Baron Larken the gentleman who reigned supreme in all matters. In truth, the earl was little at his family seat. He possessed an excellent steward which allowed him to spend time in London with his political affairs, and he knew the baron to be a fair and just man.

Lord Larken, like much of his generation, was much obsessed with his own pleasures. For some men that was gaming, while others preferred women, and some desired both. But for the baron, his life was much consumed with his hounds, his horses, and the hunt. He cared nothing for Society and, save for one visit to London many years earlier to procure a wife to secure an heir, he'd turned his back on all else.

His lady wife had properly produced three offspring in as many years, then died, leaving Larken with two sons and a daughter. With the help of his servants, he nicely managed to ignore his progeny until each child grew to an age that enabled him or her to ride and therefore join the hunt. The gentleman made little exception for his daughter, Lorissa. Truth be told, she owned the best seat of the three and could out-shoot her brothers any day.

Local Society was at first scandalized to see little Lorissa Mathis in breeches, riding astride all over the neighborhood with her brothers and the earl's two sons when they were in residence. Several well-meaning ladies attempted to convince the baron that the young girl needed a proper governess, but received only a tongue lashing for their efforts. The only person who'd ever gotten through to Lord Larken had been the Countess of Crossley, during one of her infrequent visits.

Perhaps it was fate that had ordained her to approach the gentleman on horseback. He so much admired her riding, he'd listened as she declared Lorissa must be dressed properly and instructed how to behave or she would grow up only to be left on the shelf for her unacceptable conduct. Little the baron cared about the matter, but much taken with Lady Anne, his one concession had been to inform Lorissa she must order several gowns from the village seamstress and make certain she dressed properly when her ladyship was in residence.

Being only twelve at the time, Lorissa had thought the countess just an interfering gadabout, and so she had informed her friends, Lord Justin and Adam. But all that had garnered her was a dousing in the River Windrush by an angry Adam. Lord Justin had come to her rescue, giving his brother, only a year older than Lorissa, a scold. Then he kissed her wet cheek and called her nothing but a graceless hoyden, and issued a well-meant warning to heed his mother.

That day beside the river had been a revelation for little Lorissa. She had been only a child, but she very much disliked Justin thinking badly of her. She'd made a promise to herself as she stood there wet and shivering, to try and behave more like Lady Anne.

Much changed in the intervening seven years. The Andrews brothers' visits to Crossley Court had become fewer, and then Lord Justin had gone off to war. Lorissa had not seen either since she was fifteen, but still she held Lord Justin Andrews as her ideal of what a young man should be.

Unfortunately Lorissa's efforts to turn herself into a proper young lady had met with derision from her father and brothers. There had been no female to whom she could turn save the housekeeper, Mrs. Kerr. That lady had done her best, but within a short time Lorissa found it much easier to fall in with her brothers' demands that she join them in riding and hunting. Otherwise she suffered their jibes about playing at "Lady of the Manor."

Now nineteen and much aware of the frowns of the

local matrons, Lorissa began making more of an effort to behave as she thought was proper. Despite her brothers' derision, she'd purchased a habit and mastered the art of the sidesaddle. Soon her family became used to her in feminine attire, but only her younger brother made an effort to compliment her on her looks.

Lorissa began to wonder if all the work was worth the effort. It wasn't as if her father would allow her a Season or even take the time to see that she met anyone other than his hunting companions. The very possibility of being married to a younger version of her hunt-mad parent almost made her give up the idea of trying to behave like a genteel young woman.

When she'd almost given up hope of ever escaping from Larken Hall, a letter arrived in the post from Lady Anne, inviting Lorissa to the annual Valentine's Ball at Crossley Court. The countess had informed her that it was high time that Miss Mathis enter into Society and asked what better place than a country ball.

In a frenzy of excitement, Lorissa had wheedled Mrs. Kerr into taking her to Cheltenham when the housekeeper went for supplies. There the young lady had found a modiste and, for a shocking sum, had been measured for a ball gown, which would arrive in time for the ball.

This morning Lorissa sat counting her remaining funds, trying to determine if she had enough for new silk stockings and ribbons for her hair. After examining the coins several times she realized that she would have to give up her plan for new stockings and purchase only ribbons instead.

A sudden knocking at her bedchamber door caused her to spill several farthings on her bed. Covering the money, she tugged her wrapper tight and called for the visitor to enter.

Dermot Mathis, her younger brother, stuck his head in the door. Upon seeing his sister still in her bedclothes, he frowned. "Are you not dressed yet, Lori? Clive is wanting to go to the Red Hart to meet Sir Lucas Millsbury and Mr. Percy Forster."

"Oh, I care nothing for meeting Clive's gaming friends. You must go without me today, for I have things I must attend," Lorissa said airily as she moved to her dresser and picked up a brush to tame her auburn curls.

The young man pushed the door wider. "But you must come. Clive has a wager riding on you and Daisy."

Lorissa turned on her brother, an angry glint in her jade green eyes. "How many times must I ask you to stop making me part of your foolish wagers?"

Dermot's cheeks blushed quite as red as his tousled hair. "Blast it, Lori, you are the best rider and a sure bet against these fellows who come into the neighborhood and doubt your skill. Besides, unless I am mistaken, you've earned a tidy sum laying down your coin on your abilities as well."

Lorissa realized her brother was right. Much of the money for her ball gown had come from wagering on her riding skills, and that might be the answer to her problem now. She went back to her bed, gathering her few remaining coins. "Very well, I shall come, if you will wager this amount on me with one of the gentlemen."

The young man grinned as he stuck out his hands to receive her money. "You're a great gun, Lori. I'll see you at the stable in ten minutes." He turned to depart, then stopped saying, "And don't be putting on that habit you've taken to wearing. We need you in your old rig."

Warning bells sounded in Lorissa's head. "What has Clive wagered I can do this time?"

"Nothing too difficult. You must ride from St. Andrew's Church through the village and end at the Hart." He paused; then, seeing her arch one delicate brow, he added, "While standing on Daisy's back."

As Lorissa gasped, her younger brother grinned, then closed the door without a backward glance. It had been years since she'd been foolish enough to pull that stunt, and now they wanted her to repeat the trick without so much as a day to practice. Her first thought was to go down and tell them she wouldn't do it. Then she thought about new silk stockings. How she wanted to look her best when she went to Crossley Court to see Justin for the first time in four years, for her ladyship had told her he was coming to the ball.

Could she still ride on Daisy's haunches without falling? She'd been very good at the trick at one time. Logically once the skill was learned, the ability to perform remained, she decided. With that she went to her wardrobe and pulled out the breeches and coat she used to wear, tossing them on the bed. She would go with her brothers and double her money with the wager on her riding ability, even if that required that she stand on the horse's back.

While Crossley Court lay a mere five miles beyond Naunton, it was customary for the countess to stop on her way to the family seat at the Red Hart for refreshment, as well as a bit of local gossip with the innkeeper, Mr. Summers, and his wife. The ancient but well-maintained posting house lay on the outskirts of the village, well away from the noisy crossroad in town.

Lord Justin and Adam, on horseback, galloped ahead of their mother's coach along the road, which was lined by fieldstone fencing. They would warn the Summerses of the arrival of the Crossley carriage so that all might be ready and her ladyship would not even have to step down from her coach.

The brothers slowed to a trot as they entered the busy coaching yard. Justin's gaze was drawn to a rowdy crowd of fashionable young gentlemen gathered at the far end of the yard, near the west gate. After a brief inspection of the group, he went about his business, caring little what had brought them to the small country inn. They appeared to be waiting for something as they all kept peering down the busy street of the village.

Handing his rein to an ostler, Justin turned to his brother as he drew off his gloves. "Adam, go warn Mrs. Summers that Mother will soon be here. I shall go and await the carriage by the road."

Adam disappeared inside the inn and Justin made his way to the entry they'd just passed through. Naunton was such a quiet village that the party of young men made him curious, so he stood where he could watch what was about to happen on the village street.

When Adam returned, he peered down the road from which they'd just come. "What are you doing out here on the street?"

Justin tipped his head in the direction of the young men. "Just curious what that lot is doing out here. Looks as if something is about to occur."

Adam's brown brows rose in doubt. "In Naunton? Highly unlikely. A London cemetery has more activity than this town."

The brothers laughed, but before either could comment, the sound of their mother's carriage approaching from the east reached them. They moved away from the entry to allow the coach to draw up near the inn door. About to join their mother in some refreshments, a movement up the street caught Justin's attention. He lay his hand on his brother's arm to halt him.

"I think we are about to see a stirring of the dead in Naunton."

Justin lifted his hand to shield his eyes from the afternoon sun as he stared at the sight. It appeared some young fool in a badly cut coat was standing on the back of a prime bit of cattle, galloping down the middle of the village street.

He heard his brother gasp, then mutter, "By Jove, the fellow's a wonder."

Like Adam, Justin was impressed with the young man's skill. Or should he call him a boy, for the fellow didn't look to be much above seventeen, if that old. His feet appeared to be positioned on the horse's back just behind the saddle, but, with knees bent, the lad was in perfect rhythm with the horse. With great intensity etched on his finely drawn features, the rider held the reins and guided the animal through the streets at a rapid gait.

The crowd of young men who'd been awaiting the event shouted and whistled as the rider weaved through the busy streets. Some were offering words of encouragement, while others were saying the lad would fall. Clearly blunt had been wagered on this foolhardy event.

As the daredevil drew near, Justin was struck by the notion that he knew the boy. The face was decidedly familiar. But it had been years since he'd been in the neighborhood, so his memory was a bit hazy. Then a long auburn curl jarred loose from under the wide-brimmed hat and recognition dawned.

"Damnation! It's Lorissa Mathis, and she's still as much the little hoyden as ever."

Adam gave a crooked grin as his gaze lingered on the slender yet shapely legs of the rider. "Not so little anymore, dear brother."

Justin felt a sudden urge to box his brother's ears. Somehow it didn't seem proper for him to be leering at the young girl from Larken Hall. But as she thundered past her cheering companions, Justin realized Adam was right. A pair of gray breeches did encase very rounded hips and feminine limbs.

Appalled at where his thoughts were lingering, Justin removed his gaze from the alluring sight. He suddenly found his gaze locked with a pair of fine green eyes that widened with recognition.

"Justin!" the young lady cried with delight as she straightened, then tore off the hat to wave at him, auburn curls flying in the wind. But the flamboyant gesture caused her to lose her balance. The shift of her weight sent the wrong signal to her horse. The animal veered to the stone fence, but not having enough speed to go over, Daisy came to a grinding halt. To Justin's horror, Miss Lorissa Mathis went head over heels into the open pasture across from the Red Hart and disappeared behind the stone fence.

CHAPTER TWO

A sharp pain pierced Justin's chest as he watched Lorissa tumble from her horse. In an instant he was across the street. He vaulted the stone fence and landed just inches from the girl, who was lying face-down in a pile of dried leaves that nature had collected at the edge of the fence.

"Lori, are you unharmed?"

She rolled onto her back and smiled at him. "Will you teach me to dance?"

Thinking the fall must have disordered her brain, he repeated, "Are you hurt, child?"

"Of course not." She sat up and began to brush leaves from her coat, but with a coquettish grin, she added, "And I am not a child or I would not have been invited to your mother's Valentine's Ball. But I cannot dance."

Taking her hands, Justin pulled her to her feet, then grasped her shoulders and gave her a gentle shake. "You may have left your childhood behind, my dear, but not your childish pranks. Have you not learned anything about proper conduct for a lady? Are you determined to be the oldest living hoyden, Lori?"

A pink flush settled on the young lady's cheeks and she tilted her chin upward as she pulled free. "You know nothing about me and what I have learned in the past four years, sir. Kindly mind your own business, for you are neither my brother nor my father. And remember I have not given you leave to call me by my Christian name."

Justin's brows rose. "But I have always called you Lori or Brat."

"Well . . ." Lorissa straightened her vest as she turned toward the inn to avoid the twinkling gray eyes that gazed at her. "Things are different now that we are grown."

"Grown?" Justin said, then laughed heartily, which only seemed to make the young lady angrier.

Just then the Mathis brothers arrived, having taken the time to collect on the gaming debt before coming to see how their sister fared. Adam, who'd followed his brother but not jumped the barrier, helped her climb back over the fence as her elder brother greeted his old friend. Lori marched away, her back rigid with indignation, going straight to her horse without a backward glance.

The men exchanged pleasantries even as Justin watched Lori go to her horse and run her hands over the animal's legs. Adam, a bemused glint in his eyes, joined her, and they fell into conversation like the old friends they were.

In an undertone, Justin addressed himself to Baron Larken's heir. "What can your father be thinking to allow Lori to continue to dash about the county in this mad fashion?"

Clive Mathis stared at Justin with surprise. "Why, I daresay he only gives Lori a thought when she rides across his path at the weekly foxhunt, and then it's only to yell at her to get out of his way."

That was the problem, Justin decided. There wasn't a man at Larken Hall who had ever given Lori a thought. No doubt, none had noted that the girl had grown into a passably pretty chit with a very fine figure.

To them she was just a rousing rider upon whom they might wager.

As his gaze swept over the girl in her masculine attire, which did little to conceal her shapely curves, he suspected that it was only by the grace of God that one of the sporting gentlemen who stayed at the Hall for the weekly hunts hadn't taken advantage of her. The very idea that someone would lay a hand on such an innocent made his blood boil.

Then, with a shake of his head, Justin came to his senses. The chit really was none of his concern. But for an old friend's sake he gave her eldest brother one final warning. " 'Twould be unfortunate if she were to end up on the shelf simply because no one took the time to teach her the way a lady should behave." With that he bid the Mathises good day and crossed the road to the inn, leaving Clive Mathis behind, scratching his head in thought.

In her carriage in the inn yard, Lady Anne had been enjoying the lemonade and biscuits that Mrs. Summers had provided even as she watched her son and Miss Mathis across the street in conversation. She had been astonished to see Justin angrily shake the girl for the foolish riding trick. But then she remembered how it had been when her boys were younger. When she thought one was hurt, she was terrified, but once she knew they were all right, there was always that strong desire to wring their necks for having given her such a scare. Was that how it had been for her son when he'd seen Lorissa take a tumble? Did he still hold the girl in such affection?

In the countess's mind, the most frightening thing evident from this whole event was that she had seen more emotion from Justin in those few moments with Lorissa Mathis than in all the time he had been seeking a wife in London.

Lady Anne began to fear that her son's heart had not been touched by either Miss Norris or Lady Kate.

Was he about to make a dreadful mistake by offering for one of the ladies, just to follow the Andrews tradition of giving the Ruby Heart before he turned six-and-twenty? She sincerely hoped not.

At that moment Justin arrived at the coach, bringing the lady out of her worrisome thoughts. "Is Miss Mathis unharmed?"

Justin gave an affirmative nod, but the look on his face was troubled. "Do you believe that Lord Larken has made no effort to tame that child?"

"She is hardly a child, Justin. By my reckoning she must be near twenty. That is why I invited her to our ball."

He turned to eye the young lady, who appeared to be having an enjoyable conversation with Adam. "Well, I doubt that her father can be persuaded to put out the blunt to make certain she is properly attired. She will likely arrive in a dress made of old foxtails sewn together, for I am certain that is all the old gentleman can spare the time to give her."

The countess was suddenly struck with an idea. "Then let us invite her to join us at once. If she does not have a proper ball gown, I can send her measurements to London, and we shall have her looking all the thing before the ball."

Justin turned back to his mother and smiled. "You are quite the most kindhearted person I know, dear Mother. But you do know that it will take more than a fancy gown to turn Lori into a proper lady. She has been left to run wild these many years without the care and instruction of a lady of Quality. She is very likely to embarrass you before your friends with her unconventional conduct."

"All the more reason for her to stay at Crossley Court for the entire week before the ball. Now go fetch the dear girl here so that I may invite her, and I think her youngest brother must accompany her."

With that Justin left his mother in an effort to coax

Lori and Dermot to the coach. The countess knew it was a risk to be putting an untried miss like Lorissa Mathis in the company of two polished and sophisticated ladies of the *ton*. Especially when the pair were vying for her son's attention.

A frown touched her brow. There was nothing like feminine competition for a gentleman's attentions to bring out the worst in females. But some instinctive maternal sense told her that Miss Mathis might trigger a beneficial reaction, if not from Justin, at least from one of the two prospective brides, to help her son become aware of what he truly wanted.

Miss Mathis and her brother came to the carriage and properly greeted the countess, even as Lorissa gave Justin occasional glaring glances. It took some time for the countess and her son to bring a smile to the young lady's lips, but at last she had become the engaging girl Lady Anne remembered. The invitation to Miss Mathis and her brother was issued and graciously accepted on the condition that they gained their father's approval. It was settled that they would arrive on the morrow if all went well.

After catching up on all the news of happenings in the shire, the two families parted. As her carriage made its way to Crossley Court, the countess felt a twinge of guilt. She was using her neighbor's daughter to bring about some response from her son. Then she reminded herself that Lorissa would very likely benefit from her week of rubbing shoulders with the elite of Society. So, in truth, everyone would gain.

The following afternoon a steady stream of carriages passed through the gates at Crossley Court and came up the drive to the beautiful Jacobean manor house. In order to keep the two young ladies in whom Justin was interested from being too much in each other's

company, the countess had invited some ten other
guests to stay for the week prior to the ball.

The first of the guests to arrive were Lady Katherine
Dailey, her mother, the marchioness, and her brother,
Horace, Lord Rayburn. Lady Longford was a quiet,
friendly lady with little to say, or so it seemed when she
was in the presence of her vivacious daughter. As to the
siblings, they were much alike with their fine features,
dark blond hair, and deep blue eyes. But there the simi-
larity ended. The sister was much in control of her emotions and her plans—she wanted to be Justin Andrews's
wife and own the Crossley Ruby Heart and was determined to make it happen, come what may. Whereas the
brother, with little to occupy him while he waited to
inherit his noble responsibilities, had become much involved with the more raffish elements of the sporting
crowd and, at thirty, was a hardened gamester.

Lord Rayburn had only accompanied his mother
and sister to Crossley Court in the hopes of purchasing
a stallion that Lord Justin owned, which was reported
to run like the wind. With such an animal he was convinced that he might win so many races that he would
at last climb out of debt.

The Daileys had scarcely been seated in the Rose
Drawing Room when Major Dandridge and Sir Aubrey
Brooks, the latter accompanied by his wife, arrived.
Quickly to follow were the Dowager Baroness Parmenter, a regal matron, and her thirtyish unmarried
daughter, Miss Parmenter, who appeared frail and
sickly despite avowals of good health. Then Lord and
Lady Buckman, a middle-aged couple, arrived, and on
their heels was Mr. and Mrs. Paul Lansing and their
son Vernon, the young man sporting a garish striped
blue coat with oversized shoulder pads.

Several hours passed before Miss Belinda Norris and
her father, Squire Herbert Norris, arrived. By the time
they entered the drawing room, that gentleman was
fuming, announcing to the others that his daughter

had dithered so long in dressing that morning that he thought he would be forced to pay for a second night at the posting inn. Miss Norris had blushed prettily, but the countess assured Mr. Norris that his daughter was in such fine looks it was well worth the wait. Still, the irate father was not to be appeased, especially when he saw Lord Justin seated beside Lady Kate and seemingly enjoying himself.

The squire had amassed a vast fortune through wise investments and he fully intended to use his money to make certain that Belinda married a title. The girl had the beauty to see his dream to fruition, but unfortunately she had little taste for Society. The chit was forever longing to return to their home in Surrey, but with the arrival of Lord Justin on the scene, Herbert Norris's hopes had soared. He was convinced that the earl's son would make a satisfactory husband and one day Belinda would be a countess.

With his goal in mind, he ushered his daughter into the room. He guided Belinda to a chair beside the earl's heir, then set about distracting Lady Kate.

Some minutes later, when most of the guests had retired to rest, save Lady Kate, Miss Norris, Mr. Vernon Lansing, and the major, who remained in the drawing room with the countess and her sons, the doors opened. The butler, Flanders, announced Miss Lorissa Mathis and Mr. Dermot Mathis.

Justin looked up from the lively debate that Lady Kate and Mr. Lansing were having about the merits of summering at Brighton. An arrested expression settled on Justin's face as he took in his old childhood companion. Miss Hoyden from next door looked anything but. She was dressed in a pale green muslin gown with a dark green velvet spenser, a white ruffle at the collar. Her auburn hair, which had been a tumbled mess after her fall yesterday, was pulled back into a plain chignon, with spiraling curls left to frame her face. She appeared the epitome of the proper country miss.

Then Justin took note of the look of sheer terror in Lori's green eyes as they swept the assembled company. Knowing Lord Larken, Justin suspected that this was the first time the girl had ever been present at such a genteel social gathering.

He quickly excused himself from the small circle of guests, who'd paid scant attention to the new arrivals, then went to the brother and sister standing uncertainly in the doorway. In a low voice, as he extended his arm to her, he said, "Well, Brat, I must say you *have* learned a few things since last I saw you. Your servant, Dermot."

Young Mathis bowed to Justin as Lori clutched at his arm as if her life depended upon him. Strangely, the feel of her warm hand upon his arm sent a disturbing sensation racing through him. He had always been her protector when they were children, and he was surprised to find that he still liked that she saw him as such.

"Oh, Justin, I am terrified I shall make some social blunder and never be invited anywhere ever again."

"I see we are once again on a first-name basis." He grinned at her.

She blushed but smiled back. "I am sorry about yesterday. 'Tis only that I hadn't seen you in four years and the first thing you must do is scold me, just like when I was twelve."

"Well, you must forgive me for such impertinence. I fear all those years I was soldiering, the image I held of you was that little girl soaking wet beside the river."

"Do you expect me to believe you gave any of us a thought while you were fighting the French?" Lorissa scoffed, but her smile showed clearly that she was pleased that she had been in his thoughts, even if his memories were some years out of date.

A faraway look settled in Justin's eyes for a moment. "On nights after a battle sometimes only those delightful childhood recollections helped one forget the horrors of the day's battle." Seeming to come out of his trance, he took note of the serious expression etched on both their faces as they watched him. Realizing he was being a poor host, he said, "But that is all in the past. Come let me introduce you to a few of our guests."

As the introductions were being made, both Lady Kate and Miss Norris took a long look at the young lady to whom Lord Justin had just shown such marked attention. He stated that she was an old friend. The marquis's daughter saw little to fear. Miss Mathis was a green country girl in an unfashionable gown who would prove little competition for Lady Kate's blond beauty.

From the squire's daughter's perspective, here was a pretty young girl whose eyes glowed each time they rested on Lord Justin. Miss Norris suspected that Miss Mathis might not have realized it as yet, but she showed every sign of being in love with her old childhood friend.

Soon the gathered departed to their assigned rooms to dress for dinner. The countess held Justin back for a moment's private conversation. "Well, what say you about our Lorissa now?"

Justin drew his mother's arm through his as he led her toward the stairs. "I say she turned out rather nicely once she was properly attired, but the young lady still is going to have a difficult time mingling with your guests. Did you not see the fear in her eyes when she first stood at the doorway? I was afraid if I didn't go to her at once she would take fright and run."

"I cannot say that I did, my dear. But then, one look at that coat young Lansing was wearing was enough to make any reasonable person take flight." The countess referred to the young gentleman's dandyish attire.

Justin chuckled. "We can only pray that Adam did not admire the garment greatly. People would be able to hear Father's roar all the way back in London if my brother started fashioning himself a Tulip of the *Ton.*"

Lady Anne merely nodded her head, her thoughts

already on another matter. At the upstairs landing, her hand dropped from his arm as she turned to face him. She made one last request before departing. "About Miss Mathis—I think you might want to stay close at hand to help guide her through these first few gatherings. You can direct her as to how to go on. Or perhaps I should have Adam take her under his wing. He seems much taken with her."

Justin frowned at the notion that his brother was smitten by Lori Mathis. Why, they were both little more than children. "Adam is too much the greenling himself. I shall see to the girl."

With that he kissed his mother's cheek and made his way to his own chamber to change. To his surprise, Justin found he did not dislike the idea of still watching out for little Lori in the least.

Lorissa paused at the drawing room door, her knees knocking as she faced the entire assembled company. Dressed in a white silk evening gown trimmed with Brussels lace and green ribbon, which she'd had made several years earlier in Cheltenham, she'd thought herself in looks until she surveyed the finery of the countess's guests. She felt herself under the scrutiny of the London ladies. They scanned her from head to toe, and their expressions ranged from near pity at her provincial attire to total dismissal of her. She suddenly wished she hadn't come. Then she spied Justin coming toward her and she no longer cared what anyone thought.

"You are quite lovely this evening, Miss Mathis. Allow me to introduce you to those guests you have yet to meet."

Lorissa held back. "Must I? I don't think they like me and I would much rather talk to you."

Justin took her hand and drew it though his arm. "Don't worry, Brat, no one bites. Besides, I am the host until my father arrives, so duty calls. I shall, however, find you someone with whom you may converse comfortably."

Scanning the room, Justin's gaze landed upon Lady Brooks, and he knew at once that this gentle lady would do well for Lori's first social encounter. After a new round of introductions, he led her over and introduced her to the baronet's wife, who immediately patted the sofa beside her, insisting that Lorissa sit down and tell her all about herself.

Lorissa liked the stout matron with the kind smiling eyes, but she knew a sudden urge to rush after Justin as he excused himself to continue circulating about the room. Soon Lady Brooks's kind questions about Lorissa's life at Larken Hall helped her relax. When that subject had been thoroughly examined, the woman startled Lorissa by her next statement.

"Have you seen it, my dear?"

Not having any idea what the lady referred to, Lorissa said, "Seen what, my lady?"

"Why, the Crossley Ruby Heart, child. My husband tells me that the odds are running very much in Lady Kate's favor in the betting books at White's. Still, if I were his mother I would recommend he take Miss Norris, for in my opinion, she is by far the better behaved young lady."

Lorissa's heart began to hammer. "I do not understand."

Lady Brooks turned to look at her companion with surprise. "Why, surely you know that Lord Justin is to announce his betrothal at the Valentine's Ball. Since he has shown no particular partiality for one lady or the other, it's anyone's guess which one will arrive wearing the engagement necklace."

The lady beside Lorissa on the rose damask sofa continued to chatter, but Lorissa was so stunned she heard little. Justin was to marry. The idea that her old friend was in love with one of the two beautiful women who stood beside him in front of the fireplace made

Lorissa's heart ache. In that moment she'd known that she'd always thought that Justin was hers. It had been a childish notion, and she must remember she was grown now and put such ideas from her. But when her gaze settled on her dear Justin, she knew that she wanted him still.

Lorissa spent the remainder of the evening trying to hide her disappointment, knowing she had little chance of changing the course of Justin's intentions. He would never consider her for his wife. Why, he still called her Brat and, compared to the two ladies he was pursuing, she appeared childish and unworldly. Worse, she felt gauche and unprepared for her first social outing. How could she even consider competing with the likes of Lady Kate or Miss Norris?

The only bright spot in Lorissa's evening came at the end. As the guests prepared to depart for their beds, Justin announced that there would be mounts prepared in the morning at ten for anyone wishing to ride. The one place she was confident was on the back of a horse.

About to depart, Justin took her hand and drew her aside with a worried look in his gray eyes, but he gave her a gentle smile that only made Lorissa's heart behave in an extreme manner. "I know you will be disappointed with our rather tame gait, but most of the ladies lack your excellent seat on a horse. No showing off, Brat, no trick riding."

"What, no jumping the crumbed tower near the river? No riding mounted backward with a blindfold?" she teased.

Justin's brows shot up. "Can you do those things?"

"Not in a sidesaddle."

"Good, then we should have a pleasant ride without a cross word. Sleep well, Brat." With that he kissed the hand he still held, and Lorissa floated up to her room on a cloud of euphoria.

CHAPTER THREE

"Good morning, Miss Mathis." Belinda Norris, a smile on her pretty face, came down the main staircase dressed to ride.

Lorissa looked up from where she stood waiting impatiently in the marble-paved hall for the others to rise. "Good morning, Miss Norris."

"You are much like me, I see. When there is a chance to ride, I am always the first to arrive."

Lorissa eyed the squire's daughter with caution. The lady had no reason to befriend her, yet her smile appeared genuine. She was a vision in a maroon riding habit of exceptional cut. Atop her black curls sat a Hussar-style black cap with a long maroon scarf, which at present was draped over the lady's shoulder.

Unlike last evening, however, Lorissa was confident in her new emerald green velvet habit with its gold military-style frogging and low crown black beaver hat. "Do you ride a great deal in Town, Miss Norris?"

The lady sighed. "Unfortunately not. That was why I was so delighted that we were to visit the country for Lady Anne's party. I was certain we would ride every day here."

Just then Lord Justin arrived and greeted the ladies, complimenting them both on their looks. Lorissa delighted at the look of surprise and approval reflected in his eyes as his gray gaze swept over her. She found herself puzzled, however, as she watched her old friend converse with Miss Norris. There was nothing loverlike on either of their parts. It seemed unthinkable to Lorissa that one could know Justin and not love him.

Soon the company in the front hall swelled to eight people, and after a wait of a quarter of an hour, Justin decided it was time to set forth. The Andrewses' vast stables provided the mounts for everyone but Lorissa and Dermot, who'd brought their own horses from Larken Hall.

The party included four ladies—Lorissa, Miss Norris, Lady Kate, and Lady Buckman, a pretty blonde near forty—as well as four gentlemen—Justin, Adam, Major Dandridge, and Dermot. They set out at a gentle pace, but soon it was determined that everyone was an accomplished rider, so they increased their gait and cantered along a small road that bordered the estate.

Coming to a crossroad, Justin halted the riders and asked what they preferred to see. To the right they would find a small hermitage built on the river's edge by the second Earl of Crossley, to the left across the river in the hills they could visit a beautiful triple waterfall. At once Lady Kate expressed an interest in seeing the hermitage, but Lady Buckman would have none of it, preferring nature's beauty instead.

Having watched his brother flirting with Lorissa since the ride began, Justin came to a quick decision. "I think we are such a large party, it would be better if we parted. Adam, you escort Lady Kate to the hermitage, along with the major and whoever wishes to go. I shall lead Lady Buckman to the falls."

An angry flush settled on Lady Kate's cheeks, but she made no scene. "Come, Major Dandridge, we shall enjoy the hermitage. Pray, don't drag your heels, Mr. Andrews." With that she set her horse in motion, reaching a full gallop within seconds.

Adam gave a last look at Lorissa, then shrugged his

shoulders as he put his crop to his horse to catch the lady and the major, who'd followed her.

Dermot hesitated a moment, thinking he should accompany his sister. But he knew Justin would be adequate escort for the other ladies. Being much enchanted with Lady Kate's blond beauty, he tipped his hat to the remainder of the party and quickly followed the three already disappearing down the road.

Justin led the way and he, as well as his three companions, headed west. Some fifteen minutes of steady cantering brought his party to a beautiful waterfall that meandered down a rocky slope. The area's uniqueness was that the flow of the water changed angles three times as it cascaded down the hill.

No sooner had they drawn their horses to a halt, than Lady Buckman announced, "I should very much like to climb to the top, Lord Justin. Will you accompany me?" With that she slid from her saddle unaided and began advancing on the hillside.

Justin sighed, then asked the others, "Would you ladies care to join us?"

Before Lorissa could inform her old friend that she would follow him to the ends of the earth, Miss Norris spoke.

"I think not, sir. I do believe that Miss Mathis and I shall stroll beside the river's edge and get to know one another better."

He looked at the two women and wondered what a complete hoyden and a paragon of good conduct might have to discuss. Then the thought occurred to him that such a friendship might be a good thing, if Miss Norris took Lori under her wing. "An excellent notion. Lori can assure you there is little to see atop the falls."

After helping the ladies down, Justin hurried to catch up with the intrepid Lady Buckman, who'd scaled nearly a third of the hill already. Lorissa and Miss Norris watched the gentleman rapidly ascend the rocks; then the squire's daughter turned to her companion to ask, "How long have you known Lord Justin, Miss Mathis?"

Despite the friendly tone, Lorissa eyed the beauty with a certain amount of hostility, knowing that the lady might win Justin's heart. "Why, all of my life, Miss Norris. Our fathers' estates border one another."

"Please call me Belinda. Shall we walk to the river? I have something I should like to discuss with you."

Curiosity overcame much of Lorissa's enmity, and she followed the lady to the swiftly flowing water. They turned to the east, moving away from the waterfall. Silence reigned for some minutes before Belinda spoke again.

"I hope you will forgive my presumption in approaching you on this matter, but I need an ally and I think so do you."

Lorissa halted. Every fiber of her being wanted to tell this woman that she would never assist any lady in capturing Justin's heart. But some instinct told her to remain silent, since the lady had proven far kinder than Lorissa had expected a fashionable London miss to be. She simply stared at Belinda.

The raven-haired beauty gave a soft, tinkling laugh. "Do not glare at me so, Miss Mathis. Despite my father's ambition, I have no designs on Lord Justin."

"But I thought . . ." Lorissa trailed off, puzzled yet relieved to hear the news.

Belinda gestured to nearby rocks, and the ladies settled upon them. They could see Justin and Lady Buckman still climbing near the top of the falls. The incline had grown steep and the viscountess now required the gentleman's assistance.

"Like you, I have an old childhood friend who is near and dear to my own heart, Miss Mathis. One, I might say, that I love to distraction." Belinda gave a heartfelt sigh.

Lorissa's cheeks warmed at the realization that she'd been so blatant about her feelings for Justin that this

stranger had seen it at once. "Please call me Lori."
She hesitated a moment, then asked the question
burning in her breast. "Why, then, have you allowed
Justin to court you, even come to Crossley?"

Belinda sighed again, as if the injustices of the world
rested upon her delicate shoulders. She turned her
sad gaze back to the river. "My father is determined
that I shall marry a titled gentleman, and Torquil is
but a genteel landholder. Until now most of my suitors
have been such obvious fortune hunters that I had no
trouble convincing my father they would not suit. But
Lord Justin is quite another matter. I must own, had
I not already cherished my Torquil, I would not have
been displeased to be paid such attentions by such a
kind and likable young lord. Still, I am aware that I
have not touched his heart."

Lorissa's delight at the information was tempered by
one other possibility. She hesitated for a moment, but
she had to know. "Do you think, then, that he loves
Lady Kate?" Lorissa was afraid to breathe as she waited
for the answer.

"I pray not, but you must remember I have not been
much in their company together. I can only say that I
think she will make a dreadful wife."

There was so much vehemence in the lady's voice,
Lorissa wondered why, if Belinda was not in love with
Justin, she did not wish him to make a match with
the marquess's daughter. Lorissa took note of the
lady's concerned expression. "You . . . do not like
Lady Kate?"

Belinda turned and look at Lorissa, her face serious.
"I do not think she is at all kind." She looked down
at her hands clutching her crop before she added, "I
have heard that she was the one who first started calling me the 'turnip farmer's daughter.' "

Lorissa could see the humiliation Belinda felt at the
cruel title. " 'Twas very unkind, but perhaps she only
did it out of fear that you would win Justin's heart."

"There is more. I know I shouldn't listen to servants' gossip, but my maid told me that belowstairs all London knows that Lady Kate's maid often appears in the servants' hall with bruises on her arms and face when the young lady is in a temper."

A gasp escaped Lorissa's lips. The very idea of abusing one's servants, or anyone for that matter, shocked the country-bred girl to her very core. Her gaze trailed back to her dear Justin. He and Lady Buckman had begun their descent, but it was far slower than the climb had been. "One would never guess such of Lady Kate to see her in polite company."

Belinda took one of Lorissa's hands in hers. "That is true, for I think she is clever enough to make certain few see the shrew under that carefully created mask of gentility. The question is, dear girl, will you save our friend, Lord Justin, from her?"

"Me?" Lori was stunned. "How can I do anything against such a fashionable and sophisticated beauty?"

"Because, dear child, you already have an edge. I see a great deal of affection in the gentleman's eyes each time they rest upon you."

That was not news to Lorissa. But she was neither blind nor wanting in wits. "Do not mistake his affection for anything more than old friendship, Belinda, for I have not. He still thinks of me as that little hoyden he pulled from the river years ago. Why, he still calls me Brat. Hardly the words of a gentleman in love."

"The words, my dear, of a gentleman who has yet to realize that you have grown into a very lovely young woman."

A blush warmed Lorissa's cheeks. "Thank you, but I cannot hold a candle to Lady Kate, with her beautiful gowns, her golden curls, and her ease in company."

"In my opinion, golden curls are much overrated." Belinda laughed as she patted her own raven locks. Then, seeing the amusement in Lorissa's eyes, she added, "And as to the gowns, you are much my size.

Would you allow me to have the dressing of you during the house party, or do I presume too much?"

"Oh, I could not. You are too kind, but I don't think it would be proper." Lorissa wanted more than anything to appear before Justin in looks, but how could she allow a complete stranger to provide her clothes?

"You must not think it mere kindness, Lori. We are fighting to save Lord Justin from the clutches of a female I am certain will only bring him unhappiness. As in any war, one must use all within one's ability to win the day."

Lorissa was torn. Her gaze trailed back to Justin, nearing the bottom of the hill. He looked up at her at that moment and gave that old, familiar grin, then waved. Her heart fluttered in her chest. She loved him, and Belinda was offering her a chance to win her heart's desire. How could she say no?

"I am not certain it will do any good, but I shall agree to your kind offer."

The squire's daughter grinned, then hugged Lorissa. "Excellent. After we return to Crossley, you must come with me to my room. My maid and I shall have you looking your very best by the time we dine this evening. The gentleman shall be quite amazed to see you when we are done."

The pair had been so engrossed in their conversation that they were startled when Justin stepped up to them. "Are you lovely ladies ready to return to the estate?"

Two sets of guilty eyes looked up at him. What had these two been plotting?

Belinda recovered herself first and rose. "Why, in fact we are quite ready, sir. Lori and I have made plans for this afternoon and we don't wish to be late." With that she smiled at Lorissa and moved toward Lady Buckman and the horses.

Suspicious, Justin grabbed Lori's hand and pulled her up from the rock. "Why the guilty looks? What have the pair of you been discussing?"

"Guilty looks? D-don't be ridiculous, Justin. We were just . . . discussing what to wear this evening." Lorissa's heart was hammering as he pulled her close to him.

"I shall be quite angry with you, Brat, if you have convinced Miss Norris to go along with one of your childish pranks."

Anger that he continued to perceive her as a child made Lorissa jerk her hand free. "Sir, we were merely discussing matters of dress. Have I not behaved properly since I arrived at Crossley Court? If you think I have embarrassed your mother by my presence, I shall take my leave and return to Larken Hall at once."

Justin felt like a great beast for having falsely accused his old friend. Yet he didn't blame himself overly, considering how well he knew the girl's history. Still, he knew he must apologize. He didn't want her to leave and miss the first truly social event of her young life.

On impulse, he took her face in his hands and kissed her forehead. "Forgive me, Lori. I am just cross as an old bear this week, weighed down with duty and decisions. Please don't leave." He could see that his apology only slightly thawed her rigid expression. Knowing her deep affection for the countess, he added, "You know my mother would never forgive me if you decamped because of my odd humors. Say you will stay."

Lorissa, savoring even the brotherly kiss, gave him a smile. "I cannot ever stay mad at you, Justin. I shall not go home."

Much in harmony, the couple returned to the waiting ladies. They rode back to Crossley, where the other half of the party awaited them in the stable yard. Lady Kate was at Justin's side within minutes of his dismount, begging for a stroll through one of the gardens.

Manners demanded that he accommodate the lady, so he invited everyone to join them. The other gentlemen declined, and so did the ladies. Justin experienced a strange pang in his chest as he watched Adam in conversation with Lorissa as they followed Dermot and Miss Norris back to the manor.

As he ushered the chattering Lady Kate through the well-trimmed yews into the Riverside Garden, Justin's mind was on his old friend. That guilty look in her eyes beside the river kept haunting him. She kept vowing she was grown up and would commit no mischief here, but he couldn't quite forget her standing on the back of that horse in Naunton. Nor could he forget the lovely curve of her slender hips in those breeches.

Appalled at where his musings had strayed, Justin suddenly put himself to the task of entertaining the lady beside him. She was where his interest should be, not having such thoughts about a veritable child like Lorissa. He only wished that Lady Kate was half so interesting to converse with.

"Why are you wasting time here?" Lady Kate hissed through clenched teeth at her brother while he made another selection from the tray of chocolates on the small table. The entire company was gathered in the Willow Drawing Room, awaiting the tea tray after dinner. The elder members of the party were playing whist, while Lady Buckman played softly on a pianoforte. The remaining guests were scattered about the room in conversation.

Thinking her voice might have been overly loud, Lady Kate looked over her shoulder. She pasted a false smile on her face when Lady Anne glanced toward their position at the far end of the long gallery. When the countess looked away, Kate continued to berate Horace. "Stop gorging on sweetmeats. You know they make your face spotty, and that does not suit my purpose. You must go and amuse that little country nobody, or I shall never get a moment alone with Lord Justin."

Horace, Lord Rayburn, licked the chocolate from his fingers as he looked back up the room to where

Justin, Adam, and Major Dandridge stood in conversation with Miss Mathis. "Wondered when you'd notice the little nobody has been transformed into a Diamond of the First Water."

Lady Kate gnashed her teeth. Even she had been amazed at the transformation of the girl in a mere matter of hours. But never would she admit that a country miss might be competition for her own beauty.

"Diamond! Hardly, dear brother; merely a pretty nuisance at the moment."

Horace selected another sweetmeat from the tray and popped the treat into his greedy mouth. "Don't make no difference to me. She wasn't part of our bargain. A hundred pounds to distract Miss Norris, not some little provincial puss who has aspirations above her station."

Kate very much wanted to strike the smirk off her brother's face, but she needed his help. Time was running out and Lord Justin was showing even less interest in her here than in London. At first she'd attributed it to his duties as host, but she'd finally come to realize that he appeared to have some chivalrous notion concerning his old childhood friend. He went to such great pains to see her entertained or lingered at her side much longer than was prudent.

"Then we shall make a new arrangement. I shall settle your gaming debts and give you two hundred pounds if you can not only distract Miss Mathis but discredit her in Lord Justin's eyes as well." The marquess's daughter had never been one to go into anything by half measure.

Horace frowned. "Don't mean for me to ruin the girl, I hope. Her father's a baron and likely would insist I marry the chit. Not ready to be leg-shackled even to have my debts cleared."

Lady Kate rolled her eyes. "Are you a complete ninny? Of course I don't mean for you to create a scandal. Justin would likely call you out, and I can hardly marry a man who killed my brother. We shall come up with a plan, but for now try to get the girl away from Justin."

"You come up with a reasonable ploy to discredit the girl that don't have me facing anyone at twenty paces and I'll do it. But I want something else. You must put in a word for me about that cursed racer I've come to purchase. Andrews won't give me five minutes to make an offer on the stallion. He just keeps saying that the animal's not for sale."

Lady Kate didn't give a fig about any horse, but she knew she must agree. "Very well, I shall do my best. Come to my room in the morning. By then I shall have come up with a plan to get rid of Miss Mathis."

As the lady was about to leave, her brother grabbed her arm. "Don't be so obvious in your pursuit of the gentleman. Let Andrews see you being kind to the less exalted members of the party, like that spinsterish Miss Parmenter, or flirting with that young fop Lansing."

That was the last thing Lady Kate wished to do, but she knew she must be careful. After eyeing the two diversions her brother had suggested, she chose Miss Parmenter, thinking she didn't want to risk alienating Lord Justin by a show of interest in Mr. Vernon Lansing.

While the marquess's offspring plotted at one end of the Willow Drawing Room, Justin stood at the opposite end trying to keep his brother and his oldest friend from making cakes of themselves over Lorissa. Ever since the girl had waltzed into the room looking like she'd stepped from a fashion plate in *La Belle Assembleé,* the two had hovered about her like bees around a hive.

Even Justin had to admit he could scarcely take his eyes from her, she was so changed. Her rich auburn locks had been trimmed and fashioned into a soft cap of curls that were held back from her face with pearl-studded combs. Her fashionable sea-foam green silk gown with a shimmering white sarcenet overskirt revealed a great deal of the girl's feminine assets. Upon first seeing his old friend, Justin had suggested to his mother that she urge Lori to change into something more appropriate for her age. But the countess had merely laughed, saying Miss Mathis looked perfect. Still, he didn't like the warm glances she was receiving from the gentlemen.

The countess suddenly appeared at Justin's side. "Pray, forgive us, Major, Miss Mathis, but I must steal my son away from you." With that she led Justin back toward the center of the room. Once away from the small circle of friends, she spoke in a low tone, "I think it time you circulated more, my dear. You have monopolized our lovely neighbor quite enough. I do believe Miss Norris expressed an interest in the portraits upon the wall."

Justin knew his duty. He went to Miss Norris and offered her a tour of the room. The lady accepted his arm and he led her to the huge painting hanging in a center alcove. He began to give her the history of the picture and she asked interested questions.

As he took her arm to lead her to the next work of art, the lady startled him. "My lord, I was hoping for a moment alone with you."

He paused and looked down at her, one dark brow raised. She was very pretty and he liked her a great deal, but he knew he could not call what he felt love.

As he stood silently staring at her in thought, the lady interrupted his musing. "What think you of Lori's new appearance, sir?"

His gaze immediately moved to the lady under discussion. A frown wrinkled his brow as he noted that Lord Rayburn had joined the circle around Lorissa. He thought he must warn his old friend not to pay the noted gamester much heed. "You are responsible for her transformation?"

"I am. She is lovely, is she not? Over the course of the afternoon I have come to know a great deal about her. 'Tis unfortunate that her father has made so little effort to prepare her to be presented to Society."

All Justin had to do was think of Lorissa's situation at Larken Hall and he became angry. Still, his only comment was, "The baron has taken little interest in any of his children, Miss Norris."

Belinda surveyed Lord Justin's face as he watched the gentlemen flirt with Lorissa. It was clearly not a sight that pleased him. She had been about to ask her companion to assist her to teach the girl to dance the following afternoon, but fearful he would refuse her, she decided on another tact.

"Well, I think it dreadful that the man never hired a dance instructor to teach her how to perform even the simplest of country dances."

Justin's brow rose in surprise. Then he remembered Lorissa's strange beginning to the conversation when she'd fallen off her horse in Naunton. He'd been so upset with her that he'd paid little heed to her ramblings. "I do believe she mentioned that she cannot dance."

"Not even a little. I was thinking, if you did not object, I would take her to the ballroom tomorrow and I shall play while Adam partners her."

"Adam! Why, that young cub is likely to trample her feet unmercifully."

Belinda suppressed a smile. "Then who would you recommend to help, sir? I must play the pianoforte, so I shall need someone who can instruct her in the steps."

Justin stood silent for a moment, then said, "I suppose it shall have to be me, since the major still limps from his wound and I doubt Rayburn's seen the inside of a ballroom these past ten years, if ever."

"That is an excellent suggestion, sir. I am certain Lori will be less shy with her old friend."

Just then Lady Kate arrived and Justin offered her his other arm as he invited her to join them in their inspection of the room's paintings. As he led the ladies down the room, his thoughts drifted to Lorissa. It would be a nuisance to spend the afternoon instructing the chit in the art of dance, but somehow he was looking forward to the simple task.

Learning of the proposed dance lesson from her son the following morning, Lady Anne instructed the servants to halt their decorating for the afternoon and put a pianoforte at Miss Norris's disposal. Lori and Belinda arrived some thirty minutes after nuncheon to find the parquet floors gleaming and half the room bedecked with red and white ribbons streaming from the top of the main chandelier to the outer walls to form a colorful canopy above the ballroom floor.

Justin soon arrived and found he couldn't take his eyes off Lorissa. She was utterly feminine in a simply fashioned blue lutestring gown cut low over the bodice, which was trimmed with a small ruffle of blond lace. As his gaze lingered at her lovely neck, he had to remind himself that this stylish beauty was his old friend.

Belinda took her place at the piano and announced that they would begin with a simple country reel. She played a few bars of the music. "Perhaps you should walk Lori through the step's first, my lord."

Justin grinned as Lori looked puzzled. He took her hand and led her to the floor. "Face me, Brat. And don't look as if I mean to eat you. This is a simple dance."

" 'Tis not your teeth I fear, Justin, but your feet. I worry about the state of my toes under your boots if I make a wrong turn."

"You pierce my heart with such slander, Brat." His grin belied his words. "I'm no caper-merchant, but I think I can manage a lesson without destroying your slippers or your toes."

Lorissa spent a delightful afternoon learning several dances. The uncomplicated country reels she felt confident with, but the more intricate quadrille she feared might be beyond her at the ball.

At last Justin announced, "I think we have done enough for one day."

Belinda, at the pianoforte, shook her head. "One more of the simpler dances, then we shall be done. She must learn the waltz."

Justin hesitated. He didn't like the idea of anyone holding Lorissa in such an intimate matter, then realized he was being ridiculous. Everyone danced the waltz these days. "Very well."

With that he stepped closer to Lorissa. Taking her hand, he put his other at her waist. He heard her issue a small gasp, then she gazed up into his eyes with alarm. Soon her expression melted into one of total trust. The music started and they began to move gracefully into the three-count rhythm as if she had been born waltzing.

Justin twirled her slowly about the room, but his mind was not on the dance. For the first time he really saw his old friend. Gone was the child of memory. Here was a beautiful, tempting female. What startled him the most in his revelation was the rush of desire he experienced for her. How could this be? She was little Lori. His gaze swept her. The child he'd fished from the river had passed into history. Before him stood a woman, and a very desirable one.

That she wasn't yet married was a wonder to Justin. Then he realized that her family, no doubt, was as oblivious to her now as they had been throughout her life. But one day her brothers or her father would awaken to her loveliness as he had, and then what would happen to her?

Like most females of good family, she would be sold to the highest bidder with little thought to her happiness. That was the way it had been for centuries in noble families. The very notion made Justin furious.

His anger made him falter, which in turn caused
Lorissa to trod on his boot. "Oh, I am sorry, Justin."

Still in a rage at what Lord Larken could do to this
innocent in his arms, Justin was in no mood to dance.
He moved away from her. "That is enough for one day,
Lorissa. We are both grown tired. You were excellent
in your first lesson, but I must go see to our other
guests."

With that he bid the ladies good day, leaving Lorissa
wondering if her clumsiness had displeased him so
greatly, for he never called her Lorissa. Was he afraid
she would embarrass him at the ball?

While Lorissa was full of uneasiness, Belinda was well
pleased with the afternoon's progress. She'd seen the
sudden revelation on Lord Justin's face as he'd circled
the floor with his partner.

She rose and went to Lorissa. "We have had an excellent afternoon, my dear."

"Do you think so?" Lorissa's gaze still lingered at
the door through which Justin had hurriedly exited.

"I do. We accomplished two things: You now can
dance and I think Lord Justin no longer sees you as
a little girl."

Lorissa brightened. "Are you certain?"

Belinda might be an innocent, but she'd seen that
look in a man's eyes before—her own Torquil's when
he gazed at her. "As sure as I am that your father will
fox hunt this week."

Lorissa smiled. Why, that was a positive certainty, for
her father had never missed a week of fox hunting that
she could ever remember. For the first time since coming to Crossley Court, she began to have hope that
Justin might open his eyes to what was right in front of
him.

"Come, my dear, we must make certain you look
your best this evening. Shall we go see which of my
gowns will do for tonight?" With that Belinda locked
arms with her new friend and led Lorissa upstairs.

CHAPTER FOUR

Lady Kate and Lord Rayburn held their meeting in the lady's bedchamber the following morning. Horace sat in amazement and listened to the information his sister had gleaned from young Adam Andrews the previous evening, and the devious method with which she intended to use it.

But the gentleman was no fool; it was going to be an all-or-nothing gamble, but then he liked the exhilaration of the risk. If Kate's plan worked, she would likely end up the future Countess of Crossley. If it did not, Horace might be forced to rusticate in the country well away from Lord Justin's wrath.

Rain pattered on the breakfast parlor windows as the viscount arrived looking for his prey. He was convinced that the weather was a good omen, since it meant they would be house-bound much of the day and looking for ways to amuse themselves. But Mr. Dermot Mathis was late down that day, so the morning was well advanced before Horace ran him and Mr. Andrews to ground in the billiard room.

Wisely, the marquess's son played several games with the young gentlemen before he slyly suggested that they amuse themselves with something a bit more entertaining. Within thirty minutes, Rayburn had the two greenlings ensconced in a small, rarely used parlor, engaged in a high-stakes game of dicing.

Adam was the first of the two pigeons being plucked to realize they were in over their heads. He asked Horace to tally the amount of their losses. The combined total came to nearly five hundred pounds. The two old friends exchanged bleak looks, for each knew the other was at low tide financially.

Rising rather shakily, Adam announced, "Sir, I know a debt of honor must be paid, but you must give me until next quarter, for I haven't the ability to pay at this time."

Dermot nodded. " 'Tis the same with me, Lord Rayburn." He'd made the remark, but even on quarter day the youngest of the Mathises knew he wouldn't have half so much as was needed.

Horace struggled not to grin at his success. He scooped up the dice, dropping them into his pocket. It would never do to have someone examine them closely. "Well, lads, I am in sympathy with you, but a debt is a debt and I'm not likely to see either of you again before summer."

Adam straightened. "You will get your money, sir. Word of an Andrews."

Dermot made no comment, knowing his father would likely kill him for having gamed away such a sum. He was more likely to find himself shipped off to the navy, for that was his apathetic parent's usual threat to either of his sons on the occasion of any wrongdoing.

Horace allowed the two young men to stew for several moments as they awaited his decision. He looked from one to the other and knew what terrors they were facing. He'd been under the hatches much of his life. But it didn't sway him from his purpose.

Leaning back in his chair, he gave them an understanding smile. "I have a way you lads can pay me back and not surrender a single flimsy."

Adam and Dermot exchanged a hopeful look, then

Dermot eagerly asked, "How, sir? We would do almost anything to clear the debt."

"Your brother"—Horace looked at Adam—"owns a horse that I am greatly interested in. I believe the animal is called Mercury. I wish to match the steed against my own Hannibal before I make an offer. If you can arrange for the best rider to race the animal against me, I shall discharge both your debts."

Before either young man could comment, Lord Rayburn added, "And I understand the best rider in the county is Miss Mathis. Yes, it must be a race against the lady to prove the animal's worth."

Shock was evident on Adam's boyish face as he shook his head. "My brother would never allow the lady to damage her reputation in such a manner. You must think of—"

Dermot, far more desperate than Adam, placed a hand on his friend's arm. "She can do it. Lori is game for anything."

"But Justin won't allow—"

Horace interrupted. "I think it best your brother not be informed of our arrangement, Mr. Andrews. If Mr. Mathis can convince his sister to ride, we shall do the deed at dawn on the morrow. By breakfast you both will be debt-free. No one need be the wiser."

Adam was torn. He didn't like going behind his brother's back, but neither did he want to face the earl's censure for having lost such a sum gaming; it was above all things something his father abhorred. There was also his worry about Lorissa. The stallion had proven to be high-strung and difficult to manage. Justin swore the horse would likely never be manageable enough to take to the race course. Could a female handle such a beast? But the prospect of eliminating the debt dangled just in front of him. With salvation so close at hand, Adam couldn't resist.

"Are you certain your sister can handle such a high-bred racer?"

Dermot again grabbed his friend's arm. "She can do it, Adam. She is fearless when it comes to horses. There has never been one to best her."

Pursing his lips in disgust at the path they'd chosen, Adam bowed to Lord Rayburn. "Then, sir, if the lady is agreeable, we shall meet you at sunrise just outside the gates of the estate."

"Excellent." Horace rose. "And remember, not a word to anyone but Miss Mathis. Don't want your brother putting a spoke in our wheel, so to speak." With that the young lord went off to tell his sister that her plan was well in motion. She would have to do her part.

"Absolutely not!" Lorissa glared at her brother, then turned back to her mirror to finish removing the last of her jewelry, a pearl necklace that was the one remaining possession of her mother's. "My days of involving myself in you and Clive's little wagers are at an end."

" 'Tis no wager, and I'm desperate, Lori. You must race that horse, or I shall have to go to Father and tell him I have lost a great deal of money gaming."

She saw her brother's reflection in the mirror, and the despairing look on his face shocked her. The matter seemed of far greater importance than she'd first thought.

"How much have you lost?"

"Five hundred pounds." He gave her the full amount of his and his friend's catastrophe, knowing the sum would likely do the trick.

Lorissa's eyes grew round with awe as she breathed the words, "Five hundred pounds."

Desperate, Dermot fell to his knees and grabbed his sister's hand. "You know what will happen if I go to Papa and ask for even half that amount. I'll be shipped off to the navy, never to see you or Larken Hall for years on end."

Long familiar with her younger brother's stoic nature, Lorissa knew he was truly frightened to have humbled himself in this matter. She reached out to stroke his red curls. "I would do anything to help you, dear Dermot, but how can I engage in a race? Justin and Lady Anne are forever telling me I mustn't behave in a manner that brings undue attention to myself." She was certain that Justin would never agree to such a spectacle.

"You don't understand. The way I perceive the matter, Justin *wants* to sell Lord Rayburn this horse. But that gentleman demands to see how the racer performs against his animal. He's heard what a bruising rider you are and wants you to race him. Leastwise, that is his tale. I'm thinking perhaps he has a *tendre* for you and desires you to know how much he esteems you above all others."

"A *tendre!*" Lorissa's green eyes widened in shock. The young viscount was a likable enough fellow, but no gentleman at the party compared to Justin. "Don't be silly. He hardly knows me. I would guess there is some other reason he might—"

"Will you save me from being sent to sea?" Dermot interrupted, not wanting his sister to give the matter too much thought or she wouldn't agree.

She gazed into her brother's frightened eyes. Yet there was still one thing that held her back. "Has Justin given his approval for this race?"

Dermot averted his eyes from his sister's as he spoke the falsehood. "Of course he has. 'Tis his horse that will be sold, and for a very fine price. Besides, he knows you could ride any prad in his stable. The only thing he demanded is that the race be done in a quiet manner. The match is to take place at dawn on the morrow on the road in front of the estate. Once all is finished, there is to be no discussion of the race with the other guests."

Lorissa sighed. She would not have thought Justin

would have approved, but if there was one thing she'd learned early on, it was that men were such odd creatures when it came to buying and selling bits o' blood. It seemed almost as important to them as home and hearth. Looking down at her brother's bowed head, she knew she couldn't let him face their father's wrath when she owned the ability to save him.

"Then off to bed, for we must both rise early if we are to go to a race. See if Adam can furnish me with breeches, for I shan't undertake such an adventure in a sidesaddle."

Dermot seized his sister's hand, giving it a grateful kiss, then rose. He stared at her intently for a moment, then whispered, "I don't think we've any of us ever truly valued you properly at the Hall." With that he bid his sister good night and departed.

Deciding that fear of his fate at their father's hands had made her brother so philosophical, Lorissa rose and slipped into a nightrail before she climbed into bed. She gave her sibling's situation more thought as she blew out her candles. A rush of excitement surged through her at the idea of such a match. She still found the notion that Justin had agreed to the race very peculiar, but she was quite willing to assist him in the sale of his horse to Lord Rayburn.

Still, it seemed curious that he hadn't mentioned the matter to her this evening. But then, with his duties he'd had little time to engage her in conversation, although she had noted him watching her on several occasions as she conversed with other gentlemen.

Was he a bit jealous? Belinda thought so, and Lorissa hoped it was so, but she knew she mustn't discount the persistence of Lady Kate. The lady seemed to have the talent to be wherever Justin was, amusing him with her chatter.

Then Lorissa smiled in the darkness. On the morrow, she would be the center of attention. Justin would have eyes only for her. The idea pleased her prodigiously, and with images of her triumphant win and Justin's approval, she drifted off to sleep.

A footfall on the marble entry of the library startled Justin from his musing about Lorissa and why he'd spent much of the night thinking of her instead of the two ladies he'd had his mother invite. He looked up to see Lady Kate looking lovely in the Grecian robe of soft pink muslin she'd worn that evening.

"Pray, forgive me for interrupting your solitude, Lord Justin."

He rose and bowed warily, wondering why she'd approached him alone. Then he saw a footman hovering at the door. She could not claim to have been compromised, so he relaxed and smiled, feeling foolish that he'd suspected her of such a ploy. "Is there something you require, my lady?"

Lady Kate dimpled prettily at him. "I have a very unusual request. I hope you will agree. Would it be possible for you to join me for a ride at dawn tomorrow? There is a matter I wish to discuss privately with you. We need only take a groom for propriety."

Justin was puzzled, but curious as well. "Do you not wish to discuss this matter now, Lady Kate? I am at your disposal."

The lady shook her head, making her golden-blond curls sway. " 'Tis late and I am quite fatigued. My thoughts will be better ordered in the morning."

"Very well. Shall we meet at the stables at seven?"

"Would it be possible to have the horses at the front door?"

The lady's requests all seemed to get stranger and stranger to Justin, but he merely said, "Of course, it shall be as you wish."

She stepped forward and extended her arm. "You are too kind, my lord."

He took the proffered hand and brushed an obligatory kiss upon it. "Good night, Lady Kate. Until dawn."

After the lady departed, he again settled in front of the fire to finish his brandy. His mind full of the mystery of the morning ride, he wondered why it was that Lady Kate's beauty hadn't completely bowled him over after having known her as long as he had.

She was a toast of London, much pursued, and she'd shown him that he was her preference. Yet still he hesitated, even going so far as to turn some of his attentions to Miss Norris. Perhaps it was that Lady Kate too often allowed her remarks about others to pass beyond the line of what was pleasing. But then, didn't much of Society gossip about their neighbors and friends in just that manner? Still, he'd never heard an unkind word pass Miss Norris's lips. But in that lady he'd found a want of enthusiasm for his suit.

With the two ladies' names swirling in his head, Justin put down his brandy and rose to retire. By George, he would far rather think about Lori and her changed appearance. She'd been perfectly ravishing this evening in an ecru gown with blue ribbons. His mother had urged him to stop hovering at her side or she would never gain the courage to converse with ease with the other guests. So despite his wish to guide and protect her, he'd kept his distance. To his delight, he'd found himself staring at her in wonder as he watched her spread her wings and learn to soar in such a social setting.

As he made his way to bed, he decided that he would ride with Lady Kate as she'd requested, but he would be certain to join Lorissa and the others when they rode later. He wanted to know if she was enjoying herself at her first house party.

The cold morning air nipped at Lorissa's cheeks as she made her way down the front drive in the gray light before dawn. She craned her neck to see who awaited her in the misty daybreak beside the stone pillars of the front entry. She could see the two horses, saddled and ready for their match, but dancing restlessly at the ends of the leads.

To her disappointment she realized that the group consisted of only three gentlemen and two grooms. Lord Rayburn, her brother, and Mr. Andrews were discussing the merits of the two animals even as she approached. Her gaze swept over the two huge stallions, one gray and one black.

"Good morning, Miss Mathis," Lord Rayburn called to her, his gaze lingering on her slender figure.

For the first time Lorissa was uncomfortable in a man's costume. The look in the gentleman's eyes suddenly made her wish she'd never agreed to this race.

On seeing the expression on his sister's face, Dermot came and took her hands, leading her to the gray horse. "Thank you for doing this for us. Are you quite ready?"

Lorissa nodded, then asked, "But where is Justin?"

Dermot looked at Lord Rayburn, who had a ready response. "I believe he is to ride with my sister this morning, Miss Mathis. He had no fear for your safety, knowing your riding skills, so he was content to leave matters in our hands."

Disappointment overwhelmed her. Justin hadn't cared enough to come watch her race his horse. Instead he'd chosen to ride with Lady Kate. She was fooling herself if she thought that changing her appearance and behavior would make a difference in Justin's decision about marrying another.

Adam stepped forward, taking her hand. "Are you quite well? If you are not feeling the thing . . ." He didn't finish what he was about to say, since the young lady's ride meant so much to them all.

Stiffening her spine, Lorissa realized that Dermot

needed her. "I shall be fine. Shall we begin, Lord Rayburn?"

The groom stepped forward and gave her a leg up into the saddle as Rayburn mounted his animal. Justin's horse sidled away from the group nervously, and it took her a moment to get the highbred animal under some measure of control.

From the ground Adam called, "The length of the race shall be three miles. All the way to the bridge at Little Bend. I shall follow behind." He pointed to a bay standing quietly, tied to a branch.

Lorissa nodded her head, even as she struggled to control the fidgeting horse. She hoped once she gave the animal his head, much of the nervous energy would go into his speed.

The pair moved the animals even, then a groom lifted a handkerchief. "Ready?" After both acknowledged that they were, the fellow swept downward with the white fluttering linen and shouted, "Go!"

Mercury's nostrils flared and he reared in fright, but Lord Rayburn's horse was off. Lorissa gritted her teeth with determination. Never willing to be bested by another, she dug in her heels and hunched low over the animal. The gray stallion flashed forward and the race was on.

Coming through the gates of Crossley at just that moment, Justin came to a halt with Lady Kate at his side, curious about what he'd stumbled upon at his front gate. All he could see were two riders hunched over their horses riding neck or nothing down the road, a trail of dust kicked up behind them. Then he spied Adam and Dermot at the edge of the drive.

"What is happening here?" Justin barked, his gaze again riveted on the riders.

Adam's face blanched white. " 'Tis a race. Rayburn's Hannibal against Mercury."

Justin swore softly under his breath. That stallion was too unreliable in his opinion to be tested yet. "I told you I didn't intend to race that animal. He's dangerous. Which groom did you cozen into riding that widow maker?"

Adam looked at Dermot, and that young man responded, "Have no fear, sir. 'Tis Lori on the animal. She'll manage him well enough."

"You're a damned fool, Mathis! That horse is likely to kill her!" With that he put his own animal into a hard gallop chasing after the racers, but Lorissa and Rayburn were already disappearing round the bend in the road.

Justin rode as if his life depended on it, but it was, in truth, Lorissa's life that might depend on him. He was on a well-ribbed young Arabian, but he was only able to close the gap just a bit. The horses in front of him were bred for racing, and the best he could manage was to keep the riders in sight.

Once again he found himself praying that Lorissa wouldn't be hurt. He could see that she'd pulled a little ahead of Rayburn and was winning. Uncertain about the length of the course decided upon, he prayed they didn't intend to race all the way to Naunton. The busy streets would make Mercury uncontrollable.

Things seemed to be going without a hitch at present. Mercury was performing just as he should, and winning to boot. Justin began to hope that all would end safely. That way he could enjoy ringing Lorissa's neck personally for this prank.

The horses thundered along the country road unimpeded, then from nowhere a great brown-and-white hound dashed out across the lane in pursuit of a hare. Justin's worst fears became a reality right before him. Mercury reared, trying to unseat his rider, even as Lord Rayburn raced past.

Justin could see Lorissa struggle to once again get the animal under control, but the stallion was in a frenzy of terror, heeding none of his rider's efforts.

The animal turned and dashed headlong into the woods and, using a low-hanging branch, knocked Lorissa from his back, then disappeared among the trees.

Eyes riveted on the still form on the ground as he rode full tilt toward her, Justin suddenly knew that life wouldn't be the same if something dreadful happened to Lorissa.

CHAPTER FIVE

Stunned by the impact of the fall, Lorissa lay on the ground unmoving. Every inch of her hurt, even as she struggled to draw a breath. The thundering of a horse's hooves approached, but until sweet fresh air once again entered her lungs, she was too paralyzed to think or care who was there.

At last, with a gasp, she breathed once again and the world seemed to come into focus. Gently she moved her limbs to make certain they were all still working. To her surprise, she appeared to have survived the spill without major injury.

With an effort she sat up. Her world spun a moment, then righted itself. She gazed in the direction that Mercury had disappeared, hoping the animal wouldn't come to any harm in the woods.

"Miss Mathis, are you unharmed?"

Lorissa looked up and saw Lord Rayburn, still seated on his horse but eyeing her with concern. Before she could answer his query, however, he glanced to his left and seemed to spy something that struck terror in his heart. His eyes grew wide, then he yanked his reins, wheeling his horse around to gallop away from her, as if determined to win the race despite her accident.

Again she heard pounding hooves, but coming from the opposite direction than the viscount had ridden.

Within minutes the horse came to an abrupt halt and Justin jumped down. Seconds later he was beside her, running his hands over her arms, searching for broken bones.

"Are you injured, Lori?" His tone was tight with anger.

"Of course not. I have taken worse spills than this." When he moved to testing of her legs she took exception. She shoved his hands away, despite liking the sensation of warmth that surged through her body. She couldn't understand why he was mad at her. "I merely had the wind knocked from me. I am fine."

Justin rocked back on his heels as she rebuffed his efforts, his eyes glittering with outrage. "If only you could have some sense knocked *into* you so easily. Has nothing I've said to you over the past few days gotten into that head of yours? Have my mother's entreaties fallen on deaf ears? What do you mean, to be out here racing Rayburn on the open road like some common baggage?"

Anger gave Lorissa a sudden surge of strength. She gave him a shove causing him to fall backward into the leafy turf. "How dare you say that to me? I was out here for you."

He glared back at her as they both now sat sprawled on the ground. "Don't use me as an excuse to justify your improper and flighty behavior, young lady. Did I request you to make a spectacle of yourself before your neighbors? Did I beg you to ride that cursedly uncontrollable stallion? Did we ever have a conversation about you riding one of my racers? I think not."

"But I did it because—" Lori tried to explain, but Justin wouldn't listen.

"You did it because you are a childish hoyden who thinks she can fly about the county from one scandal to another without the least thought in her flighty little head. I warned my mother how it would be if she invited a hey-go-mad chit like yourself to her Valentine's Ball."

Humiliation flooded Lorissa. Justin hadn't even wanted her to come to Crossley. All her efforts over the past few days hadn't made one wit of difference. She ignored him, avoiding his censuring glare as she rose and brushed the leaves and dirt from her clothes. From the corner of her eye, she could see that he too had risen, but he stood watching her in rigid silence. Clearly he was not going to listen to any explanation she would give him. Her shoulders sagged with dejection.

She turned her back on Justin, not wanting to think about this disaster. At that moment her thoughts turned to Dermot. She was more angry with her brother than she had ever been. He had lied to her and ruined, perhaps forever, her chances with the man she loved.

Adam galloped up on his horse, reining to a halt but not getting down. "Did you take a spill, Lori? Are you hurt? Where the devil is Rayburn? What's going on, Justin?" The young man was full of questions that came in rapid succession, but the two standing on the ground had little to say.

Lorissa moved to stand beside him. "I have been unseated. Will you take me back to Crossley, Adam?"

Behind her Justin snapped, "I'm not finished with this yet, Lorissa. I shall take you back after we have fully discussed your conduct."

She tossed a snappish, "No, you shan't, my lord. I ride with Adam," over her shoulder, then extended her hand to the young man.

Adam avoided looking at his brother. He knew he and Dermot were the villains in this piece, but Justin and Lori's quarrels always passed quickly, or so he tried to convince himself. He took her hand and pulled her up in front of him, then settled his arms around her.

She smiled radiantly at him. "You have become

much the gentleman, Adam." Without a glance at
Justin, she turned her gaze forward.

Adam experienced a rush of pleasure at her words,
but then he heard a strangled sound from his brother.
He hesitated a moment, waiting for either Lorissa or
Justin to speak to one another, but silence reigned. At
last Adam spoke into the frosty silence between his
brother and the lady in front of him. "We shall await
you back at the house, Justin."

With that he put his horse into a gentle trot heading
to the Court.

Adam wasn't certain, but he thought he detected a
sniffle from Lorissa, yet that was hardly possible. She
was not one of those missish females who turned into
a watering pot at the slightest provocation. "Are you
certain you are all right?"

The lady gave a terse nod of her head, but continued
to face forward. Still, she gave a heartrending sigh that
only heightened Adam's guilt.

On the ground, watching his brother and Lorissa
ride away, Justin was still furious, but with whom he
wasn't certain. Was his anger for Lorissa for once again
engaging in a foolish prank despite all he'd said to
her, or with Adam for holding the young lady in his
arms in that too-familiar manner. Justin had wanted to
go and yank her away from the intimacy of her position on Adam's horse but had stopped himself, knowing he would appear the fool.

Then it dawned on Justin that he was most angry
with himself. He'd allowed his disappointment in her
conduct to get the better of him and not listen to what
Lorissa had tried to tell him.

Justin stood deep in thought, chiding himself for
having not allowed her to explain. What could have
induced her to do something so rash as to race one
of his prime stock?

Then he shifted his gaze in the direction in which
Rayburn had vanished. That gentleman had behaved

very oddly. Had the viscount been the instigator of this little adventure? Did it have something to do with the fact that the man had mentioned buying Mercury upon first arriving? But why had the fellow ridden away like the dogs of Hades were after him? Justin knew that if and when he saw the fellow again, he wanted to plant the cad a facer for leaving Lorissa after her accident. But for his mother's sake he would resist.

The whole thing was a puzzle, but Justin knew he'd get no answers standing here. First he must go find that cursed stallion. Mercury was too unstable to be left to wander the countryside unfettered, not to mention too valuable as a stud.

As he mounted his horse, he knew that once he'd returned the racer to the stables, his next task would be to make things right with Lorissa. In all fairness he must at least allow her the chance to give whatever explanation she might have. He gave a soft laugh. It would, no doubt, be something totally outlandish, but she would be certain to think her reasoning had been right. With the certainty that he could set things with Lorissa right by dinner, Justin turned his horse toward the woods to follow Mercury.

Lorissa's hand hovered just a moment before she knocked on Miss Norris's door. The door was opened by the lady's maid and Belinda called her to enter, but seeing the gowns across Lorissa's arm, the young lady frowned.

"Did Molly not alter them properly, my dear?"

Lorissa gave a disheartened smile. "Oh, no, that isn't why I am returning your lovely gowns. I shall have no need for them after all."

Belinda rose from the daybed where she'd been resting. She came to take Lorissa's hands after the lady had passed the gowns to the young maid. "Have you merely given up hope, or has something happened of which I'm not aware?"

"Both." Lorissa's voice sounded shaky and a hint of tears welled up in her green eyes.

"Molly, bring us tea." As the maid hurried away, the lady put her arm round Lorissa's shoulders. "Come, my dear friend, tell me all about what has you so upset. I feel certain we shall be able to resolve whatever problem has arisen."

Lorissa allowed herself to be led to the nearby sofa, but she shook her head as she sat heavily on the pink damask furniture. "There is no point in my pretending that pretty gowns will make Justin see me as I truly am. I am going home."

"You mustn't give up, Lori. What has happened to make you lose heart?"

Lorissa quickly told the tale of being tricked into the race by her brother and Mr. Andrews, for she was now certain that was what had occurred. A single tear rolled down her cheek as she described Justin's rage at her conduct and his declaration that he'd not wanted her at Crossley in the first place. Clearly he saw her as being too tactless to mix with polite company.

With a sigh she brushed the tear away, straightening her back. "I'm going home. There is no reason for me to stay."

"Pray, don't leave. If not for your sake, stay for mine. Surprisingly my father doesn't see you as a threat. He is not forever pushing me at Lord Justin when you are with him."

Lorissa lifted her sad gaze to her new friend. "He sees me as Justin does, just some graceless child being guided by a more experienced older friend."

Belinda couldn't deny the truth in the girl's statement. "Men are so blind, my dear. But I am certain that with time—"

"I cannot stay. It would be too painful for me when

Lady Kate arrives at the ball wearing the Crossly Heart." Lorissa jumped up. "I couldn't bear it."

With that the young lady fled the room. Belinda considered going after the distraught girl, then realized that nothing she could say at the moment would change Lorissa's mind.

Miss Norris sat lost in thought, pondering what she must do to help Lord Justin realize his true feelings, since she was more certain than ever that he cared about Lorissa. Why else would he storm at her in such a manner? Why would his intent gaze follow her at every gathering? And why did he bristle with jealousy when Adam or one of the other gentlemen paid too much attention to Miss Mathis?

The whole affair was proving more difficult than Belinda had thought, but she was still determined to make Lord Justin listen to his heart. The problem was that she was at a standstill as to how to proceed. The Valentine's Ball was two days away, so she knew she still had time. But with no clue as to what to do next, she would simply have to wait and see what the young lord did upon discovering Lorissa's defection.

Adam stormed into the parlor, where he'd been told Dermot had taken refuge. Without any greeting, the earl's youngest son launched into a tirade on the dastardliness of their conduct. "We should be drawn and quartered for getting Lori into this mess."

Dermot looked up. "Was Justin mad as blazes when he caught up to them?"

"Them, ha! Rayburn was nowhere to be found after Lori took a spill."

"Is she unhurt?" Dermot sat up, awaiting the answer.

"Physically, yes, but I fear Justin flayed the skin off her with his tongue-lashing about her conduct. We must do something."

Dermot's conscience had been bothering him, but

still he was reluctant to own up to their treachery. "Must we? Justin and Lori always get past their little tiffs. By this evening, I feel certain all will be as before."

Adam shook his head. "I have never seen your sister in such a way. I may be wrong, but I think she was crying as I brought her back to the manor. And Justin had been bellowing like an angry bear. 'Tis a serious matter."

"Crying?" Dermot sat up. He didn't think he'd ever seen his sister shed tears. "Are you certain?"

"Nearly. I tell you, it goes against the pluck to allow a female to take the blame for our misdeeds. We must go to Justin and confess our role in this ugly affair."

Dermot rose with resolution. Lorissa had raced to save him; how could he do anything less for her? "Indeed you are right. My sister must be exonerated of any wrongdoing in your brother's eyes. Shall we go find Justin and tell him all?"

The two young men gamely set out to find the young lord, but that gentleman was still roaming the countryside looking for the missing Mercury. After ascertaining that their prey was not in the Court, the two went to while away the time in the billiards room, but neither had much interest in the game.

It was nearly six o'clock and the sun had set by the time Justin arrived back at Crossley, tired and out of sorts after his long search. After leaving the troublesome horse with a groom, he went straight to the library, where he poured himself a good measure of brandy. As the clock struck the hour, he knew he must hurry to dress in time for dinner.

A knock sounded at the door, then Adam and Dermot entered the room, looking like green recruits about to face a column of French soldiers. Adam halted just inside the room. "May we speak with you for a moment?"

Justin had intended to seek out Lorissa at the earliest

possible moment, but seeing the look on this pair's faces, he decided to see just how these two were involved in Lorissa's adventure. He gestured to a group of leather-bound chairs before the fire. As the young men settled, Justin tossed off the last of his brandy before saying, "Just the two I would most like to hear from at this moment. Can you explain how it happens that, without my permission, one of my prime animals was involved in an impromptu race? And why, Mathis, was your sister on his back?"

Adam quickly told the disgraceful tale of gaming and loss. Of Rayburn's offer to dismiss the debt if Lorissa would race Mercury against him.

Justin sat forward at that. "He specifically asked that Lori ride the horse?"

Dermot nodded, taking over the tale. "Thought it strange myself, but he said he'd heard of her skill in the saddle."

A thoughtful expression settled on Justin's face as the memory of Lady Kate's strange morning ride came to mind. Had there been some plot against Lorissa between the Daileys? But to what purpose? He decided he would have to sort that out later, for now he must hear the rest. "Continue."

Dermot blushed as he recounted how he'd convinced Lorissa that Justin wanted her to race Mercury to benefit the animal's sale. Seeing the look on the young lord's face, Mr. Mathis stuttered, "I-I was desperate. Adam might get a rare trimming for his losses, but I'm certain my father is likely to ship me off to the navy for such an offense, were he to find out."

Justin wondered if the navy might not be a place that the young man should be to keep him out of trouble, but he knew that was between the baron and his son. For now, Justin's remorse was great over his conduct to Lorissa. He would have to seek her out immediately and beg her forgiveness.

At that moment the library door opened and the

Earl of Crossley entered. The three young men rose. Justin advanced toward the gentleman. "Father, I am glad you have arrived."

The earl's gaze traveled over each of the three faces. "Is there some difficulty?"

Justin wouldn't betray his brother. There was almost an unwritten law regarding sibling loyalty. "Why, no, sir, nothing that I cannot handle. I am merely glad to surrender my duties as host to you."

The older gentleman arched one dark brow but made no comment. "Why are you lads not dressing for dinner? Is it not scheduled for seven?"

Dermot and Adam exchanged a relieved glance. "We were just leaving to do so, Father."

As the young men all made for the door, the earl said, "Justin, a word with you, if you please."

The heir turned toward his father as the two younger men exited the room. "Sir?"

The earl fingered the quizzing glass that dangled from a black ribbon around his neck. It was no affectation, his eyesight having weakened with time. "Have you come to a decision about which lucky lady will wear the Ruby Heart at the ball?"

Justin ran his hand through his black hair, mussing it uncharacteristically. "Sir, I must own that I have been so busy keeping Lorissa Mathis out of trouble this week that I've had little time to think of anyone else."

Lord Crossley's hands grew still. "Anne invited Larken's girl?"

"The very one. Out of kindness, Mother asked her to stay the week and attend the ball. 'Tis her first house party, as you know, and I felt the need to guide her through our treacherous social waters."

His father's eyes became hooded. "Very wise." The Ormulu clock on the mantel chimed half past the hour. "I shall delay you no longer, my boy, or we shall both be late down and your mother will be quite cross with me."

Justin grinned. "I doubt that, sir. She has been missing you as ever." With that he left his father in the library.

The earl walked to the fireplace, looking down into the flames. Speaking out loud, he pondered, "What have you been about, my dearest wife? Sweet little Lorissa Mathis here? What a sly maneuver to add a new beauty to the party." He hadn't seen the girl since she was fifteen, but even then she'd been a blossoming beauty, though his sons had paid little enough attention to their childhood friend, taking her very much for granted.

The gentleman looked up at the clock and knew he must hurry, but he was determined to have a private word with his wife as soon as possible. He was curious whether it had dawned on the lady that instead of the estimable Miss Norris or the vivacious Lady Kate, she might well end up with Lorissa Mathis as a daughter-in-law.

The earl gave a soft laugh. What was he thinking? Of course Anne had considered the possibility. His wife was awake on every suit. Besides, she'd always had a fondness for the child and would welcome her to the family, as she would anyone Justin loved. With that thought, the gentleman strode from the library, determined to be ready for dinner on time.

Justin shrugged on his dark blue superfine evening coat as he hurried down the hallway toward Lorissa's room. His valet had taken exception at the hurried affair of his master's dressing. Justin wanted to see his old friend and had grabbed the jacket from Becket's hand, assuring him that he could manage on his own.

Coming to the door, Justin knocked and awaited her response. But there was none. Debating the propriety of such an act, he opened the door. Her bedchamber stood empty. What's more, there was nothing in it to indicate that she was staying there. No ribbons or pelisses on the bed or hairbrushes casually tossed on a dresser.

Closing the door, Justin spied a passing maid carrying a tin of hot water to one of the other guests. "Have you seen Miss Mathis about?"

"Saw her earlier, my lord, knocking at Miss Norris's sitting room door." The maid pointed back up the corridor. " 'Tis the first door on the left." With that the girl hurried down the hall.

Justin guessed that was where Lorissa had gone. After all, the two young ladies had become good friends. He hurried to the room, then knocked sharply. He was certain Miss Norris would leave them alone so that he might make a proper apology.

The door was opened by a maid, who eyed the gentleman with censure, as if to say he had no business coming to a lady's apartments. Beyond the servant he saw Miss Norris sitting with a book in her lap.

She looked up and smiled. Suddenly, Justin realized that he might be giving her false hopes about the reason for his visit, since she was one of the two expecting to be offered the Ruby Heart.

"Lord Justin, come in."

He took a single step into the room, then in a rush asked, "Have you seen Lori . . . er . . . I mean, Miss Mathis?"

Justin would have sworn the lady's smile widened for a moment, before it settled into a normal position. "Why, so I have, sir."

He looked about the room curiously when she didn't continue. "Is she here? I wish to speak to her most urgently."

Miss Norris rose and walked to the gentleman. "I am sure you do, my lord."

The lady gave him a knowing look, leaving him in

little doubt that she was aware of his tirade against his old friend.

"I thought you knew, sir, that the lady is gone from Crossley Court."

CHAPTER SIX

Justin's gray eyes reflected the full shock of his disbelief. "You cannot mean the foolish child returned to Larken Hall because of a simple misunderstanding."

The lady shook her head. "Child, my lord? Lorissa ceased to be a child some time ago in everyone's eyes but yours."

Remembering the way Lorissa had looked as he twirled her about the ballroom, Justin opened his mouth to protest that he was not unaware of the changes. But suddenly he bit off what he was about to say. Despite his response to her as a woman, he had treated her like a recalcitrant child after the race. He looked up into Miss Norris's observant eyes. "I must own that since we've returned, it seems I've fallen back into my old ways of acting like her big brother."

The dark-haired beauty looked down at her hands. "But you are not her brother, my lord, nor does she see you as one. In truth, she has returned home because she prefers the role of ignored daughter at Larken Manor to that of incorrigible madcap child as only you seem to treat her at Crossley."

A pain seized Justin's gut. After the race he had spoken to her as one would an unruly child forever into mischief, yet now he knew she'd been innocent of his harsh charges. Good heavens, his damnably sharp tongue had driven Lorissa from the very premises. He paused a moment, but that was very odd, for she'd never been so craven before. "I still don't understand her running back home. Even when she truly was a child she was never afraid to stand her ground in a disagreement with me."

"But she is no longer a child, and as such she suffers as a woman." Belinda hesitated for a moment, then decided she must do all in her power to help bring the two together. "When a woman is in love, sir, she is much more aware of all her emotions."

"In love?" Justin suddenly remembered the smile Lorissa had bestowed on his brother as he'd lifted her upon the horse. The way she'd settled comfortably into Adam's arms. The very notion that Lorissa was in love with his brother filled Justin with anger. *He* had always been the one to whom she'd run with her hurts, her joys, and her confidences. He was surprised at the possessiveness that filled his heart.

Lorissa Mathis belonged with him, not Adam. At that moment Justin knew that he couldn't bear losing her, couldn't tolerate having his beloved brother possess what Justin realized he wanted so desperately. He was madly in love with Lorissa and he might have lost her because he'd been unable to see what was right before his eyes.

Belinda, seeing the sick expression settle on the gentleman's face, asked, "Are you well, my lord?"

Justin, holding his raw emotions in check, asked in a strangled voice, "Is Lori in love with my brother?"

"With Adam?" The lady shook her head.

Overjoyed, Justin grabbed the lady's hands. "Tell me, Miss Norris, that I may hope."

Belinda laughed. "Sir, I think she has loved you from the cradle, but your conduct over the past days has not made your suit prosper."

Justin dropped the lady's hands and began to pace. "I have been such a fool, Miss Norris." He paused and looked back at her, his gray eyes full of guilt. "The worst of it is raising your hopes for a possible alliance—"

The young lady gestured for him to stop. "I do assure you, my lord, my heart is elsewhere engaged and has been since before I first came to London."

For a moment Justin looked puzzled, then a dawning light appeared in his eyes. "Parental displeasure with your choice."

"Just so, but there is little we can do about that. We must concentrate on you. My only wish is to make certain that you get your heart's desire."

Justin breathed the single word: "Lori." Then the gentleman stepped forward, and taking Miss Norris's hand, he brushed a quick kiss upon it. "I cannot thank you enough for your help and your understanding." With that the gentleman turned on his heel, heading for the door.

"What are you planning to do, sir?"

"Why, go to Larken Hall at once."

Belinda wasn't sure that was the best thing. "Are you certain she will see you? She is dreadfully hurt and disillusioned at the moment. Do you not think she needs a little time to reflect?"

Justin grinned confidently. "She will not turn her old friend away."

As the gentleman disappeared down the hall, Belinda hoped he was right. But she also hoped that Lorissa didn't fall too easily into his arms. A man never seemed to appreciate what came easily.

Some two hours later, the gentlemen were just joining the ladies in the drawing room after their brandy when Justin returned to Crossley looking as if he'd been struck by a bolt of lightning. He made his apologies for being away during the meal, then made straight for Belinda, much to Lady Kate's chagrin.

He turned and faced the curious gazes of the guests, settling his face into a neutral pose. Despite his calm appearance, his tone was angry as he whispered, "She wouldn't see me. Sent word by that prunish old house-keeper that she was indisposed, as if Lori has ever been sick a day in her life. Didn't even get a chance to tell her how I feel."

Belinda struggled to keep her composure. "I tried to tell you, my lord. You keep thinking of her as little Lori, yours to command. But she is Miss Mathis now, and so she must be beguiled as you would any other woman whose heart has been wounded."

"Should I go back and demand to speak with her?"

Belinda placed a hand on his arm, taking note of the frightened look that leapt into Lady Kate's eyes at the intimate gesture. "Allow me to visit her in the morning, to encourage her to return to Crossley."

Justin turned to the lady, taking one gloved hand in his. "Do you think you can convince her to return?"

Belinda placed her other hand atop his and smiled. "I shall try my best, but remember, I couldn't persuade her to stay this afternoon. And you must promise me not to badger her to accept you if she does not wish it at present."

The gentleman nodded but gave a hopeful grin. "I feel certain she will return."

At that moment the pair found that a quiet had fallen over the room as all eyes were riveted on them. Everyone seemed to be waiting for some great revela-tion from the couple. Belinda schooled her features to one of bored indifference. "I do believe we have fostered a bit too much hope in everyone's heart for the moment." Not to mention the dark looks Lady Kate was giving them.

Justin knew she was right. "Allow me to escort you to Major Dandridge. He is always amusing." With that he led the lady across the room, and they were soon in conversation with the soldier.

All present were convinced that the private *tête-à-tête* between Lord Justin and Miss Norris implied that the gentleman was leaning toward choosing the raven-haired beauty.

Lady Kate was frantic but not ready to give up yet. After the gentleman left Miss Norris's side, Kate became a permanent fixture on his arm. She even weathered a piercing question about her brother's race and subsequent disappearance, swearing no knowledge of any of Horace's dealings. The dawn ride, she'd vowed, was merely a wish to see him alone, no more. It had taken some doing, but he'd seemed to accept her story.

Her mother inadvertently helped, when she joined her to complain that her son was quite irresponsible to have abandoned them once again. The lady vowed that his father would hear of the viscount's conduct.

As Lady Kate retired to bed that night, she was more convinced than ever that Justin wasn't in love with the turnip farmer's daughter. The little country nobody had disappeared as well, which was all to the good. That meant Kate still had a chance to get her hands on the Ruby Heart.

Lorissa ran her fingers over the mare's white blaze. She'd risen late, being unable to sleep until near dawn. Her mood dark, she'd wandered to the stables to see how her favorite mare had spent the night. Stevens, the head groom, assured her that the horse still had another good month before she dropped her foal, but Lorissa knew how often the man had been proven wrong before.

The stable was nearly empty, her father and his guests having already departed on their morning hunt long ago. He'd paid little heed to the fact that his daughter had returned, other than to ask if she would ride with them, to which she had replied no. It seemed things rarely changed.

Once again she questioned the wisdom of turning Justin away the previous evening. But in her heart she knew that little would have changed if she'd gone down to receive his apology. He would have gone back to treating her like his old friend, and insist that she come back to the Valentine's Ball. That she would not do. It would be hard enough to know that he was lost to her forever, but she couldn't have borne to witness Lady Kate's triumph, for she was certain Miss Norris wouldn't accept an offer.

Giving the mare a final pat and a few soothing words, Lorissa decided to stroll in the garden to put the matter from her mind, since all her worrying wouldn't change a thing. As she exited the open door of the stable she ran straight into her brother and Belinda.

"There you are, Lori. Why didn't you tell me you were leaving Crossley yesterday? Felt the fool to come down to breakfast and have her ladyship inform me you'd hied off the day before with little explanation." Dermot's tone was subdued despite his words.

Lorissa politely greeted them before she responded. "There was no reason for you to leave because I did." She smiled sadly at Miss Norris, who was looking lovely in a dark blue riding habit trimmed with white swansdown. " 'Tis good to see you, Belinda, but I hope you have not come to try to persuade me to return to the Court."

"I fear I have." The lady smiled, then looked around. "Shall we stroll in that small garden we passed so I might tell you about my conversation with Lord Justin?"

Despite her hurt, Lorissa couldn't resist knowing what had transpired after she left. "Very well. Do you join us, Dermot?"

The young man nodded, then fell into step behind the ladies. He had something important to tell Lorissa, but he decided to allow Miss Norris to have her say first.

Belinda told of Justin's determined search for

Lorissa. How he'd reacted when he learned she'd left and his dejection when he'd mistakenly thought her in love with his brother.

Still Lorissa hesitated. She stopped and looked deeply into her new friend's eyes. "I have always known Justin had a brotherly affection for me, but I'm not certain what he feels now is any more than that." Her gaze dropped to the ground as she asked, "Did he tell you he intended to ask me to marry him?"

"Not in so many words, my dear, but it was implied. You will never know if you don't return to Crossley. Besides, I understand there must be an engagement announced tomorrow night by tradition. Do you want him to marry the wrong woman?"

Dermot, who'd been silent during much of the conversation, interrupted, "You surely don't want that scheming Lady Kate to get her claws into him."

Lorissa looked sharply at her brother. "What do you mean?"

"Didn't expect it of a gentleman, but I think the dice were fuzzed when Adam and I played with Rayburn. Told Justin so this morning, and he said it was very likely, for the man's reputation is a bit disreputable. Then it occurred to me that it isn't likely that purse-pinched scoundrel came up with such a scheme to discredit you on his own. Nothing in it for him, since he would have preferred our money. If I was a wagering man—which I ain't after this experience—I'd put money on Lady Kate being the one who wanted you and Justin to be at daggers drawing. She was the one who brought him to the race."

An angry glint appeared in Lorissa's green eyes. "Did she?" Her female instincts were all alert. To lose a man to the love of another woman was one thing, but to lose him due to a trick, she wouldn't allow. Straightening, she announced, "I shall return to—"

Just then there was a great ruckus in the stableyard. Thundering hooves echoed on the afternoon air as several members of the hunt party galloped in, shouting for a doctor. There had been an accident during the morning hunt.

To Dermot's and Lorissa's amazement, they discovered that their father had taken a spill from his horse. A young man named Baxter assured the siblings that their father was not seriously injured, for he was awake and roaring like a lion, but was being brought to the manor on a gate.

Belinda, realizing that Lorissa could not leave at present, begged to help in whatever way she could. Lorissa thanked her, and the ladies hurried to the kitchen to make ready for the arrival of the injured baron.

At six that evening, a message was sent to Crossley Court from Miss Norris to Lord Justin. She informed the young man of Lord Larken's injury, which proved to be a sprained wrist and bruised hip, then begged to be excused for the evening. It was her intention to stay at Larken Manor.

Justin's heart plummeted at the news. Lorissa would not be back at the Court that night. Then he read the postscript. *Both Lorissa and I shall return in time for the ball. Take heart, my lord, for the lady is most anxious to hear what you have to say.*

He folded the letter, then picked up the box with the Crossley Ruby Heart. Lifting the top, he stared at the red stone with the white diamonds twinkling on the black velvet. He prayed he would get the chance to see what it would look like around Lorissa's lovely neck.

The morning of the ball dawned and the servants at the Court were up before times cleaning, polishing, and arranging fresh flowers in the ballroom. The kitchens were bustling and the air held a variety of enticing scents.

Lady Anne, despite her busy morning, had taken

note that her eldest son was especially nervous as he stood staring out the window. She wondered if he'd made a decision, but she didn't press him. She had done all she could to help him, but the final choice must be his. She only hoped he made the right one.

By midafternoon, Justin was certain he would go mad if Lorissa and Miss Norris did not arrive soon. He made a halfhearted effort to entertain his mother's guests, but always with an eye to the front drive.

It was with a deep foreboding that he went to his room to dress. Where were the ladies? What had happened? Should he go to his father and tell him that he just couldn't give the Ruby Heart at tonight's ball because the woman he loved wasn't there? Or should he get on his horse and go to Lorissa immediately?

Duty to his family won the day. Arriving at his chamber, Becket awaited him with a note. The ladies had arrived some thirty minutes earlier, having slipped in quietly through the rear. Justin immediately rang for a footman, informing him that he was to wait outside Miss Mathis's door. When the lady was ready, she was to be taken to the yellow sitting room. That taken care of, Justin was in a rush to dress.

In her bedchamber, Lorissa nervously played with the folds of her white shot-gold silk ball gown as the maid put the finishing touches on her hair. The servant had pulled Lorissa's auburn locks back and run a string of small pearls through the coiled knot. When the girl was finished, Lorissa was amazed at how sophisticated she looked, for inside she was as frightened as a ten-year-old.

A waiting footman led her to a small drawing room to which she'd never before been. The room was empty and Lorissa nervously began to pace, wondering where Justin could be and what would happen when he arrived.

As she moved to look out the window at an arriving carriage, her gaze fell on a small table on which a glass-topped wooden box sat. Curious, she moved to look into the case. Then she gasped. There lay the famous Crossley Ruby Heart on display.

The door to the room opened, startling her. Lorissa turned and to her surprise Lady Kate marched in dressed in a deep red gown, clearly designed to go with a ruby necklace. "Miss Mathis, I could not believe my eyes when I saw you in the hall just now. I am all amazement to see you back at Crossley Court after your scandalous conduct of the other day. Do you think Lord Justin will be so forgiving? I do not believe he shall."

Lorissa moved back to the window. "Justin was the one who asked me back. As to forgiveness, I am wondering how much he shall have, should he learn that you were the one behind your brother trying to cheat two innocent young men out of a great deal of money." She had no proof, but deep inside Lorissa was convinced of the fact. She turned her back on Lady Kate, staring out into the night and wishing Justin would come.

Lady Kate's anger and fear made her reckless. She would not be thwarted in her wishes. She moved closer to Lorissa. "There is no proof of that, and my brother is likely in Scotland at our country estate by now. I have convinced dear Justin that I wasn't—" The lady's gaze suddenly fell on the wooden case. Her voice was full of avarice as she breathed, "The Crossley Heart."

In an instant, the marquess's daughter threw open the case and yanked the necklace from the mounting on the blue velvet. She hurried to the mirror over the fireplace, clasping the jewelry about her throat as she went. She preened, enjoying her image in the looking glass, muttering, " 'Tis mine now."

Just then the door to the drawing room opened and closed. Both ladies turned to the new arrival. Justin stood, handsome in his black evening coat. His gaze traveled to Lorissa. In the gray depths was such love and longing, the young lady nearly dashed across the room and threw herself into his arms. But not in Lady Kate's presence.

At the mirror Lady Kate, so much enjoying what she thought was her moment of triumph, called, "Does the necklace not go well with my gown, my lord? We shall be gloriously happy."

His voice cold, Justin asked, "Why are you wearing my fiancée's ruby, Lady Kate? Please remove it at once."

The lady's eyes narrowed. "What are you saying? I shall be your wife. I have come all the way here for this necklace and I intend to keep it." With that the young lady dashed for the door, throwing it open as she ran away.

The sounds of her footsteps pattering on the marble hall echoed in the room as Justin moved across the room and took Lorissa in his arms. "Are you unhurt?"

"Yes, but I do believe she is quite mad. You must go after her and retrieve your family's heirloom."

Justin grinned, but shook his head. "I have the only thing of value here that I care about, my love." With that he lowered his head and claimed her lips. The searing kiss lasted several minutes and left Lorissa without a thought but of Justin.

He lifted his head, saying, "I take it you have forgiven me for my overbearing conduct of the other day." Then he drew her back to him. "Oh, dearest Lori, I do love you to distraction. Will you marry me?"

Lorissa's joy knew no bounds. "I love you, and yes, I wish to marry you." She gave a soft laugh, causing him to draw back and look at her. "I don't even care that I shall not be able to wear the Ruby Heart for the Valentine's Ball, for I shall have you for eternity."

"But you shall have both, my darling Brat." With that he drew a box from his pocket and opened it. There lay another ruby necklace of equal beauty as the one Lady Kate had stolen. "You didn't think my father was so foolish as to leave such a valuable item just sitting in a glass case for any thief . . . or thoroughly mad miss to steal. Lady Kate just purloined a paste copy. Here is the true Crossley Heart."

With that he took the sparkling ruby and diamond heart and placed it around Lorissa's neck, then kissed the soft white skin upon which it lay. After he ceased distracting her, she looked up at him as her fingers traced the stone. "It's beautiful, but if I never saw it again, I wouldn't care, for I would have you."

Justin kissed her with all the passion the lady could have wished, leaving her in little doubt of his feelings. But a knock sounded at the door.

The butler entered, eyeing the pair with suppressed curiosity. "The earl's compliments, my lord, but all are waiting in the Willow Drawing Room."

Justin pulled Lorissa's arm through his and followed the servant back to the closed set of double doors of the main drawing room. The trio paused, and the butler looked a question.

Justin grinned down at Lorissa, saying, "Flanders, you may announce my fiancée to the gathering."

Despite years of training to show little emotion, the faithful old retainer grinned. "Very good, my lord." Then he turned and opened the doors. "Lord Justin Andrews and his fiancée, Miss Lorissa Mathis."

As the lovers stepped into the drawing room, the company surged forward to offer congratulations to Justin and Lorissa. The only disappointed faces were on Lady Longford and Squire Norris. There was such excitement and pleasure among the friends and neighbors of the earl at his son's good fortune that no one gave a thought to the missing Lady Kate, save her mother.

Out of kindness, Justin pulled the lady aside and gently told the tale of Lady Kate finding the paste copy and running off. The marchioness, color elevated in her cheeks, offered her profound apology, declaring that it was all the marquess's fault for having denied his son and daughter nothing. The humiliated lady begged to be excused.

Lady Longford, on reaching their rooms, soundly boxed her daughter's ears, something she'd never before done, and vowed the girl would not go to London this Season or ever again unless she mended her ways. Then they packed and left while the other guests were in the ballroom, dancing and celebrating the engagement.

The Valentine Ball at Crossley Court was considered a smashing success by all who attended. But the judgment had little to do with the elegance of the decorations or the excellence of the food or even the cordial company. Instead, for years to come all anyone remembered was the look on Lord Justin Andrews's face as he twirled Miss Lorissa Mathis around the floor, her adoring green eyes locked with his. Everyone agreed that only Cupid could have made such a perfect match on Valentine's Day.

More Zebra Regency Romances

__A Noble Pursuit by Sara Blayne $4.99US/$6.50CAN
   0-8217-5756-3

__Crossed Quills by Carola Dunn $4.99US/$6.50CAN
   0-8217-6007-6

__A Poet's Kiss by Valerie King $4.99US/$6.50CAN
   0-8217-5789-X

__Exquisite by Joan Overfield $5.99US/$7.50CAN
   0-8217-5894-2

__The Reluctant Lord by Teresa Desjardien $4.99US/$6.50CAN
   0-8217-5646-X

__A Dangerous Affair by Mona Gedney $4.50US/$5.50CAN
   0-8217-5294-4

__Love's Masquerade by Violet Hamilton $4.99US/$6.50CAN
   0-8217-5409-2

__Rake's Gambit by Meg-Lynn Roberts $4.99US/$6.50CAN
   0-8217-5687-7

__Cupid's Challenge by Jeanne Savery $4.50US/$5.50CAN
   0-8217-5240-5

__A Deceptive Bequest by Olivia Sumner $4.50US/$5.50CAN
   0-8217-5380-0

__A Taste for Love by Donna Bell $4.99US/$6.50CAN
   0-8217-6104-8

Call toll free **1-888-345-BOOK** to order by phone or use this coupon to order by mail.

Name_____

Address_____

City _____ State _____Zip_____

Please send me the books I have checked above.

I am enclosing $_____

Plus postage and handling* $_____

Sales tax (in New York and Tennessee only) $_____

Total amount enclosed $_____

*Add $2.50 for the first book and $.50 for each additional book.

Send check or money order (no cash or CODs) to:

Kensington Publishing Corp., 850 Third Avenue, New York, NY 10022

Prices and Numbers subject to change without notice.

All orders subject to availability.

Check out our website at **www.kensingtonbooks.com**

Put a Little Romance in Your Life With
Fern Michaels